Novels by Matthew K. Isaac

Broken Chains
Touched by Redeeming Love

Extraordinary Acclaim for Matthew Isaac's
BROKEN CHAINS

"*Broken Chains*" is a tale of forbidden love and the fight against systemic oppression. I was immediately captivated by the first sentence of the novel. It was hard to put down, and I learned a great deal about the foundations of caste superiority and societal ostracization in India during the 1950s and 60s. This book is a deeply moving narrative that critiques casteism, religious bigotry, and societal oppression while celebrating the transformative power of love, resilience, and truth. It is a poignant tale of two individuals who suffered religious bigotry, violence, and marginalization as they break free from the chains of tradition and prejudice, advocating for dignity, equality, and shared humanity. Well done, Matthew Isaac. I would love to see this turn into a major Hollywood film." –Ms. Brenda Pickleman, Hollywood Actress and Artist, Chicago, Illinois.

"*Broken Chains* is not merely a love story or a political novel. It is a moral investigation into how freedom is defined, who grants it, and what it ultimately costs. It confronts religion, caste, patriarchy, and institutional power with fearless honesty. It moved me, disturbed me, and reminded me that the work of liberation—anywhere—is never complete. It deserves to be read widely. It deserves to be argued with. And above all, it deserves to be taken seriously. I thoroughly enjoyed reading *Broken Chains*." –Dr. Henry D'Souza, Professor of Social Work, Grace Abbott School of Social Work, University of Nebraska at Omaha, Omaha, Nebraska, USA

"Matthew Isaac's novel *Broken Chains* is a profoundly moving work that exemplifies the transformative method, a distinguished form of novelistic expression. It is an impressive, gripping, and epic tale of forbidden love, an eloquent fusion of age-old injustices such as untouchability and religious bigotry, woven into a powerful exploration of the tensions between bigotry, faith, and science, and the deeper truths of the human condition that resonate with a universal audience." –A. K. B. Pillai, Ph.D. (Columbia University, NY), Former Professor of Anthropology and Comparative Literature at the New Jersey University System of Higher Education, Medical Anthropologist, Former Fellow of the National Institute of Mental Health and Diplomate of the American Board of Medical Psychotherapists, and Founder and Chairperson of New York Institute of Integral Human Development, Inc., New York.

"Matthew Isaac has fashioned a classic forbidden love story complete with fascinating character development, intriguing and insightful dialogue, and an examination of the impact of rigid cultural traditions on the attempt of two individuals from different backgrounds to forge a life together. Though set in a particular cultural context, this challenging and provocative work raises questions of universal importance such as class discrimination, religious arrogance and bigotry and the relationship between religion and morality as well as the intellectual and academic collision between religion and science. Ultimately though, it is an uplifting story of the victory of true love and dedication over a myriad of obstacles." –Dr. Dale Lanigan, Former Pastor and Asst. Professor Emeritus of Sociology and Criminal Justice, Lourdes University, Sylvania, Ohio

"One of the most artfully empathetic and inspiring forbidden love stories of our time, *Broken Chains* confronts the bigotry of untouchability, the existential struggles of Dalits, and their physical and emotional oppression, as it exposes these injustices through the lens of evolutionary biology and illuminates society's collective moral blindness, all rendered in a lucid and graceful style." –Mr. Bala Sriraghavan, CEO/Co-Founder of Datanetiix Solutions, Inc., a global software development/ Services company based in Irvine, California.

BROKEN CHAINS

A Novel

MATTHEW K. ISAAC

VERITAS
VINCIT
PRESS

VERITAS
VINCIT
PRESS

Published in the United States by Veritas Vincit Press
www.veritasvincitpress.com

First Edition

Library of Congress Control Number (LCCN): 2025946301
ISBN 979-8-9998600-2-6 (E-book)
ISBN 979-8-9998600-0-2 (Paperback)
ISBN 979-8-9998600-1-9 (Hardback)

Book cover design by Datanetiix Solutions Inc., Irvine, California
Printed in the United States of America

For Bina, Shawn, Sonya and Rohit, and Adriana

CONTENTS

PART ONE

"Forbidden Love"
In Paradise

THE MALABAR COAST

CHAPTER 1

S ome lovers are not doomed merely by fate but by the ancient myths and superstitions their cultures continue to uphold, as they are haunted by cursed stars, bound by tradition, and left to navigate stormy seas with nothing to guide them but the power of love.

Sam picked up Devi's wedding invitation card with trembling hands and stared at it poignantly once again. Holding it helplessly in despair, his eyes welled up with tears, and he sobbed quietly in the privacy of his room. The love of his life, Devi, would be married the following day—but he was not the lucky man.

Warm, salty teardrops fell on the card, bleeding into spidery streaks that warped and curled the paper, leaving behind physical marks of his grief. His chest tightened with pain; his breath hitched. The flicker of hope that once lit his eyes had faded, but the unrelenting love he carried for Devi still pulsed within him. He had never stopped loving her, even with the crushing realization that she would be another man's wife within hours.

Devi's fearful but wise words and her sobbing reverberated in his ears: "Sam, I love you, but I'm forbidden from falling in love with an upper-caste Syrian Christian man like you. Abjectly poor Untouchables like me, living in the shackles of servitude and yoke of oppression, in their sane minds, don't fall in love with younger, upper caste men and marry them without grave consequences. You're like a younger brother to me. If your parents and our community find out that we're in love, my parents and I'll be thrown into the cold streets since we are untouchable vassals, and we'll lose our livelihood and become vagrants."

Sam clenched his jaw tightly and ground his teeth quietly with tears still in his eyes; Sam thought, "Low caste Dalits (Untouchables) of polluted origin don't even have the right to fall in love with a person of upper caste origin. Falling in love with someone of an upper caste like me is impermissible, forbidden, and comes with dangerous societal and religious consequences."

Feeling the weight of the moment of truth, Sam got up from his desk and threw the biology book he had been trying so hard to read onto a pile of others he needed to review for his master's comprehensive exam. He couldn't concentrate. The grief of losing Devi—the love of his life—to another man was too heavy a burden, one he had to bear alone. He couldn't share it with his family, as he had kept their forbidden love a secret from his parents.

Devi's wedding was set for the following day. Since Sam's parents were oblivious to his long-standing emotional connection with her, they vacuously expected him to go with them, smile, and congratulate Devi and her new husband. The thought of losing her to another man twisted in his gut like a knife cutting deep. He imagined the music, the garlands, the fire—and Devi standing next to someone else, looking beautiful, looking lost to him forever.

He had told himself for months that he'd be ready. But now, just hours away, he couldn't breathe without his chest tightening. The weight in his stomach wouldn't lift. His thoughts were jagged, his hands cold. The closer the moment came, the less strength he seemed to have.

It had been several days since he'd had a good night's sleep. He glanced at his reflection in the wall mirror with shock: sleepless nights had sunken his eyes. The sweaty pajamas clung to his body and smelled of his body odor from the sweat. He was dirty, smelly, and in need of a shower and a shave. His mouth was dry from the sadness and anxiety of losing Devi forever to another man.

It was Sunday, but, as usual, he hadn't woken up to attend church with his parents. Sam was thirsty and strolled past his father's office to the kitchen for a drink. His father was busy preparing a lecture for the next day's class. Seeing Sam, he called out, "Son, are you okay? You look unkempt, tired, and sad. Are you alright? You'll do fine in the exam—you're the top-ranking graduate student. Don't worry too much. You'll be okay," said Johnnie, Sam's father. He didn't know what was truly ailing his son, or what had stolen all his joy.

After regaining composure and wearing a smile, Sam quickly peeked into his father's office, "*Appa* (Dad), I'm exhausted from staying up late and studying. I'll be fine," Sam reassured his father and headed toward the kitchen.

When Sam gently opened the kitchen door, he was shocked to see a young woman in a sari, her head bowed, wailing, standing beside his mother, Elsy. The loose sleeve of her sari covered her mouth—a typical gesture of someone in servitude—as she struggled to regain composure while confiding something to his mother. They were lost in the moment, waiting for the agony of her news to pass, unaware of Sam's startled presence at the doorway.

The wailing woman seemed to be in such agony that she could not articulate her sadness and release it from her system. She was heaving, and Sam's mother, Elsy, was trying to calm her down so she could contain her emotions and explain why she was wailing. The intensity of her sobbing and heaving suddenly waned when she saw Sam in the doorway as if she had seen a ghost in her distress and wanted to regain composure to protect her very being.

When the sleeve of the sari she held against her face suddenly dropped, Sam recognized the wailing woman. As he suspected, it was Devi, the love of his life, who he had been losing sleep over the past several days. She was visibly embarrassed to see Sam and abruptly tried to exit the kitchen through the other door when Sam turned around and left. He could hear his mother trying to stop her from leaving and asking her to stay.

Elsy yelled, "Sam, please shut the kitchen door behind you." He could still hear his mother's conversation as he slowly closed the door behind him.

"Okay, Devi. Please tell me why your wedding, scheduled for tomorrow, has been canceled," Elsy asked.

"My fiancé had a motorbike accident last night on his way back from a dinner party with his friends in town. He was pronounced dead at the scene. *Ammachi* (ma'am), my marital future is being wrecked by the malefic influence of *Mangal Dosha* (Mars defect). I'll never have a normal married life because of my unfortunate horoscope. Any man who dares to enter into a marital relationship with me will be in imminent danger of physical harm." Devi blurted out the gist of her uncontrollable grief.

The shock of Devi's tragic news made Sam frozen for a moment in time. He was startled with fear, and his heart pounded rapidly, skipping a beat; his palms became clammy, and his stomach twisted in knots. He stood there in front of the kitchen door for a moment, aimlessly to listen.

"But isn't it a baseless supposition that he met with his ill fate because of your horoscope?

He died because he got into a motorbike accident. It certainly wasn't your fault, dear," said Elsy, trying to calm Devi down.

"But, *Ammachi*, he got into the accident because of the malefic influence of my *Mangal Dosha*, as was foretold in my '*Jathakam*' (horoscope). We were warned about such effects by the *Jyolsyan* (astrologer) who prepared my *Jathakam*," replied Devi.

Sam's mouth was growing drier, and each breath stole what little moisture remained. He was thirsty for a drink of water, but his mother asked him to shut the kitchen door to safeguard Devi's privacy. As he exited the kitchen hallway, he overheard the rest of their conversation, which revealed the tragic news of Devi's fiancé's death. He heard his mother consoling Devi and her muffled sobs. Sam quietly left the hallway and returned to his room. A gut-wrenching sadness overtook him as he absorbed the emotional anguish and suffering of Devi—the one he still loved—yet he felt helpless as a young man.

Propping his pillow against the headboard of his bed, he lay down. As he closed his eyes, thoughts of Devi occupied his mind far more than concerns about his upcoming comprehensive exam. He hadn't seen her in several months because she and her family had been busy with wedding preparations. And she recently took a half-time job at the hospital as a physiotherapist assistant.

To understand the pain of Devi's tragic predicament and Sam's torment, one must grasp the complexities and nuances of their caste divide and the tangled web of the Malabar Coast's continuing saga of the caste system—deeply embedded in the ancient culture and age-old traditions of what was the Indian state of Kerala—and prevailing during the 1950s and '60s.

Devi, a short form of her full name Devika, was the daughter of Elsy's housemaid, Saraswathi. In Indian mythology, the name Devika means "goddess of beauty," symbolizing a divine woman who embodies purity, love, and grace. Devi truly represented these virtues; however, she bore the weight of 'untouchability' due to her birth to parents who were untouchable. This painful misconception marked her as inherently impure in the eyes of others.

Devi's mother's name, Saraswathi, was derived from the Hindu goddess of knowledge and the arts. True to her namesake, Devi's mother, Saraswathi, carried herself with wisdom and grace, bringing these qualities into Elsy's household as a housemaid.

Elsy, the wife of John Jacob and Sam's mother, developed severe arthritis in her early 40s, which left her unable to perform even the most basic household chores. Although an Untouchable (Dalit), Saraswathi, whom Elsy affectionately called Sarasu, was like any other member of society to Elsy and was, therefore, good enough for her household work. Although Brahmins generally didn't eat anything touched by Untouchables at the time, as a Christian, Elsy didn't have any problem with employing Sarasu to perform their household work. She was Elsy's most trusted domestic servant and essential help in the kitchen, regardless of her so-called untouchability.

Sarasu, along with her husband, Balan, and their daughter Devi, lived as vassals in a thatched hut built for them by Elsy and her husband, John Jacob, on their 10-acre coconut and sugarcane farm, which was located adjacent to their beautiful estate on the banks of the *Achan Kovil* River in *Mangalam* village. Despite their caste and societal disparities, this close living arrangement fostered a familial bond between the two families.

Affectionately known as Johnnie, John Jacob inherited the ten-acre verdant farmland from his father upon his passing. Johnnie was a professor at the Protestant Christian Theological Seminary in town and also a part-time farmer. He was independently wealthy, thanks to the income from selling coconuts and sugarcanes on his farm.

Sarasu's husband, Balan, was a full-time laborer employed by Johnnie for coconut farming. The terms of Balan's employment included daily wages, a rent-free stay in Johnnie's thatched hut on the farm as a vassal in exchange for his assistance with farming, and Sarasu's help with household chores at Johnnie's house. Balan was also allowed to cultivate tapioca (cassava) in the hut's backyard. His duties included trimming and fertilizing the coconut trees, climbing them to pick the hundreds of high-priced coconuts, and collecting and storing them in the shed each month for sale to contractors who came to buy them. This labor relationship, while providing a livelihood, also highlighted the power dynamics and labor exploitation prevalent in Kerala society.

Despite Johnnie's refusal to sell the coveted waterfront farmland, hospitality industry developers always sought it out. It lay adjacent to the boundary wall of his homestead on the West side, at the banks of the shimmering and mesmerizing *Achan Kovil* River. During the spring season (*Vasant Kalam*), his family's long-serving and diligent laborers farmed sugar cane crops for him, as had been historically done for his parents.

This beautiful farmland, which was a unique nature space enjoyed for generations by Johnnie, his father, grandfather, and now his son, Sam, was home to some 600 high-yielding tall coconut palms with spread-out leaves that crowned the farm, a wide variety of mango trees, and jackfruit trees which were planted by his father decades ago. This farmland's most beautiful and desirable feature was a lagoon, which the seasonally swelling *Achan Kovil* River naturally formed through eons of erosion from the monsoon seasons at the south side of the property's boundary, where the property met the river.

Since the property was situated at a 20-foot elevation above the river, when the river swelled from the heavy monsoon rains, the farmland and their estate property, where Johnnie and Elsy resided, never flooded. This was the most desirable feature of this piece of land, coveted by developers.

The lagoon had crystal-clear water in most seasons, except during the monsoon rains, and it trapped many fish, such as bass, snakeheads, bullheads, and silver catfish, when the river overflowed. It was also home to numerous bullfrogs. The most enchanting and therapeutic melodies of this crispy lagoon were the floating flowers of the incredibly colorful water lilies that rose from the mud at its heart, with perfection and beauty for the orchestration of the choral ensemble of the bullfrogs and the variegated butterflies to frolic in the sun, and the dwarfish guppies to hide from their predators.

When Johnnie's family went swimming, they entered the river through the mouth of the lagoon. On both sides of the lagoon at its mouth, where it opened to the river, sandy beach-like areas appeared every season due to the receding water. These areas were ideal for sunbathing, simply relaxing, or fishing for clean freshwater fish.

While Sam was growing up, he and his father, Johnnie, spent many hours together fishing snakeheads, catfish, and freshwater eels down the river. Sam loved swimming and frolicking in the lagoon, relaxing in its private sandy areas, fishing in the river, and simply lying on the sand, enjoying tender coconut juice, mangoes, and freshly cut sweet sugar cane from the farm.

Although Balan, Sarasu, and Devi were vassals, they were allowed to access the river through the mouth of the lagoon when they went swimming or bathing, but they were not welcome to swim in the lagoon itself. Johnnie had reserved this private area exclusively for his family to swim and fish.

When Johnnie's family spent leisurely days by the lagoon, they were always enchanted by its beauty and splendor. Balan and Sarasu joined them, serving freshly cut sugarcane, delicious mangoes picked fresh from the trees, and tender coconuts that only Balan knew how to choose.

Johnnie's family had created a rustic barbecue area by the lagoon, complete with earthen ovens under a thatched shed for cooking and broiling freshwater eels and catfish. These moments became the fondest and most cherished memories for Sam during his time with family, especially during the Onam harvest festival season. The lagoon's beauty and experiences, like catching adorable tropical guppies in the shallow waters with Devi, were cherished memories from their early childhood and pre-teen years.

As small children, they were untouched by the diabolical narratives of bigotry or the nuances of caste hatred and class disparity—those invisible yet rigid lines of caste and social separation that defined Sam as an upper-caste boy with privileges and Devi as an impoverished Untouchable (Dalit). Growing up together, they remained unaware of these differences until puberty and adolescence began to reshape their once-genderless interactions.

Whenever the parents were busy barbecuing fish with Sarasu's assistance, the two kids, Sam and Devi explored the lagoon. Even as a child, Devi had developed a profound intuition of "existential worthlessness" and "material deprivation" that was deeply ingrained in her mind. The profundity of this intuition was too complex for her to articulate but somehow manifested in her actions. She subconsciously seemed to have learned to please her master's son, Sam, by serving him in a manner of servitude.

She knew how to pick the sweetest and ripest sugar cane as a child, but when she brought it to Sam, peeled it, and served it to him, she did it to please him but never ate a piece herself. But it never occurred to her that, by her birth as an Untouchable lower-caste person, she was polluting Sam when playing with him as a child. To her, both Sam and Devi were like brother and sister.

Not surprisingly, Sam often gave her a piece of sugar cane or fruit and made her savor it before eating one himself, for some unknown categorical moral imperative built into his mind from early childhood, independent of his other social experiences. But Sam felt happy as a child, unaware of the age-old and well-orchestrated caste narratives.

Balan, Sarasu, and their daughter, Devi, belonged to one of the oldest and most impoverished Dalit castes on the Malabar Coast. Historically, regardless of their specific caste or tribal identity, all Untouchables were categorized as Dalits, standing outside the *Varna* system, which was a revered social order defined by a Brahmin-dominated hierarchical caste system.

In those days, the division of various castes was often based on whether a group was considered "polluting" or "non-polluting." Those castes considered non-polluting were labeled as the "upper castes." They comprised the Brahmins, Kshatriyas, and Vaishyas, three of the four *varnas* in the traditional Hindu social hierarchy. Shudras, although the fourth caste in the *varna* system, were considered "lower caste" and associated with menial labor, which led to perceptions of ritual impurity by orthodox standards.

Beyond the *varna* hierarchical system were those 'Untouchables' who were considered outside of it altogether. Those were people deemed so impure that even their touch or proximity was believed to cause pollution. Such individuals, who were labeled "Untouchables," were later labeled as Dalits (a term historically meant "the broken or oppressed people"). The euphemism "Dalit" evolved as part of a political and social movement aimed at asserting dignity and rights. However, critics of the caste system argued that changing terminology alone would not eliminate entrenched caste-based discrimination. In this sense, some see it as old prejudice in new packaging, an attempt to soften systemic inequality without dismantling its foundations.

The distinctions between the upper and lower castes were not based on race, skin color, or any genotypic or phenotypic features, as all castes shared a similar genotypic origin and skin color. Instead, they were defined by an irrational spiritual hierarchy within the Brahmin-dominated social order. According to the standards of this religious framework, Untouchables were regarded by the dominant upper castes as impure and polluting to them through contact or proximity. They were, therefore, required to live apart from each other.

Thus, as devised by upper caste people, the Dalits generally lived on the outskirts of the village, in colonies with other Untouchables, maintaining a safe distance from the higher castes in their daily lives. The upper caste liberally used sacred scriptures to justify this stratification, with the imprimatur of the existing religious establishments, just as the Christians used the Bible to justify slavery in the Americas and apartheid in South Africa.

In many regions of India, for centuries—dating back over 3000 years—a vast majority of the hundreds of millions of Untouchables lived under the yoke of social and economic bondage, effectively as enslaved people. They performed menial jobs for their brown-skinned masters within a world of "brown-skinned" people.

However, since the leftist communists came to power in Kerala in the 1950s, their radical political philosophy has changed the social status of the Untouchables to some degree. As a result of the Communist government's sway in Kerala, Dalits no longer had to observe the social rules requiring them to maintain a safe distance from the upper castes. The government relaxed the rules, allowing Dalits to work alongside the dominant castes in close quarters as laborers.

Still, they were expected to remain a subservient class within Kerala society—a reality acknowledged by Johnnie, a professor of Old and New Testament at the Theological Seminary. He argued that casteism in India was somewhat analogous to slavery in Biblical times and comparable to the enslavement of African people, who, according to specific Biblical interpretations, were believed to bear a curse. These interpretations, held by some modern-day Fundamentalist and Evangelical Christians, claim that the cursed descendants of Ham and his son Canaan were the ancestors of Africans—many of whom, centuries later, were enslaved in America. Johnnie believed that, much like the Africans who were supposedly enslaved due to a Biblical curse, the Untouchables were also scripturally set apart to be subservient, with the endorsement of religious texts.

This literal Biblical worldview of Sam's father, deeply rooted in the Pentateuch of the Old Testament, challenged Sam's reasoning as he became a rational, critical thinker and a specialized student of Evolutionary Biology. The justification of a pernicious social order embedded in scriptural narratives had been necessary for White slave traders and enslavers in America, as well as for the upper castes in India, to exploit slave labor for their comfort. However, the evils of such religious bigotry troubled Sam deeply, as they conflicted with his deeply ingrained moral imperatives, which were rooted in his Christian faith.

Furthermore, the American Jim Crow laws, which enforced racial segregation between Whites and African Americans in the Southern states during the late 19th and early 20th centuries, appeared to provide universal moral and scriptural justifications for Kerala Christian scholars and leaders. These justifications helped sustain the marginalization and segregation of Dalits. Specifically, Biblical events and verses commonly used by Christians to justify slavery in America—such as the Law of Moses and the Holiness Code in Leviticus, which allowed the purchase of non-Israelites as property—were cited as justifications for slavery. These scriptural interpretations served as unabashed endorsements of casteism, reinforcing the denial of a moral awakening to caste discrimination among Syrian Christians in Kerala, even for well-meaning, devout Christians like Sam's father, Johnnie.

The Christians in Kerala were known as 'Syrian Christians' (also known as *Nasranis*) due to their rich, ancient liturgical and apostolic connection to the Jerusalem Church, as well as their later ecclesiastical affiliation with the East Syriac Christian Church (Church of the East), which used the Syriac language in worship.

The original theological traditions of the Syrian Christians (*Nasranis*) trace back to the "Mother Church" in Jerusalem, led by James, the brother of Jesus. These traditions were established in India by St. Thomas the Apostle, who was believed to have arrived in Kerala in 52 AD. According to oral history, St. Thomas began evangelizing and converting local Brahmins, which led to the founding of several Christian communities in the region.

Due to this apostolic connection and the later development of East Syriac church traditions, the Christians of Kerala came to be known as *Nasranis*. The Syriac term *"Nasrani"* was derived from the word *"Nazarene,"* which originated from Nazareth. The Nazarenes were the followers of Jesus of Nazareth. In fact, the Syrian Christians do not have any ethnic or ancestral link to Syria apart from their theological and apostolic traditions.

Influenced by Kerala's centuries-old cultural traditions and social hierarchy, Syrian Christians who were primarily of Brahmin or upper caste ancestry in the region largely conformed to the prevailing caste system, likely due to the social and economic advantages it offered and to assert status, respectability, and legitimacy in a society predominantly made up of Hindus. As a result, they treated the Untouchables as impure and polluted, as other upper castes, strictly adhering to endogamous practices by avoiding marriage with lower castes. The dominant Syrian Christian denominations in Kerala even forbade their members from marrying Dalits, including those who had converted to Christianity.

Elsy, Johnnie, and Sam were Protestant Christians and members of the Syrian Christian Church of Malabar Coast (also known as the Church of Malabar Coast). This indigenous Protestant church was part of the One Holy, Catholic, and Apostolic Church. Known as the "Syrian Christians," this denomination was an offshoot of the ancient Saint Thomas Christian community, established by Saint Thomas, the Apostle of Christ, who arrived on the Malabar Coast in the first century.

According to legend, through divine intervention, Apostle Thomas founded seven Christian churches along the Malabar Coast, now known as modern-day Kerala. This historical conversion, supported by oral traditions and later archaeological findings, provided evidence of Apostle Thomas's influence in the region. While the Church of Malabar Coast preserved its orthodox teachings, it underwent schisms and reformation over the years, emerging with a liturgy similar to that of the Episcopal Church.

―――――――――

As expected, Sarasu's daughter, Devi, was not born under the care of a professional gynecologist in a well-equipped hospital. Instead, she came into the world in the most impoverished thatched hut of a poor Untouchable family, assisted by an elderly, untrained midwife who had experience delivering babies for Untouchables. Devi's identity as an Untouchable was preordained even before birth, and her first cry marked her arrival as, in the eyes of society, an impure and polluting human being. Yet this beautiful baby—whose essence was said to be predetermined before her existence—was an adorable bundle of joy, wrapped in her parents' love, just like any other child, regardless of caste or creed.

Her parents named this beautiful child Devika, who later became Devi. Long before attending to the needs of mother and child, Devi's family consulted a *Jyolsyan* (astrologer) to determine her Zodiac sign and the positions of the Sun, Moon, and planets at the time of her birth and develop a horoscope. The horoscope was essential for predicting future events and challenges in her life. Based on the infant's Zodiac sign, the *Jyolsyan*—a man who had failed eighth grade but possessed skills in astrology—wrote a *Jathakam* (horoscope) that foretold the ups and downs of Devi's life.

When the *Jyolsyan* analyzed the Natal Chart to write the *Jathakam*, Devi's parents were shocked to learn that Devi was born under the malefic influence of *Mangala* (Mars) according to Vedic astrology, which meant she had *"Mangala Dosha"* (Mars defect). This revelation darkened the joy surrounding her birth, as the position of Mars at that time indicated that Devi was a *Manglik*, possessing a high level of *Mangal Dosha*.

The *Jyolsyan* cautioned that if Devi married a non-*Manglik*, it could lead to disastrous consequences, including serious danger or even the early death of her spouse. Although this information was deeply unsettling for her parents, they chose to keep it from Devi until she reached her teenage years.

When Devi had her first menstrual period, Sarasu explained *Jathakam* to her. However, like many teenagers, Devi shrugged it off, not fully grasping the seriousness of her horoscope.

CHAPTER 2

W hen Sam returned to the kitchen after some rest and recovery from the shocking news of Devi's fiancé's death, his mother was reading the Bible at the dining table. Elsy read the Bible every late afternoon. By then, Devi had gone, and another maid, substituting for Sarasu, was preparing dinner in the kitchen. Sam sat beside his mother, unwittingly holding a glass of sweet lime juice on the rocks, prepared by the maid, along with some spiced-up trail mix.

After taking a couple of sips of his drink and waiting for a moment to savor his trail mix, Sam gently interrupted his mother and asked, "*Amma*, are you almost done with your reading?"

"Yes, son, I'm almost finished with my reading for today," she said, folding her well-worn Bible and the latest issue of her favorite magazine, *The Upper Room*. She turned to him, ready to listen.

Distraught yet with guarded enthusiasm, Sam inquired about Devi. He reined in his desperation and sadness, pretending not to know anything about Devi's current situation. Elsy paused momentarily and beckoned Sam into her bedroom to avoid discussing Devi in front of the other nosy maid working in the kitchen.

"As you know, Devi's wedding, which we planned to attend tomorrow, is now canceled. Her fiancé had a bachelor's dinner party with his friends last night. They insisted on taking him home afterward, but he refused, claiming he wasn't drunk. Tragically, he was riding his motorbike home quite intoxicated and crashed into a boundary wall while speeding, resulting in his instant death," Elsy explained in the privacy of her bedroom.

Sam had overheard Devi's conversation with his mother earlier that day when he walked into the kitchen and found them talking. Still, he acted shocked when he heard the tragic news of Devi's fiancé's death from his mother. He pretended not to know anything about Devi's current personal affairs and reflected on the complicated past and ongoing hardships she had endured.

"*Amma*, I'm shocked and deeply saddened. How is Devi? Sadly, I think her poverty, servitude, and the horror of her malefic *Jathakam* have made her life a living hell. Even as a child, she had to endure the ups and downs of a harsh life. Growing up with her during our pre-teen years gave me some of my fondest memories. It breaks my heart to hear her sobbing like a child. I'm so sorry for walking in on your private conversation," Sam said softly, his tone heavy with sorrow.

"That's okay, son! She is heartbroken that the dreams of her wedding, which would have been a sure ticket out of her poverty, are now quashed. But she will recover with time. Whenever Devi was distressed, she felt comfortable approaching me to confide in me. I tried my best to console her and convince her that he suffered an accident and was killed because he was drunk. I also told her to reason and disregard the superstitions and the irrational, baneful effects of her astrology as foretold in her *Jathakam*," said Elsy.

Sam shook his head and sighed. "I'm glad you comforted her and tried to reason with her," he said.

"But her experience proved otherwise, and now Devi seems all the more convinced of the harmful effects of her horoscope—especially because of the self-fulfilling, malefic spell she believes she just suffered through the tragic death of her fiancé. No matter how educated or rational we're, my intuition tells me that humans are more often driven by cultural traditions and emotions than by reason," Elsy added.

"This tragedy that struck her so suddenly may have reinforced her credulity and her eagerness to trust her horoscope unconditionally—and the falsehood written by some loser *Jyolsyan* in her *Jathakam*," said Sam, frustrated.

"As you probably heard, Devi's foiled marriage was arranged, although the boy studied with her in her pre-degree (two-year) program at college. She knew him only as a classmate, and they weren't in love! He was also a Dalit boy from her community, and because of his status as a minority, he got employment with the state government as an Excise Officer with a lucrative salary and got rich quickly from the kickbacks he received from the bootleggers," said Elsy.

Although Sam learned this information from a private conversation he had with Devi during their encounter at the bus depot many weeks ago, he stayed tight-lipped and pretended to be surprised to avoid raising his mother's suspicions.

"I see! So, even though they were classmates, they weren't in love," Sam wanted to confirm.

"Her Dalit classmate wanted to marry Devi once he achieved success because she was a stunningly beautiful and intelligent girl from his community. It's hard to deny that many would desire to marry her, given her remarkable looks and great intellect. If we disregard the superstitious social stigma attached to her unfortunate horoscope and her status as a Dalit of untouchable origin that preceded her very existence—stemming from the age-old cultural and religious traditions of the dominant castes—Devi emerges as a classy and exquisitely attractive woman, more so than many so-called privileged daughters of the upper castes," Elsy said.

"That's absolutely correct, *Amma*! I agree that Devi is a beautiful woman. Unfortunately, her caste status as a Dalit and her seemingly superstitious and bogus *Mangal Dosha*, along with the bad reputation stemming from her recent tragedy, will all drive other men in our village away from her. Defining her essence or worth by affixing such labels long before she even began to live her life renders her existence meaningless and leads us to question the validity of all values, deeming them baseless. This may ultimately push her to be pessimistic and nihilistic toward life itself," said Sam, with his face flushed.

"Devi told me that the boy directly went and asked for her hand in marriage through her parents. Her parents had forewarned him that she was a *Manglik*, born with a high *Mangal Dosha,* and the malefic curse that would result if she married a non-*Manglik* boy. As a radical leftist, he didn't care, pooh-poohed her horoscope, and told them he was an atheist and did not believe in such irrational and meaningless superstitions," said Elsy.

"Wow! I would do the same, even though I'm not an atheist. He seemed quite resolute, didn't he?" said Sam.

"Devi is heartbroken and filled with guilt now because, deep down, she believes this tragedy happened to her fiancé because of her *Mangal Dosha*. As you mentioned, this unfortunate event leaves her with a negative reputation in the community, warning potential suitors to stay away from her," added Elsy.

"How are Devi and her parents managing financially after the canceled wedding and related expenses?" asked Sam.

"They are doing okay, but they are grief-stricken. The boy had arranged everything and had already paid for the entire wedding. He didn't ask for any dowry or request any wedding expenses from her parents. Initially, Devi did not consent to the marriage proposal because she had heard from her friends that he drank a lot. However, her parents persuaded her, believing that he would change after their marriage," said Elsy.

"*Amma*, I would like to visit them if that's okay," said Sam.

"Well, that's not necessary, son. But if you happen to see her, you can always let her know your sympathy and concern," Elsy replied.

Elsy knew that, even though Devi was an untouchable Dalit girl, Sam liked her as his childhood friend, and their friendship was not colored or tainted by any social stigma. Sam's mother was reassured that Devi was almost two years older than Sam, so it was not customary and unlikely for Devi and Sam to develop romantic feelings for each other. Since Devi was older than him, she was like his older sister, whom he never had when they were growing up, and she became his protector when they played in the backyard or around the lagoon.

Because of the cultural traditions and practices of the region, and to a great extent, due to the religious traditions of the Syrian Christians, no boy rooted deeply in their spiritual values and traditions, under normal conditions, would desire a romantic relationship with someone older than him before marriage or even dare to marry a girl two years older, let alone an Untouchable *Manglik* girl with the specter of *Mangal Dosha (Mangala Dosha or Mangal Dosh)*.

Elsy and Johnnie believed that Sam was intuitively aware of the tricky situation they had found themselves in. At the same time, they recognized that Devi was the most enticing "forbidden fruit" in their metaphorical Garden of Eden. For Sam, eating this fruit metaphorically meant succumbing to temptation and disobeying both God and his cultural and religious traditions. But for Devi, engaging in a romantic affair with Sam meant eating the forbidden fruit in her own paradise—a choice that would lead to complete ruin. Still, Elsy pushed aside any concerns about Sam developing self-destructive romantic feelings for Devi, burying those thoughts in the darkest corners of her heart.

Sam was a voracious reader with a powerful memory. In addition to being a biology major, he was also a student of philosophy and religion. He was passionately interested in applying and validating the scientific facts he learned as an evolutionary biology student against the metaphysical aspects of his untenable Christian faith exclusively in light of his empirical understanding of this world. So, Johnnie and Elsy became increasingly concerned about their son's growing skepticism and irreligious worldview, which he had honed over the years. Ever since he completed his postgraduate studies and started working on his master's thesis research in Evolutionary Biology, he had become a Secular Humanist and took pride in being intellectually honest about it.

By the time Sam completed his undergraduate degree, he had read the Holy Bible several times. He became very familiar with the scriptural details and its many scholarly exegeses. As the son of a theological professor of the Old and New Testaments at the Christian seminary, Sam had easy access to theological and philosophical books that his father used at home. Naturally, he developed an interest in it. Consequently, it was Sam's favorite pastime to flip through the theological and philosophical books stacked up by his father in their small home library.

From Johnnie's conversations with Sam, he had noticed early on that Sam had an uncanny ability to comprehend and synthesize large volumes of philosophical and theological material, creating unique ideas, insights, and concepts. He drew upon such ideas, insights, and profound theological understanding—gathered from his readings in disciplines like theology and philosophy—in light of his breadth and depth of knowledge in Evolutionary Biology to synthesize a "phenomenal reality," apart from the apologetics of his father and the belief system of his faith community.

As a devout Christian, his father, Johnnie, on the other hand, was a firm believer in the inerrancy of scripture and truly believed that the Bible was the accurate word of God. There was no doubt that Johnnie was an apologist who defended the divinity and resurrection of Jesus

Christ. He also firmly believed that Jesus was the Messiah who was sent to redeem humanity from sin. However, as a professor of the Bible at the seminary, he was also aware, from his research and scholarship, that many of the books in the Bible were considered pseudepigrapha since their authors were unknown.

On the other hand, Sam held the view that not only some of the gospels and books of the Bible were pseudepigrapha, but they were also inconsistent, error-ridden due to translation and scribal mistakes, incoherent, and filled with falsities in the light of modern science.

Sam had many discussions with Johnnie about the authenticity and inerrancy of scripture, given the archaeological findings, its historicity, and modern scholarship. He also had many lengthy conversations with his father about the veracity of the scriptural stories in light of scholarly and modern-day archaeological findings. Although Johnnie acknowledged Sam's understanding and unique perspectives, he still defended sacred scripture and his Christian faith. At times, the intellectual dishonesty of his father greatly troubled Sam.

After successfully completing his comprehensive exams and earning his master's degree, Sam planned to seek a position as a Junior Lecturer at a college while also pursuing a doctoral degree to further his research in Evolutionary Biology. However, his father grew increasingly concerned. He feared that advanced education in Evolutionary Biology and Sam's commitment to the objective pursuit of truth might undermine his religious beliefs and deepen his skepticism. Johnnie was worried that the conflict between science and faith that Sam would face, as both a skeptic and a scientist, could ultimately shape his beliefs and lead him to become an agnostic.

When Sam pensively remained at the dining table, immersed in his thoughts, his mother stared at him. She knew that he was lost in some intellectual self-talk. So, she asked, "Son, how are you doing with your exam preparation?" She simply asked to shake him out of his thoughts, although she was fully confident that he was ahead of the game.

"I'm doing well and will be ready to take the exam next week," replied Sam confidently.

He hugged his mother and returned to his room, feeling a deep sense of sadness and unease about something within him regarding Devi. He was consumed by lingering, passionate thoughts of their secret romantic relationship, which at times felt one-sided because Devi was more aware of the dangers that such a forbidden love posed to her and her family. When she agreed to marry her classmate, who tragically lost his life in the motorbike accident the previous night, Sam was distraught and believed he had lost Devi forever.

After returning to his room, Sam sat at his desk and attempted to resume preparing for his exam. But Devi filled his mind, and his heart was filled with new hopes and strong determination. Sam slipped into a stream of consciousness about his failed romantic attempts to fall in love with Devi. But he was hurt that Devi, acting like an older sister to him, rejected all his overtures for fear of the dangers inherent in such an unseemly and forbidden relationship.

Sam's crush on Devi began when he was a teenager in the 10th grade, and Devi was in her 12th...

That afternoon, Sam was fishing at the river by the lagoon when Devi was taking a bath at the river a few yards away from him in a secluded area, but partially in his view from a distance. He noticed that she was an excellent swimmer, even against the strong water currents. Sam had never had a similar occasion to see and admire Devi's gorgeous looks and her slender, supple, sculpted, fully-developed body as a woman. She was well endowed with big breasts and a very sexy physique.

After her bath, when she walked by his side, he was so physically attracted to Devi's flawless and beautiful stature that he could not take his eyes off her. For the first time in her life, Devi felt shy in the presence of her childhood friend, who had an admiring gaze, so she quickly pulled her bath towel tightly over her bosom to cover herself entirely and walked past him quickly.

Suddenly, they both experienced an intense emotional high and an undeniable mutual attraction that drew them closer for the first time in their lives. The golden rays of the setting sun reflected off Devi, creating a stunning silhouette against the lagoon's green water. This moment evoked a sense of ethereal magic, reminding him of the promise of a new day. Neither of them had ever felt this kind of attraction before in their entire lives.

Sam fondly recalled another cherished moment like this from his past...

One day, he was walking around the field near Devi's home while the workers were harvesting sugar cane. In the distance, he could hear Devi singing a Christian hymn beautifully. She may have learned the song while assisting his mother with the Bible Study group's retreat a few weeks earlier. Sam was captivated by her mesmerizing, crisp voice. He was so emotionally moved by her singing that day that he yearned to hear more of her melodies.

When Sam saw her another day while walking through the sugarcane fields near her home, he called out to her,

"Devi, the other day, I was walking by your house, and I heard you singing a Christian hymn in the fields. You have such a melodious voice—you sang so beautifully, dear," Sam said, gazing at her.

"Sam! I don't sing that well," she replied modestly, then ran off.

As an Untouchable, she felt guilty even for singing, as though joy or expression through music were forbidden—some unwritten rule she dared not break. But the song lingered in Sam's ears, and he found himself wanting to hear her voice again and again.

He often walked around her thatched hut, pretending to tend to the crops for his father, all the while hoping to hear her sing again. Unfortunately, she had stopped singing.

One day, he bravely told his childhood friend that he wanted to hear her voice once more. That day, he encouraged her to walk with him to the lagoon, to sing and spend some time there, just like they did in their childhood. Devi felt uncertain about it, but he insisted, and she reluctantly agreed to go to the lagoon with him.

"Sam *Kunju*, our parents will get angry if they see us together here," said Devi. She called him Sam *Kunju* (baby) with the utmost respect and as a person living in servitude.

"Why? You're my older sister! Aren't you? Did we do anything wrong?" asked Sam.

"Yes, please remember that we're not small children anymore. We're teenagers growing up—a boy and a girl. Furthermore, I'm an Untouchable girl, while you belong to a higher caste: a Christian. I shouldn't be in your presence or talking to you in private. My life is destined for servitude to our master's son," said Devi.

Devi had matured beyond her years. At 17, she looked like a voluptuous young woman, while Sam was a nearly 16-year-old boy. Though they seemed unlikely playmates now, they often met at the lagoon.

One day, during one of their secret meetings, Devi's father, Balan, surprisingly interrupted them while he was fertilizing the coconut trees.

"Devi, what are you doing here with our master's son?" asked Balan.

Devi caught off guard, replied, "I lost my earrings at the riverbank while bathing. I came to look for them and found Sam here, so we were talking about it."

"Did you find them?" asked Balan.

"Yes, I have those now." She cleverly handled a suspicious situation and left.

Ever since Sam's brief romantic encounter with Devi in her bathing dress at the lagoon many moons ago, he had become eager to see her regularly after her baths. To catch a glimpse of her, Sam began arriving at the lagoon early, ahead of Devi's routine swim and bath in the river. He would hide quietly, ensuring she didn't notice him, and wait for her to return from her bath so he could speak to her on her way home. Sam cherished those moments of seeing Devi after she had finished swimming and bathing. He would stealthily make his way to the lagoon, making sure that Balan or anyone else was not around, and he would hide among the thickest sugar cane until she completed her bath.

Devi felt awkward about Sam's private meetings, not by the lagoon, but now around the dense area of the sugar cane crops, where others could not see them. They began sitting comfortably under a jackfruit tree and discussing school and other topics. Devi repeatedly told Sam that her little brother should not come there often to see her, fearing that her parents would find them there. But Sam's ready-made answer was always that they were not doing anything wrong other than talking. After every meeting, Sam wanted to make sure that Devi would come again the next day at the same time and told her he would be waiting for her.

Although Devi also loved seeing Sam there, she was very uncomfortable and guilty about their secretive meetings and his extreme excitement about seeing her daily. As an older girl than him in her sweet seventeen, she had this intuitive sense of vulnerability about being alone with someone of the opposite sex, no matter upper or lower caste. But she reassured herself that Sam was younger than her and was an upper caste boy, and any romantic relationship was beyond the pale, for which the consequences were losing her home and his family's entire livelihood.

Yes, if Sam's parents found out about their secretive meetings, Johnnie would throw her and her parents out of their beautiful paradise, which would end Devi's parents' income. As a teenager, Sam was too driven by his attraction to Devi and desire to see her often. While Devi enjoyed meeting him there and talking to him, it didn't sink in Devi that Sam was all out in love with her, the forbidden fruit in his beautiful world.

Understanding her vulnerability and wanting to protect themselves from the dangerous situation they were both facing, Devi decided to switch her bathing routine from the late afternoon to the early morning. Sam began to miss Devi desperately; he was utterly taken by the "love bug" that was Devi.

One day, in a fit of desperation, Sam showed up at her home, an unthinkable act for an upper-caste Christian boy to visit an Untouchable girl's residence in search of her. Sam knew very well that Devi's father was sorting coconuts for the contractors at the storage shed that Saturday. He knocked on Devi's front door, and Devi was shocked to see him standing there.

"Sam *Kunju*! You're here at my house? My parents are absent, and I'm unable to speak with you now. Please kindly leave. You shouldn't be coming here for *Bhagavan's* (God's) sake." She was startled, keeping her door partially closed while sticking her head out to tell him to leave.

"Devi, I haven't seen you in a few days. Where have you been?" Sam asked.

"You're an upper-caste Christian boy and shouldn't be coming to our poor shack looking for an Untouchable girl like me. Don't you know you're forbidden from seeking me out, and I'm forbidden from spending private time with you, Sam?" Devi blurted out with courage. Her words reverberated with fear.

"But you aren't an Untouchable Dalit or a low-caste person to me. You're my childhood friend; I just wanted to see you and catch up with you. We aren't doing anything wrong," Sam retorted.

"Yes, we were childhood friends, but we're grown-up teenagers now. Your parents will be upset if you come here to see me. They will throw my family out into the street, and we will lose our home and livelihoods. We'll end up roaming the streets, begging for food and shelter. We're impoverished Dalits. Please leave before they find out you came looking for me. If you like me, please let us live our lives peacefully as poor Untouchables." Devi poignantly told Sam.

"Okay, I'm sorry for causing you distress. I'll leave," said Sam.

He was profoundly disappointed and distressed, and for the first time, he cursed himself for being an upper caste boy. This was the first moment he became keenly aware of the social distinction between them—an upper-caste boy and an Untouchable girl. He struggled to accept that his childhood friend, whom he had come to love as a teenager, was forbidden to him. There was a looming danger over his innocent attraction to Devi and their close friendship.

He was agitated and spent much time either in his room or by the lagoon, hoping that Devi would come by so he could see her. He began to realize the ignominious consequences he and his parents would face and felt powerless as a teenager overflowing with love for Devi.

Yes, he was smitten by Devi, but the social disgrace of falling in love with an Untouchable in Kerala culture would lead to dangerous consequences for her family. Sam and his family would experience ignominy and ostracization from his faith community. Such a forbidden relationship would tarnish his father's reputation as a respected Christian theologian and leader, potentially leading to his excommunication from the Church he loved so much, as well as ostracism from his social circles.

Although Devi might have sensed the love in his eyes and actions, Sam never had a chance to overtly express his love in words. Aware of the consequences of a romantic relationship, Devi continued to pretend that she was unaware of his feelings and chose to ignore them. Sam, on the other hand, was too timid and afraid to tell her that he loved her and wanted to be with her forever.

Devi stopped accessing the river through the mouth of the lagoon; instead, she took the long route to get to the river for her bath.

As an impoverished Dalit in abject poverty, they did not have the luxury of a stand-up shower or modern bathroom facilities in their rustic thatched hut, which did not even have running water or a bathroom. They were fortunate to have a tube well with clear green water in front of their hut for sustenance. Her father had built a makeshift thatched toilet with a hole in the ground in their backyard, away from their dwelling, just for the family. They used the river for bathing and cleaning clothes, just like all other impoverished people who lived by the river in their village.

Sam saw Devi occasionally by the river, but she was very reserved yet warm and seemed to be building a boundary around her. She appeared friendly in their conversations but seemed to have grown cautious. Her eyes reflected sheer fear, though deep down, she desperately missed Sam's company.

She understood very well that she could not desire what she did not deserve and what was forbidden to her. From her short life, she had intuitively learned that wanting something forbidden was like holding onto a beautiful, fragrant fruit that was also toxic—it was appealing but dangerous. For Sam, Devi represented the lovely, ripe apple in his paradise that he was not allowed to enjoy. If Sam pursued her, the community would devastate Devi's Dalit family and her in the process. This would bring unbearable shame upon Sam and his family. However, Sam had not yet fully grasped the complexity of this reality.

Sam spent leisurely hours by the lagoon with his fishing rod and books when he attended his two-year pre-degree program in college. On weekends, he read philosophy and theology books by the lagoon and occasionally ran into Devi. At other times, he saw her from afar and hoped she would come his way.

Those days, Devi was like a mirage in the desert—breathtaking, mesmerizing, and beyond reach. When he tried to get closer to her, she disappeared. So, he often found her elusive and thought he was chasing something that existed only in his imagination. But her presence, even at a distance, no matter how elusive it was, still promised him comfort. Devi was a misbegotten moon, and he was too diffident to approach her.

Sam once again slipped into memory lane, vividly recalling other incidents from his teenage years, when Devi had completed her two-year college program and was seeking employment or considering pursuing further studies...

During the two years following Devi's graduation from her pre-degree program, she actively searched for a job. As a member of a backward caste, she was eligible for employment under the government's reserved quota for minorities. However, despite her efforts, she was unsuccessful. Sam often saw her at home while walking near the sugarcane fields, and they would occasionally engage in brief, casual conversations.

A couple of years after her graduation—and after repeated failed attempts to find a job—a new Physiotherapy Training School opened in town. The first program they offered was a two-year diploma course designed to train Physiotherapy Assistants, leading to certification upon successful completion of all requirements. The program was coordinated and taught by a Christian missionary physiotherapist from England, affiliated with the local Protestant Christian Hospital. This was the first program of its kind in the state, as physiotherapy was an emerging field within allied health. Hospitals had only recently begun to recognize the importance of physiotherapy, albeit in a limited capacity, for rehabilitation purposes.

Devi sought Elsy's advice regarding the job prospects after completing the physiotherapy program. After consulting her brother, who was both a physician and a hospital administrator, Elsy strongly recommended that Devi enroll in the training program as a pathway to stable employment.

Following Elsy's recommendation, Devi applied to the two-year Physiotherapy Assistant program. As a lower-caste student with excellent academic performance, she was immediately admitted and began the rigorous training.

She traveled to town every day to attend classes and clinical rotations. After two years of hard work, she successfully completed the program and received her diploma.

When a half-time Physiotherapy Assistant position opened at the Christian Hospital, Devi was selected for the role. Thanks to her strong academic record and her status as a member of a scheduled caste from a minority group, the government offered hiring incentives to her employer. And so Devi began her career as a physiotherapy assistant.

That same year, Sam entered his final year of undergraduate studies in Biology. He became absorbed in his classes and lab work, though he occasionally saw Devi at the bus depot or around town. At the same time, he also had several opportunities to meet Devi and speak with her privately by the river.

From those few interactions at the depot and by the river, he gradually came to accept a painful truth: a romantic relationship with Devi was impossible. Devi was acutely aware of the social, religious, and economic consequences of falling in love with someone from an upper caste like Sam. Despite his efforts to nurture their connection, every attempt he made ultimately failed.

Eventually, Devi became busy with her job, and Sam moved on to graduate school at the university in the capital city, Trivandrum, where he lived in a graduate dormitory. Occasionally, he saw her at the bus depot, waiting to catch a bus back to their village when he returned home during university breaks.

During one such break in his final year of graduate school, Devi told Sam that her parents had arranged her marriage to a well-placed classmate—someone she did not love. Sam was devastated. The news of her impending wedding shattered his dreams.

CHAPTER 3

L ife offers no syllabus or study guide. For Sam, its tests arrived like unannounced quizzes and the many academic examinations he had taken—pages filled with questions no amount of preparation could fully anticipate. He could prepare, yes, but only in the broadest sense. The real questions came cloaked in surprise, and the answers had to be discovered at the very moment of being tested.

Love was no different for Sam. Its trials and tribulations never announced themselves in advance. Stormy days descended without warning, and no guidebook could chart a course through them. He could not rehearse for heartbreak or miscommunication, for absence or doubt. He navigated by instinct, improvised at every turn, and held on—not because he was ready, but because something deeper compelled him to.

That late afternoon, after hearing the tragic news of Devi's fiancé's death from his mother, Sam struggled to focus on preparing for his master's comprehensive examination. Thoughts of Devi and of his own painful failures to nurture and sustain their relationship consumed him. He lay in bed, adrift in memory.

Instead of studying for his exam, he once again was uncontrollably lost in memories from a few years earlier, when Devi had completed college and was mostly at home searching for employment.

In those days, he would walk around the sugarcane fields intentionally, hoping to catch glimpses of Devi, who often sat on the mud floor of her hut's verandah, using a wooden stool as her makeshift desk to fill out applications and other correspondence related to her job search.

Whenever he walked around the farm under the pretext of checking on the crops, he would, driven by some inner persuasion, find himself near her home, subtly hoping to catch a glimpse of her. Since the wooden stool wasn't high enough, she would kneel and bend forward to write, her long, silky black hair cascading over the stool, her sari clinging to her sculpted body. Most often, he stood there silently, watching her from afar without drawing her attention. Her very presence seemed to comfort Sam.

If Sam greeted her or tried to engage in conversation, she remained guarded and seemingly petrified of being seen talking to him or spending time with him—because he was an upper-caste boy. He remembered those weekends during his first year of college when he longed for even the slightest interaction—a whisper, a glance—as he yearned for her grace, gently and subtly, without pushing her further away.

Sam was increasingly frustrated and growing intolerant of the meaningless traditions and social taboos that prevented him from interacting with Devi. Even carrying on a casual conversation with his childhood playmate was forbidden by certain social norms. Around that time, he vividly remembered an incident one afternoon when his mother was sitting at the dining table, reading her *Upper Room* devotional.

As usual, she was in her best mood after reading the Bible and the devotional. Sam took a deep breath, gathered his courage, and asked her, "*Amma*, why is it that upper-caste Christians can't fall in love with or marry Dalit girls or boys?"

This surprised his mother. "Why do you ask, son? I'm curious," she asked.

Sam hesitated before speaking. "I just don't understand why," he replied.

"Well, there are major cultural and religious differences between upper-caste Christians and Dalits of untouchable origin, who are Hindus.

First and foremost, our faith defines us as Syrian Christians. The first of the Ten Commandments we observe says, 'Thou shalt have no other gods before me.' As you know, we are monotheists, not monolatrous. The second commandment says,

'You shall not make idols.' These two commandments prohibit us from worshiping other gods or practicing idolatry. On the other hand, Hindus view the statues and images of gods as earthly representations of their deities. While that is acceptable for them, it is considered idolatry for Christians."

"Okay, so?" Sam impatiently interrupted.

"As Hindus, the Dalits—though from the untouchable caste—also practice idolatry. Historically, Dalits have been considered a polluted group, and their presence causes *Ayitham* or *Asudham* (impurity) for upper-caste Hindus. This belief, rooted in our collective cultural traditions, has also influenced us as Christians," Elsy explained.

"But aren't we Christians redeemed by the love of Jesus Christ?" asked Sam.

"As Syrian Christians, we have traditionally practiced endogamy for generations due to cultural customs, much like the upper-caste Hindus. We do not marry outside our Christian denomination. Even if someone were to marry a member of another Syrian Christian denomination, such as Catholic or Orthodox, the bride or groom must first be baptized in the Church of Malabar Coast, receive our religious rites, and formally join our Church before marriage. Under no circumstances do we marry outside our Christian faith—especially not into Hindu groups, including Dalits. If we did, we could be excommunicated from our Church and ostracized by our community," Elsy continued.

"That's ridiculous! If what you're saying is truly our traditional practice, then why do we have issues marrying people from other Christian denominations? Are we really the only righteous ones? It seems hypocritical and self-righteous for our Church to impose restrictions even on marrying someone from the Catholic or Orthodox Churches," Sam exclaimed.

"Son, let me finish answering your question. Our forefathers believed that the woman, or mother, is like the 'field' that receives the seed, and the man is the giver of the 'seed.' When the seed grows in the field, it determines the nature and quality of the offspring. According to our traditions, Dalits are considered a polluting caste, and that is why we do not marry among them," Elsy explained metaphorically, illustrating why their particular sect of Syrian Christians didn't marry Dalits.

Still confused, Sam asked, "So, what if a Dalit or untouchable converts to our Christian denomination? Can we then marry them?"

"No," Elsy replied. "Even if a Dalit converts, they are still a neophyte Christian. The 'seed' is still that of a polluted untouchable. Their religion may have changed, but not their caste—or their inherent nature."

"Well, what if it's the field, the woman, who is redeemed by the love of Christ and converts to our Christian denomination and proposes to marry a Syrian Christian boy with the 'right' Christian seed? Do we then enter into a marital relationship with that neophyte Christian?" Sam asked.

"No, the woman from a polluted caste would still corrupt the 'seed,' and the offspring would be tainted as well," Elsy responded.

Sam was stunned at the inherent bigotry of this practice. "Wow, that sounds incredibly convoluted, bigoted, and un-Christian, especially considering the teachings of Jesus, who fought for the poor and disenfranchised. What surprises me is that there are no evident genotypic or phenotypic differences between a brown Dalit and a brown Syrian Christian. In other words, there are no inherent racial or biological differences, except for the clever classification of a homogenous society into upper- and lower-caste and untouchable by the dominant caste, all for their own convenience and comfortable living conditions," exclaimed Sam.

Sam was seething with frustration, unable to contain his anger any longer. He could not accept the age-old bigotry and the arbitrary, inequitable classification of individuals even before they were born. To Sam, what his mother called their traditional belief was an "essentialist doctrine." This meant that, by belonging to a lower or Dalit caste, a person's worth was predetermined and deemed compromised without any evidence or scientific basis.

Sam could not accept the notion that, simply because Devi was born into a Dalit family of untouchable origin, her "essence was predetermined before her existence." Guided by his philosophical convictions, he rejected *essentialism* as a valid way of categorizing free-willed and intelligent human beings. Rooted in his deepening convictions of Jean-Paul Sartre's *existentialism*, Sam believed that for rational and intelligent individuals, "existence precedes essence" rather than "essence precedes existence."

"Why are you asking all this now, son? You're still in your senior year of college. You have a couple more years before you earn your master's degree and find a job. Only then should we talk about marriage. Customarily, that's when we arrange a marriage for you with a good Christian girl who shares our customs and traditions," said Elsy, her tone practical.

Suddenly, a thought crossed Elsy's mind like a flash of lightning in the dark. "Sam, are you in love with a Dalit girl in college?" she asked, the words unsettling her.

"No, *Amma*, I'm not in love with anyone in my class," Sam replied, though his heart felt heavy with the truth. He was deeply disappointed by his community's bigoted and inequitable cultural and religious beliefs. His mother was merely the messenger of a system of practices accepted by their moral community, of which he was still a member. The realization left Sam deeply disturbed.

It never occurred to Elsy, or perhaps she chose not to entertain the thought—that Sam might have fallen in love with Devi. But she trusted her instincts and beliefs, and the possibility never crossed her mind.

Sam remembered another unforgettable romantic pursuit of Devi from his past, one that left indelible and painful scars on his psyche. Despite being rushed to the local hospital emergency room, he nearly lost his life that day. His parents believed that without their fervent prayers at his hospital bedside and the intervention of skilled medical professionals, he wouldn't have survived.

That incident occurred during a summer recess. Sam's favorite summertime pastime was wandering through the sugarcane fields, treating himself to sweet stalks of sugarcane and ripe mangoes, then swimming in the lagoon.

One day, feeling playful and impulsive, he walked to Devi's house, fully aware that Devi's mother, Sarasu, was working at his home, and her father, Balan, was out running errands for Sam's father. From a distance, Sam spotted Devi sitting on a wooden stool, reading a magazine. He called out to her. She was delighted to see him but also visibly fearful. If any of the laborers saw them together, rumors would spread like wildfire, ruining her reputation.

"Devi, I'm so happy to see you. Why don't you come for a walk with me? I want to tell you something important and give you something," Sam said, trying to persuade her.

"Sam *Kunju*, I'm scared someone might see us. If our parents find out we're meeting in private, it'll cause a lot of mistrust and suspicion. Okay,

I'll come with you this time, but I need to take some dirty clothes for washing and bring a towel as well. I'll go to the river afterward to bathe and do laundry," she replied, her tone cautious and defensive.

"Let's go to our usual spot under the jackfruit tree. No one will see us there, and we can talk for a few minutes," Sam suggested.

When they reached the spot, Sam said, "I want to tell you something, but I'm scared... nervous... I don't know how to say it. Please come a little closer, Devi." Under the shimmering shade of the jackfruit tree, she looked breathtakingly beautiful to him.

"What is it, Sam *Kunju*?" Devi asked.

"Devi... I love you. And when I finish college, I want to... I want to..."

"Want to what, Sam *Kunju*?"

"I want to marry you," he finally confessed, a truth he had carried in his heart for years.

Devi was overjoyed. "I could never dream of someone like you marrying me... but are you out of your mind? You're almost two years younger than me, and you're an upper-caste Syrian Christian boy, our master's son! No boy around here marries a girl older than him. They all marry girls two to five years younger. And above all, I'm an Untouchable girl, cursed for life with a *Mangal Dosha*. If you marry me, you'll be in danger. If your parents find out you're in love with a poor, untouchable Dalit girl like me, they'll be furious and throw my family out of this farm. My parents would lose their only livelihood. We'd be homeless and penniless—do you want us begging in the streets?" Devi asked, her voice trembling.

"I know it sounds scary, but I'll beg my parents not to throw you out for something that's not your fault. Now, please tell me what it is that you fear about your *Mangal Dosha*, Devi." Sam asked.

"You see, according to my horoscope, I was born when *Mangal* (Mars) entered its eighth house. Therefore, I have *Mangala Dosha* or Mars Defect, which meant any man who marries me will have the malignant influence of *Mangal*," Devi explained.

Sam chuckled, unable to hold back. "You must be crazy to believe that, Devi. Mars is a huge, lifeless planet made of dirt and minerals, hundreds of millions of miles away. It doesn't live in a house or enter one—it's in constant orbit around the Sun. How could it possibly enter or leave a house? That's absurd. Mars is just a red rock, half the size of Earth. No human has even set foot on it. It doesn't have a mind or magical powers to dictate someone's fate," said Sam.

"But my *Jathakam* says that anyone who marries me, if they're not *Manglik*, will face danger, maybe even death, or suffer due to incompatibility," she replied.

"You're telling me the red planet, Mars, will put whoever marries you in danger? That's ridiculous. Mars has no consciousness, no intellect, and no divine powers. And I'm surprised you believe such things, especially being an intelligent, college-educated girl," Sam said.

After four years of studying biology and immersing himself in philosophy and theology, Sam had become a critical thinker. His scientific education and rational outlook allowed him to dismantle superstitions with ease.

"You don't understand, Sam. Misfortune has happened to others with the same *Jathakam*. My *Jyolsyan*, who wrote my horoscope, warned me. I'm under a malefic spell; being a *Manglik* is dangerous for the man who marries me," Devi said softly.

"What is a *Manglik*?" Sam asked.

"A person born with a *Mangal Dosha* is a *Manglik*," she explained.

"And how does your *Jyolsyan* know that? Is he God? Has he traveled to Mars to study its influence on you? There's no empirical or scientific basis for astrology, Devi," Sam countered.

Devi looked heartbreakingly innocent, being an oppressed village girl of untouchable origin. Yet, in that moment, she radiated a rustic, unspoiled beauty that overwhelmed Sam. Nervously, he rose from the fallen tree trunk on which he was seated and locked eyes with Devi. Hesitantly, he pulled her closer, embraced her tightly, and kissed her cheek passionately.

A warmth and sense of worth Devi had never known washed over her. She embraced it, embraced him, melting into the moment. But just as suddenly, she froze. Fear surged through her. Overwhelmed and trembling, she pulled away and hurried toward the river with her clothes, terrified by the consequences.

As Sam stood there, stunned by his impulsive action, he watched Devi walk away in fear. In the distance, he spotted her father, but the thick sugarcane leaves shielded them from Balan's view.

Gripped by guilt and fear, Sam ran nervously toward his home, feeling that what he had done was impermissible. As he dashed through the thick wild grass on his property, he accidentally stepped on a cold, slithering reptile that bit him on the calf. The intense pain made him realize he had been bitten by a venomous snake. The excruciating pain debilitated him momentarily, and panic set in. He knew that unless he was rushed to the hospital, he was going to die.

One of the laborers working in the fields heard Sam's cries for help and immediately rushed to carry him home. Another laborer, who arrived at the scene, identified the snake that had bitten Sam as a Russell's viper. He killed the viper and took it with him to show the doctors so they could identify its species and administer the appropriate antivenom. As a biology student who had studied indigenous snakes in his zoology classes, he knew that the Russell's viper was highly venomous and potentially deadly.

Sam was quickly transported to the Christian Hospital in town, with Elsy accompanying him and visibly upset. Johnnie, who was at work, was rushed to the hospital upon receiving the shocking news and was devastated. He stayed by Sam's side to offer comfort.

The specialist who identified the snake administered the appropriate antivenom. However, Sam developed an anaphylactic reaction to it. Less than an hour after the injection, he experienced life-threatening anaphylaxis, which caused severe hypotension, bronchospasm, and altered consciousness. Sadly, his condition worsened, and he was in grave danger of losing his life.

Johnnie and Elsy knelt before God at his bedside, praying desperately for mercy to save their only son from death. It took four days of intensive medical care and agonizing pain before Sam finally began to recover from the venom. Fortunately, he survived—but was not yet out of the woods.

Devi did not know what had happened to Sam until Sarasu came home from work at Elsy's and broke the news. Devi trembled upon hearing it, as if she had played a part in Sam getting bitten. She repeatedly asked her mother when and where it had happened. Sarasu, however, was beginning to grow impatient with her daughter's constant probing.

The puncture wound from the viper's bite, combined with the toxic venom that had damaged his muscles, caused severe swelling and necrosis in his calf. The doctors noted that the venom had already begun to damage muscle tissue by the time Sam reached the hospital. After four days in the Intensive Care Unit, he was discharged, though he required several more days of rest before fully recovering. Eventually, the wound healed, the swelling subsided, and Sam returned to normal health.

When Sam returned home from the hospital, Devi went with her mother to see him. However, due to customs and traditions regarding interactions between upper-caste individuals and Dalits of the opposite sex, she could only observe him from a distance. As a Dalit girl, she was not permitted to approach or sit beside him. Sam saw her eyes welling with tears as she tried to wipe them away with the sleeve of her sari.

Once Sam had recovered, Devi sought him out to share something with him. One afternoon, she went to bathe in the river but couldn't find him at the lagoon. Due to the caste, class, and religious differences that separated them, she could only speak to Sam in secret. As an untouchable Dalit girl, she was not allowed to be openly close to a Christian upper caste boy.

One weekend afternoon, she waited by the river, washing her clothes while keeping an eye out for Sam. As she was returning, she saw him sitting under a large mango tree by the lagoon, reading one of his favorite books.

When Devi passed by, Sam looked up and was overjoyed to see her. She stopped to speak with him, but feeling guilty and heartbroken, she held the tip of her bath towel over her face and began to sob softly.

"Sam *Kunju*, you were bitten by a venomous snake, and you nearly died because of my malefic *Mangal Dosha*. I'm so sorry for causing this injury to you! Based on what I've learned from my *Jyolsyan* and my *Jathakam*, I'm sure this happened because you got too close to me and expressed your desire to marry me. I love you, but I can't let you put your blessed life in danger by falling in love with a cursed, untouchable girl like me. What happened is proof that anyone who gets romantically involved with me will suffer grave danger," Devi exclaimed her naïve and misconstrued version of the ill effects of her *Mangal Dosha*.

"Listen, Devi, I respect your thoughts, but trust me, I wasn't bitten by a snake because of your horoscope written by some ignorant high school dropout. I stepped on the reptile and startled it; Mars certainly didn't see me, an insignificant speck 140 million miles away, stepping on the snake. Dead planets don't have telescopic eyes that can peer through such vast distances. I'm sorry, but whoever told you that nonsense was feeding you hogwash. Trust me, when I stepped on the snake, Mars didn't send any radio signals to its brain to bite me. Think about it, Mars doesn't have any transmitting system, and snakes don't have a brain capable of receiving radio signals from Mars. The viper bit me because I stepped on it and threatened it. Biting is a natural reflex for snakes when they feel hurt or endangered," Sam replied.

"Sam *Kunju*, how come you went through that thick grass in the field many times before but weren't bitten? Why was the snake waiting at that spot right after you kissed me and told me you wanted to marry me?" asked Devi.

"Please don't be silly, Devi. It was just a coincidence. The snake was probably hungry and chasing a rat. I was running home, and our paths crossed. Your *Mangal Dosha* had nothing to do with the snake bite or the danger to my life from developing an allergic reaction to the antivenom. Trust me, you are not at fault. I still love you with all my heart and will continue to love you, no matter what consequences arise from your so-called malefic Mars defect," Sam affirmed.

"Sam, may I ask you something?" Devi asked.

"Yes, Devi," he replied.

"Sam, aren't you a Christian? Do you believe the snake in the Garden of Eden just appeared and spoke to Eve, tempting her to eat the forbidden fruit? How did the snake appear there, looking for Eve to speak to her when Adam was away? Who directed the snake to entice Eve to eat the fruit, Sam *Kunju*? Do you think the snake incident in the Garden of Eden was also a superstition?" Devi asked gently, in a respectful voice.

Sam was taken aback by her reasoning and biblical knowledge. He remembered that Devi had attended Vacation Bible School (VBS) as a child. All the village children, regardless of caste or religion, had been invited to participate in VBS, which provided a fun and engaging experience for many kids during their summer break. He was surprised that Devi drew on her religious understanding to make a point.

"Yes, I was brought up as a Christian, but I've grown skeptical of old Christian mythologies that contradict the laws of nature. I don't have any scientific evidence to support the tale of a talking serpent. The story of the snake tempting Eve in the Garden of Eden is not meant to be taken literally. According to many Christian theologians, it's an allegory. Satan took the form of a serpent to deceive Eve. As a student of biological science, I don't see any scientific basis for believing in talking snakes or that Satan could take the form of a reptile to defy God and deceive humans. Have you ever come across a talking snake, dear? Snakes are just snakes. They live by the same natural laws we do. They're not guided or directed by supernatural beings. Their tiny brains can't receive signals from gods or forces beyond nature," Sam explained.

"My dearest Sam *Kunju*, I am terrified of our meaningless existence as Untouchables. From the moment I was born, society labeled me polluted and untouchable, condemning me to a life of servitude. My future seemed predetermined, and falling in love with you won't change that. A romance between us could endanger my family's livelihood and safety. Please don't come looking for me again. I can't bear the thought of you being in danger or fighting for your life once more. You nearly died already, and it seems you haven't learned your lesson. If you ask to meet me in private again, the consequences could be disastrous for both of us. I love you, but I'm forbidden from desiring or marrying you. I'm old enough to understand that marriage between us is both impermissible and impossible," Devi exclaimed.

"I don't believe your future or essence was predetermined by anyone or by fate. Your essence, future, and meaning will be created by you. I understand the societal constraints imposed on innocent people like you, but I truly believe that if we marry, together we can help change the meaning of your life," Sam said confidently.

"Sam *Kunju*, unfortunately, I was born a polluted Dalit. We are condemned to live separate lives, and I am destined to lead a life of servitude. That is our reality. Please don't let your parents throw me and my family out onto the street from the hut your father graciously allowed us to live in. You and I are irreparably forbidden from falling in love or marrying," Devi said, her voice heavy with emotion.

Devi hurriedly walked away before anyone noticed them, leaving Sam with a sobering sense of reality, a warning that if he persisted, the consequences for her would be dire.

When Sam completed his undergraduate degree in biology, he was admitted to a master's degree program in biology at Kerala State's flagship university in Trivandrum, located nearly a hundred miles from his home. While attending school there, he stayed in the graduate student hostel, returning home only during long weekends and breaks.

Although Sam and Devi's relationship had cooled, he still thought about her every day. Then, one day during the last semester of his master's program, while coming home for the Easter holidays, Sam happened to see Devi at the bus depot, waiting to return home from her job as a physiotherapy assistant at the hospital.

When they met, Devi told Sam that she had agreed to a marriage arranged by her parents. The groom was a classmate from her two-year college program. It was an arranged marriage and they were not lovers, but the boy belonged to their Dalit community. After completing two years of college with her, he continued his studies and earned his undergraduate degree. Upon graduation, he was hired by the state government as an Excise Officer through the job reservation system provided for the Scheduled Caste (lower caste) community.

Sam was devastated and distraught ever since. His heart was broken, and his dreams were shattered. He became increasingly despondent about losing Devi forever with no recourse. However, he hid his pain from his parents and others and kept it to himself. As a well-read young man with ambitious goals, he believed he couldn't allow despair to bring him down or overpower him. He was resolved not to give in to it.

Earlier that day, late in the afternoon, when his mother told him about the tragic motorbike accident that had killed Devi's fiancé as he was preparing for his master's comprehensive exam, Sam already knew about her arranged marriage and who she was going to marry. Still, he pretended not to know anything about the engagement or the man to avoid raising any suspicion with his mother.

Haunted by the memories of his failed love affair, Sam wandered endlessly and drifted into long hours of painful remembrance, steeped in sorrow. Suddenly, a wave of dehydration and hunger snapped him out of it, and he looked at his watch; it was 7:00 p.m., around dinnertime.

Although he had tried hard to prepare for his upcoming exam, he couldn't focus on his reading or stop thinking about the tragedy that had befallen Devi. He still loved her and would have continued the relationship if not for the cruel reality of the bigotry and injustice that had shattered his world. But pursuing what was forbidden had become far too dangerous for Devi.

Hearing a gentle knock at his door, Sam got out of his bed and opened it. It was his mother.

"*Amma*, I'm so famished. Do you have something good to eat?" Sam asked.

"Yes, dinner is ready, son! Please come downstairs and join us for dinner. Your *Appa* is waiting. Take a break from your exam prep and enjoy some of your favorite dishes. The maid made special chicken curry and pomfret fish fry, which you missed at the dorm. Dinner's getting cold, let's go," said Elsy.

CHAPTER 4

S am believed that harmful traditions and superstitions persisted across generations because the older generation instilled them into the minds of the young—especially children who were still unguarded, impressionable, and naturally inclined to obey their elders and uphold inherited beliefs. Conditioned early, they carried these ideas into adulthood, perpetuating them indefinitely.

But to dismantle such inherited illusions, only *a priori* reasoning could break their hold and free the human spirit from torment. Through intellect and education, Sam came to believe that only scientific learning and empirical inquiry, combined with economic well-being, could truly liberate exploited individuals like Devi and her parents, allowing them to move forward, unshackled from the weight of oppressive systems and pernicious superstitions.

Exactly one week after the tragic death of Devi's fiancé from a motorbike accident, Sam took his comprehensive examination administered by the State Board of Exams for all graduate Biological Sciences students who completed the academic requirements of their master's degree program.

Completing the exam marked the end of Sam's hectic two-year journey to earn a master's degree in biology. The exam itself was uneventful, and as a top-ranking student, Sam felt confident he would graduate with the highest honors when the results were released in six weeks.

During the six weeks before the exam results were posted, he had the opportunity to relax, reflect, and catch up on readings on topics that interested him personally. This was also the perfect time for him to apply for teaching positions for the upcoming academic year. To gather information about available teaching opportunities at colleges and universities across the country, he reached out to his network of family and friends.

So, he took some time off to unwind and rejuvenate before applying for jobs. For Sam, relaxation meant sitting under the soothing shade of the big mango tree by the lagoon, reading books without interruption in his favorite disciplines: philosophy, theology, and evolutionary biology.

When Devi's grief began to wane, and life started to return to normal after a few days of mourning and rest, Sam approached her several times at the town bus depot and spoke with her while they waited for the bus to take her home from work. Often, she was sullen and somewhat disoriented from the tragedy of her fiancé's death and the misfortune that had befallen her. Still, she seemed determined to move forward, making a living for herself and her parents through her part-time physiotherapy assistant job at the Christian hospital.

Now that Devi was a free woman again and no longer someone else's fiancé, Sam gradually began to rekindle his friendship with her, and romantic thoughts about her filled his heart. Rather than letting the world around him dictate his worldview and future, he wanted to control his own affairs, worldview, and the future he envisioned. He decided to pursue a future that was right for him and made sense in light of his sensory experiences, intuition, and empirically based scientific understanding, irrespective of his Christian beliefs and cultural traditions.

Sam found it hard to go along with Devi's superstitions and astrological woo-woo. He strongly regretted the repressive and caste-based cultural baggage surrounding her. Although such matters did not sway Sam's rational thinking, they impeded their progress in building a romantic relationship. While respecting their world of differences, he also wanted to find common grounds for rekindling his latent love for Devi and giving it another chance to blossom. So, he was cautious and tactful in approaching Devi and did not want to display any aggressive or expedient romantic overtures that might scare her off or turn her away from him.

When he occasionally saw Devi at the bus depot or when she was walking to her usual spot to wash clothes and take a bath at the river, he would nonchalantly greet her, ask how she was doing lately, and inquire about her work and living conditions with her parents. However, he avoided any romantic expressions, overtures, and conversations about the tragic death of her fiancé, giving her more time to heal.

He often lent a sympathetic ear to her concerns about her future and the challenges she faced as a physiotherapy assistant of untouchable origin. More frequently, he listened attentively whenever she expressed worries about her *Mangal Dosha*. He showed no judgment and lavishly expressed sympathy for her indignation at the bigoted treatment she received from some of her colleagues and community members.

Sam was curious and asked Devi how her colleagues discovered that she was a Dalit. Based on her appearance alone, she was a stunningly attractive woman who could easily be mistaken for an upper-caste Brahmin or a Syrian Christian. In Kerala, a person's sociocultural background held more value as an identity for building relationships than their looks did.

Devi got preferential treatment for employment as a half-time physiotherapist assistant because of her minority status as a Dalit under the employment reservation for the Backward Class. However, such personnel information was generally held confidential by the employer, and it took time for the information to trickle down through the grapevine to one's colleagues. So, it was not surprising that the first things your coworkers wanted to know about you in Kerala were your caste, religion, and marital and family status because those were the things they wanted to know first to build a trusting relationship with someone.

In many cases, when they found out that you belonged to a Dalit class in the olden days, many upper caste colleagues stayed clear of you, kept you at bay, and avoided close friendships.

This sort of isolation based on their caste status led to workplace hostility, marginalization, dehumanization, inequitable treatment, and extraordinary stress for Dalits. What was causing anxiety and moral indignation in Devi was this hostile treatment, which she was venting to Sam.

Whenever Devi saw him at the bus depot, she often spoke to Sam without reservation, as it was a public space. The depot was invariably busy with people going to work or returning home, making it a spot for accidental and unplanned meetings. So, Sam deliberately went to town in the late afternoon to keep in touch with Devi and run his errands. He arrived at the depot early to catch the same bus Devi took to return home in the evening. He ensured he arrived at the depot 15 minutes early, knowing that Devi usually arrived there early to catch the same bus from town.

Devi started earning a steady income as a result of her professional work as a half-time physiotherapy assistant and began to feel a sense of economic empowerment from the financial benefits of a decent job and the stability it offered. This economic independence gave her greater confidence in her new identity as a working woman and in her ability to shape her own destiny—at least to some extent—regardless of her caste status.

One late Friday afternoon, the regular bus scheduled to take passengers to their village broke down and was taken to the garage at the bus depot for repair. The station master announced the delay over the PA system, initially without a timeline, but it was later updated to an hour before departure.

Sam and Devi were both waiting for the same bus. Due to the long delay, Sam asked, "Devi, would you like to go to the café for tea and some snacks? We can sit down there comfortably and talk." She was neither bashful nor afraid to go with him.

"Sure, I'm tired of standing here. Besides, there's some privacy there, and we'll still be able to hear announcements about the bus. We can return when it's ready," said Devi with a smile.

She gladly joined him. In town, many passengers didn't recognize her as a Dalit or simply didn't care about her background, unlike in her village.

While they were having their tea and snacks, Sam asked when her birthday was. He discreetly noted that it was coming up in three weeks. Their eyes met, and their gazes locked as love passed silently between their souls. In that gaze, their love found its place, and the world faded away. Devi began to enjoy Sam's company, and their meetings at the busy depot no longer frightened her.

Two weeks before her Birthday, Sam went to town and bought a gold necklace for Devi. He saw her several more times while running errands and felt reassured by their growing friendship. He listened closely as Devi shared her thoughts and struggles. They had become confidants, sharing both their hardships and small joys.

When he saw her at the depot on the Thursday before her Birthday, he asked if she could meet him briefly by the lagoon that Saturday afternoon to discuss a teaching job he had applied for. Hesitant but unwittingly, she agreed.

"I hope you don't have any surprises for me, like the time you ended up in the hospital from a snakebite," Devi said jokingly.

"I promise nothing like that this time. But I do have something more serious to share," Sam replied.

As planned, Sam waited by the lagoon under a mango tree, reading. He had the necklace nicely wrapped and tucked into his pocket.

"Devi, I'm so happy to see you, dear! I know you're uncomfortable meeting me here in private, but I wanted to celebrate this special day with you. Thank you for coming," said Sam, his face lit with joy.

"I'd have preferred to meet at the depot. If someone sees us alone here, they might gossip. As you know, it could damage my reputation," Devi replied, scanning the area nervously.

"I understand. We'll be quick. My exam results are forthcoming, and I expect to receive my master's degree in biology soon. I've applied for a lecturer position at a private Christian college in Cochin, where my father's friend is the principal. If I get the job, I'll have to move," said Sam.

"I wish you the best, Sam. I hope you get it," said Devi.

"If I do, I won't see you as often. I'll miss you. What do you think— should I take the job?" Asked Sam.

"I'll miss you too, but maybe you can visit once a month. Who am I to advise you, Sam *Kunju*? I may have a job, but I'm still a Dalit. I'm not allowed to dream of loving someone like you. My parents might arrange another marriage soon. Beggars can't be choosers," said Devi.

"Devi, Happy Birthday! Here's a birthday greeting I wrote and a small gift for you," Sam said, handing them to her. She was stunned that he had remembered and even brought a handwritten note and gift, something she had never received before.

"Please read my birthday greetings aloud," Sam urged.

She opened it and began, "To the most beautiful woman, the one who means the world to me, and the love of my life… Happy Birthday, my love. I love you with all my heart, despite and beyond all the walls of caste, religion, and horoscope that you think separate us." Tears welled in her eyes.

"No one has ever given me a handwritten birthday greeting or gift. We don't celebrate birthdays—we're too poor to afford such things," said Devi.

"Now open the gift," Sam said.

She unwrapped it and found the gold necklace. She was overjoyed but also overwhelmed.

"Sam, this is too much. I'm afraid to accept it. If your parents found out, they'd be angry."

"Don't worry. My grandfather gave me a large sum for my academic achievements, and it's in my personal account. I used that money. This is my gift to you," Sam explained.

"Sam, over these past weeks, we've grown into each other in love, like an ivy entwining itself around a lone tree—entangled before we even realized it. I tried to guard myself, but I fell. I love you, too. But this love may ruin me. I'm terrified we're on a doomed voyage. As a Dalit, I'm forbidden from loving you," said Devi.

"I understand, dear. But it's too late—we're already deeply in love," said Sam.

"I shouldn't linger here. Thank you, my dearest friend," Devi said with a trembling voice, then quickly walked away, hiding the gift in her palms and the birthday greetings beneath her sari sleeve.

After a few days, Devi's work schedule changed to the morning shift, and her hours ended in the early afternoon rather than late in the day. So, she began arriving at the depot to catch the early afternoon bus to her village. Sam adjusted his schedule to run his errands earlier so he could meet her at the depot and take the afternoon bus with her. Most often, they took the later bus and spent time together, usually going to the café for tea before returning home on the usual late afternoon bus.

That afternoon, while they were having tea, Sam shared the exciting news. "Devi, I have some wonderful news to share. I've passed the comprehensive exam with the highest honors, ranking first in the entire state. I've also been conferred my master's degree in biology. Now, I feel confident about landing the teaching position in Cochin. I believe it will take a couple more months before the school officially hires someone."

"Dear, I'm so excited and happy for you. My heartfelt congratulations, Sam!" Devi said.

During their tea at the café, Sam summoned the courage to ask Devi why she was hesitant about sharing a life together in marriage:

"Devi, you told me you love me, but why are you so hesitant about marrying me if you do love me? Once I get the job, my parents will start looking for a girl to arrange a marriage for me. I want to inform them early and tell them you're the one I love and want to marry. I know they'll oppose it at first due to us being in two different castes and religions. They'll fight it with everything they've got. But I'm not going to give up—I'll marry you unless you don't want to marry me. I believe love must be the foundation for a marriage, and the choice of whom we marry should be ours alone," said Sam.

"Because of the malefic effects of my *Mangal Dosha*, you would be in danger of losing your life if you marry me—just like the man I unwillingly agreed to marry before. I love you with all my heart, and I don't want to ruin your life or bring physical danger to your blessed future because of my *Mangal Dosha* and my status as an untouchable. I also fear that my family will face violence and retribution if it becomes known that I fell in love with someone like you," Devi said.

"You are silly," Sam smiled softly. "I don't see you as an untouchable Dalit. I love you with all my heart, regardless of your caste or your *Mangal Dosha*. There's no tangible sign or mark of a Dalit on you. I see only a beautiful soul—inside and out. You're a human being who deserves dignity and respect. You're educated, you hold a decent job as a physiotherapy assistant, and you carry yourself with grace. That's the person I want to spend the rest of my life with. Your caste and *Mangal Dosha* mean nothing to me," said Sam.

"Oh, Sam Kunju, you carry a heart that beats with so much grace and the soul of a saint full of light," said Devi.

"Devi, will you allow me to talk through your *Mangal Dosha* with you, just for the sake of discussion, so that you can see how irrational this superstition really is?" Sam asked gently.

"Okay, Sam. Please go ahead," replied Devi.

"Devi, perception is the foundation of all our knowledge. We perceive and understand the world through our five senses—sight, sound, taste, smell, and touch. But none of these senses can predict the future. We need sensory data and empirical evidence for something to be considered true. That's why astrology isn't a science. So think about it: how could a high school dropout astrologer predict what will or won't happen in your marriage? There's no scientific proof that Mars being in the eighth house at the time of your birth has doomed your future. Mars doesn't influence human lives! Can anyone seriously forecast marital misfortune based on a chart derived from the position of a distant planet?" Sam reasoned.

"Okay, Sam, your explanations make sense to me. But still, horoscopes have been used for centuries. People from all backgrounds, regardless of caste or religion, still write *Jathakams*. And sometimes, those predictions come true," Devi replied.

"Yes, but people also occasionally get struck by lightning. Does that mean lightning is predictable or caused by fate? Can you provide any scientific evidence showing that Mars affects a person's marital life? Do you really believe a lifeless rock 140 million miles away has the power to dictate your destiny? And how does your *Jyolsyan* claim to know this?

Mars is not a god. It's not omnipotent. So we can safely conclude it doesn't influence human lives," Sam explained.

"But the truth is, people from both upper and lower castes still create *Jathakams* for their children every day here in Kerala," said Devi.

"The tradition of writing a *Jathakam*, a horoscope or birth chart, comes from ancient astrological practices, originating from Mesopotamia, passed down through many cultures and through generations over the millenniums. In our neck of the woods, these charts were usually written by an astrologer (*Jyolsyan*) shortly after a baby's birth to predict the future. The custom is deeply connected to celestial bodies, rooted in spiritual beliefs, and has long been a central part of our culture and traditions. Even today, it persists despite the growing understanding that it's based on superstition," said Sam.

"Okay, I catch your drift," said Devi.

"And our culture isn't alone in this. Europe, too, held onto superstitions for centuries. One of the most fascinating was the 'sin eater' tradition. This belief even survived the Great Awakening of the 19th century and continued into the early 20th century in parts of England, Scotland, and Wales. In the 'sin eater' tradition, when a loved one died, during the wake, the family would place a plate of salt and bread on the deceased's body." Sam continued…

"The belief was that the food on the plate would absorb the sins of the dead. A professional 'sin eater'—usually an impoverished old man or woman—would then eat the bread, symbolically consuming the sins and thereby purifying the departed soul for judgment. They were paid in food and beer. This was their livelihood. The profession of the 'sin eater' continued for generations, somewhat similar to the *Kaniyars* in our society, whose traditional trade was writing *Jathakams*," Sam concluded.

"Wow, that is an eye-opening parallel," said Devi.

"Although the 'sin-eater' superstition persisted until the early 20th century, intelligent people eventually realized that salt and bread could not absorb the sins of the departed souls—and that having a 'sin-eater' consume the bread could not absolve anyone's soul. So, how did it finally die out? This superstition likely vanished because rational people recognized the absurdity and meaninglessness of such a superstitious custom," Sam explained.

Sam was careful not to let the discussion turn into an argument. Instead, he drew parallels and asked questions gently, encouraging Devi to apply the critical thinking skills she had developed in college.

To respect her feelings, Sam asked, "Devi, what if we found out that I'm a *Manglik*, too, with the same *Mangal Dosha*?"

"My *Jyolsyan* told me that a *Manglik* can marry another *Manglik* to avoid the negative effects on their marriage and prevent physical harm to the spouse. Let's assume you aren't a *Manglik*. In that case, I'd have to marry a *Kumbha* (a clay pot), or a tree like a banana or a peepal (*bodhi*) tree, or even an animal before marrying you—to protect us from the consequences of the *Mangal Dosha*," said Devi.

"If you marry a clay pot or a tree or a cow first before marrying me, then who would be responsible for removing the malefic effects of your *Mangal Dosha*? Mars or God? Have you ever thought about how that actually works, Devi? In human terms, is Mars like a person sitting somewhere with a clipboard, monitoring who marries whom and then removing the curse? So, do you believe that Mars, a dead planet, is an omnipotent and omniscient deity capable of such complex decision-making?" asked Sam.

"I don't know whether Mars is a supernatural being like a god or goddess, but it may have some powers," said Devi.

"Listen, Devi, I would like to consult your *Jyolsyan* and have him create a *Jathakam* for me too. It's possible I was also born with *Mangal*

Dosha. I have the date and time of my birth, and your *Jyolsyan* has the tools to prepare a natal chart and to find out if I'm a *Manglik*," said Sam.

"That's a good idea, but I am worried what if you are not a *Manglik*," said Devi.

"Devi, could you please give me your *Jyolsyan's* name? If possible, I'd like to ask him to prepare a *Jathakam* predicting my future," said Sam.

"His name is Keshavan Kaniyar. He lives on the outskirts of our village," said Devi.

"Oh, I have heard a lot about him! He's the high school dropout, Keshavan, the grifter, who claims to possess powers to predict the future of newborns but can't seem to lift himself out of poverty. Sadly, he has neither the knowledge nor the extrasensory powers he claims, and yet he makes *Jathakams* for every newborn in the village. Tell me, if he really had the power to predict someone's future, why hasn't he used it to better his own life? Isn't he just another fraud, surviving on clever words and exploiting people's beliefs?" asked Sam.

Devi listened warmly and attentively to Sam's reasoning. She had always admired his intelligence and insights, which made her think deeply without ever feeling insulted or dismissed. Slowly, the superstitions and irrational assumptions tied to her *Jathakam* began to unravel in her mind.

The next day, Sam went to the bank, withdrew Rs. 5,000 in cash, and visited Keshavan. Everyone in the village knew Keshavan, who lived in a crumbling two-bedroom brick house he had inherited from his father, Nilakandan, in one of the town's poorest neighborhoods.

Upon arrival, Sam informed Keshavan that he had the birth date and time of a newborn recorded in both the English and Malayalam calendars and requested that a *Jathakam* be prepared immediately.

"What is your normal fee for preparing a *Jathakam*? I'd like you to create it right away," said Sam.

"It costs Rs. 500 to prepare a *Sampurna Jathakam* (full horoscope), but if you want it urgently, there's an extra fee of Rs. 200. So, the total is Rs. 700," said Keshavan.

"Can you do the *Jathakam* today itself? It's for me—I have my birth date and time written down. Can you prepare a *Sampurna Jathakam*? I'll double your fee and pay Rs. 1,000," said Sam.

"If it's for an adult, I'll need to study the astrological charts and calendars going back several decades to see whether it's even feasible to prepare one now. That will take time. And, of course, it will cost a lot more," said Keshavan.

"Listen, to be honest, I need a *Jathakam* that specifically states I have *Mangal Dosha*, and that I'm a *Manglik*. If you can customize it accordingly, I'll pay you a much higher fee. Can you do that for me?" asked Sam.

"Sir, people come here to write *Jathakams* for their newborns. However, they never dictate what to write in the horoscope, as a *Jathakam* is typically developed based on Vedic astrology after studying the natal chart for each newborn. If you're not born with *Mangal Dosha* based on your natal chart and the position of Mars, I can't simply create one with *Mangal Dosha* and state that you're a *Manglik*. *Mangal Dosha* is called a Mars defect, and it's based on the position of Mars at the time of your birth as per the natal chart," said Keshavan.

"What if I sweeten the deal and compensate you a lot more for your troubles?" asked Sam.

Sam recalled how the medieval Church sold "indulgences" to raise revenue for the Papal office. These indulgences were offered to believers as a means to reduce divine punishment and receive remission for their sins. If the Church was motivated by money to support such baseless practices, Sam believed money could similarly persuade a village astrologer to bend the rules of superstition.

He was confident that, with the power of cash, he could fuel Keshavan's greed and convince him to write the *Jathakam* exactly as he wanted. Sam knew astrology was another form of charlatanry used to exploit the gullible by pseudo-experts. It had likely survived so long because those profiting from it were eager to pass the craft down through generations. Though many made only a hand-to-mouth living, they clung to the trade. To maintain the illusion, they invoked distant, lifeless planets like Mars to mislead the credulous and uninformed.

Sam was convinced this charlatan would fall for cash. So, he pulled out a thick envelope containing a bundle of notes worth Rs. 5,000 and showed it to Keshavan.

"Look, this is just between you and me. I'll pay you Rs. 5,000, ten times your normal fee, for writing a *Jathakam* that specifically states I was born with *Mangal Dosha*, and I'm a *Manglik*. I need this, and I promise to keep it confidential. No one will know you customized it for me. Will you do it?" Sam asked.

"Sir, I'm curious about one thing. Why do you so desperately need such a sham *Jathakam* as an adult? Tell me so I can develop it appropriately," said Keshavan.

"Quite frankly, I'm in love with a *Manglik* and want to marry her. She won't marry me unless I show her a *Jathakam* that proves I was also born with *Mangal Dosha*. I'm from a Christian family, and my parents never had a *Jathakam* made for me. She's afraid that our marriage would endanger my life unless I'm also a *Manglik*," Sam explained.

Keshavan was ecstatic at the sight of the money, an amount he'd never received in a single payment. His jaw dropped, and his eyes widened at the bundle. He lived hand-to-mouth and knew this would clear his debts and provide a cushion. In his heart, he knew that a *Jathakam* was merely hit-or-miss, never affecting anyone's actual fate. No one had ever held him accountable for inaccuracies, malpractice, or any harm caused by his predictions. Most of what he wrote came from an old, tattered chart passed down by his father, Nilakandan Kaniyar, who had taught him how to use it to earn a living.

"Sir, since you're being so generous, I'll make an exception for you based on my understanding of the science of astrology. It's even possible that you were born with *Mangal Dosha*. But please promise me not to tell anyone I did this. If word spreads, I'll lose my credibility and my livelihood. If you come back tomorrow, I'll have it ready. I'll study the Vedic charts and customize the horoscope for you," said Keshavan.

"No, I need it today. If you can't do it, I'll go to another *Jyolsyan* in town who will. Also, please mention in the *Jathakam* that, as a *Manglik*, I can marry another *Manglik* without any ill effects. If you can do that, the money is yours," said Sam.

"Sir, I'm here to help you. No need to go elsewhere when I'm here. But I need three hours to study the charts and prepare the document. Yes, I'll write that Mars was in the eighth house at the time of your birth and that you were born with *Mangal Dosha*. I'll also add that you can marry another *Manglik* without negative consequences. And yes, I'll gladly accept the money now," said Keshavan.

Keshavan took the cash from Sam as gratefully as a starving man received food. He held the bundle to his eyes in reverence, kissed it, smiled with delight, and thanked both Sam and *Bhagwan* (God) loudly.

When Sam returned later that afternoon, the *Jathakam* was ready. Keshavan presented it ceremoniously, placing it on a silver plate lined with fresh tobacco leaves, a symbol of the auspiciousness of the moment.

Keshavan assured Sam that, according to his chart, he had indeed been born with *Mangal Dosha*. There had been no need to forge it since it was all "written in the stars."

Sam knew Keshavan was lying through his teeth. He glanced at the document to confirm that it stated exactly what he had requested earlier: that he was a *Manglik* by birth and could safely marry another *Manglik* without suffering any ill effects.

That was all Sam needed for now. He was pleased to have the forged document, both as a tool to convince Devi and as potential evidence to expose the long-standing charlatanry of horoscopy if ever necessary. But for now, he kept quiet.

All he wanted was to surprise Devi with the final *Jathakam*, stating that he, too, was a *Manglik* and to reassure her that their marriage would be safe from harm or destruction, which was her deepest fear.

CHAPTER 5

U pon earning his master's degree, Sam began to enjoy his well-deserved days of rest in quiet reading and reflection, allowing leisure to mend what time had frayed. As Devi gradually yielded to the mesmerizing power of his unconditional love, a faint light of hope began to shine through the darkest, deepest tunnel he had wandered for years. It was like the first rays of dawn slipping through the cracks of a passage that had never known morning. This was the dawn of hope his soul had yearned for all these years.

He thought no golden sword, no bullets, and no torture chamber could stop a man and woman from falling in love. The love that flickers within Homo sapiens is an evolutionary inheritance, bestowed upon them after millions of years of adaptation and natural selection, unfolding like the unseen, silent movements of a clock's hour hand.

The millions of neurons shaped over eons of evolution manifest this ethereal feeling through vast networks of neural connections. This love is the most powerful force that draws a man and a woman together, a force that defies guillotines, bullets, and torture chambers. Love, though not necessarily romantic love, is the very force that led Jesus willingly to the cross, arms outstretched, to show just how powerful that feeling truly is. It is etched so deeply into the soul of *Homo sapiens* that not even nuclear bombs or weapons of mass destruction can destroy it.

The passion that developed between the sexes and survived millions of years of natural selection despite adversity is powered by the same evolutionary drive that ensures survival. It is the most potent force of nature: the propagation of species. All living beings partake in this evolutionary dance to preserve and propagate their kind, moving in harmony with nature like a grand, invisible symphony. With this newfound enlightenment, Sam began to find moral clarity in his unrelenting pursuit of Devi.

He was convinced that no human-made construct, or no caste, creed, race, or religion, can suppress this elemental force. It will play out, undeterred by cultural traditions, social taboos, or religious strictures. Sam was delighted by this awakening, which brought new meaning and purpose to his life.

The next day, Sam went to town to mail a few more job applications and to run some errands. On his return trip, he saw Devi at the bus depot and asked if she could meet him at their private meeting place, under the jackfruit tree, on Saturday afternoon.

Their designated meeting area under the jackfruit tree was so private due to the thick sugar cane growth around it, and besides, the workers did not work in the fields on Saturdays. As usual, Devi was worried about their meeting, fearing that someone might see them and tell their parents about their clandestine meetings. However, Devi did not want to miss this opportunity to be alone with him, although she was slightly scared.

"Why are we meeting there in private, Sam? Are you going to pull another fast one on me like before?" Devi asked in a humorous tone.

"No, trust me, no more kisses in public; then I don't have to run scared, although I long for one from you. I'm an adult, and I'm my own man. I'd like to see you in private because I have something important to show you. It's a document you would be happy to see," said Sam.

On Saturday, Sam went to their private meeting place under the jackfruit tree and excitedly waited for Devi. A few minutes later, Devi arrived dressed in a beautiful sari and a matching blouse. She wore a radiant red dot (Bindi) on her forehead, and her silky black hair cascaded down her shoulders. A bunch of short ringlets of hair caressed her upper body with a tantalizing melody of its own in the soft autumn breeze.

Devi brought a mesmerizing gentle breeze of warmth and an alluring presence that evoked a palpable desire in him. As she stood by him, her beautiful body in brown skin shimmered in the sunlight, not like a Dalit or an upper caste Brahmin, but with the glimmering elegance, grace, and attractiveness of a woman who took away any man's breath at first glance. Sam could not take his eyes off her. He had grown deeply in love with her beauty, warmth, elegance, and profound grace.

"You look stunningly beautiful in that sari, Devi. I thank you for meeting with me here in private. I love you more than you can ever imagine! My words are too weak to describe the depth of my love, dear. May I hug you?" Asked Sam.

"Okay, quickly, please, before someone sees us hugging each other," said Devi.

Sam gave her a passionate hug, and they held each other tightly in an embrace, where they found the bliss of their lives and longed for it to last forever. But they came to their senses quickly and sat on the white sand under the shade of the jackfruit tree.

"Devi, I went to see your *Jyolsyan* Keshavan with my birth records, such as the date and time of birth and paid him to develop a *Jathakam* for me. Here is the '*Sampurna Jathakam*' he wrote. I want you to see and read it with your own eyes. This is written by the same person who wrote yours in the same handwriting and manner and with the same signature, as you can see. Please read it to your own heart's content," said Sam.

Sam excitedly handed his *Jathakam* to Devi. As she began to read his horoscope, written in Malayalam, her jaw dropped, and she looked flabbergasted. After a moment, her expression shifted to calm joy once she finished reading the summary of his horoscope. Then, she stood up excitedly, raising the *Jathakam* as if she had just won a Rs.10 million lottery, and performed a victory jig. Sam had never seen Devi in such a jubilant mood, genuinely celebrating the moment.

"Sam, your *Jathakam* states that you were also born with a *Mangal Dosha*, so you're a *Manglik*. And, the *Jyolsyan* Keshavan states that you can marry another *Manglik* without the ill effects of *Mangal Dosha*. Hooray! I'm so relieved and happy. When you told me you wanted to marry me, I was so petrified that you would also meet with the same fate as my previous fiancé, who died in a motorbike accident. Because you were bitten by a deadly, poisonous snake after our first romantic encounter, I thought it was a forewarning of a bad omen!" Devi said.

"Not a bad omen anymore. We both are *Manglik*s now, and we can marry each other," said Sam.

"I'm not concerned now after you rationally explained to me a few days ago why *Mangal Dosha* was a superstition. But even if it is true, now we have this horoscope to prove that you're a *Manglik*, and there wouldn't be any baneful effects if we enter a marital life. I'm now convinced that nothing would happen to you if we were to get married. That was my greatest fear, which was causing so much anxiety in me," said Devi in an unprecedentedly relaxed manner, with her face flickering with joy.

"It feels like this is the moment of truth and the beginning of a new day. I love you deeply from the bottom of my heart. I want to marry you and be with you until my last breath. No caste, Mars, class, or any imperfections can stop me from loving you. You have the most beautiful and tender heart, and I adore you for it. And beyond that, to me, you're the most beautiful woman I have ever seen," said Sam.

"I love you with all my heart; every beat of my heart sings a joyful song; and every glance of yours sets fire to a burning desire in me and arouses endless dreams within me. In your smile, I find a reassuring comfort; in your presence, I find a sacred space of warmth where our two hearts become one with endless possibilities," said Devi.

Sam was euphoric. He had long awaited this moment—her whole-hearted surrender to his unconditional love. Every note in the sweet melody of his love for Devi rang true, and the exhilarating rhythm of that love pulsed through his veins. He asked for one more hug, and they embraced, holding each other tightly for several minutes, regardless of who might be watching. They seemed ready to face the world as two adults in love, undeterred by the storms of their perilous journey.

Since Devi articulated her deep love for him, he asked her to promise that she would marry him no matter what. Sam asked her to place her hand in his hand and make a promise that no matter what adversities were ahead of them in their forbidden love, she would remain faithful to him in love and no caste or creed or *Mangal Dosha* or any other superstitions or religious conditions or circumstances would separate them from their love for each other.

She placed her hand in Sam's; her hands trembled in fear. "Sam," her whisper filled with emotions, "even if the world turns against us or even if thunder splits the sky or the earth crumbles beneath our feet, I will not let go of you. Not illness, not physical threats, not even death itself can erase what we carry between us. What I feel for you isn't bound by condition or circumstance." A rush of blood made her face and eyes red with quiet fire. Apparently, in that moment, they were no longer shielded by reason; they were only carried by the raw, undeniable gravity of love.

"I love you, and I promise the same. I want to marry you as soon as I land a teaching job. I'll tell my parents about our love and commitment to each other at an opportune time and will persuade them to consent to our marriage, regardless of the consequences. If they don't consent, I'll move out, and we'll have a civil marriage and lead our lives as husband and wife in another town," said Sam.

Sam took the *Jathakam*, folded it, and hid it in his trouser pocket. He said goodbye to Devi and left before someone found them there in their secret meeting place. Sam had never been this happy in his entire life, and an unsung song was sounding through his whole being, with a melody where all words and verses echoed "Devi." He could not think of anything but Devi, and she filled his heart with joy.

Devi was overjoyed with a new hope and confidence that found a new meaning and identity in her life. For Devi, life seemed worth living every second now, with Sam's love and constant presence providing warmth, assurance, grace, and trust. She decided not to tell her parents about this life-changing decision they both made and sealed in the cement of love for now.

———————————

Sam received an invitation for an interview for the Junior Lecturer position in biology at the Christian College operated by his Church. He was told that competition for the teaching job was steep, with applicants holding doctorates competing for the job, although a doctorate was not a requirement. However, Sam already had two publications in professional journals to his advantage and therefore stood a good chance of securing the job.

His father, Johnnie, advised him to prepare for the interview well in advance because his friend, who was the Principal of the College, had given him a heads-up that the interview committee vetted every candidate for the job before the interview and grilled them extensively during the interview to find a suitable candidate.

Sam's first job interview at the College went swimmingly well. The Committee selected three candidates for the final interview, which was scheduled with another committee comprised of the Chair of the College's governing board, the Principal, the Head of the Department, and the Chair of the First Interview Committee.

During Sam's final interview, one of the interview committee members leaned forward and said, "Our College's mission is to help young men and women grow not only academically but emotionally, spiritually, and intellectually, rooted in Christian values. Do you see yourself working toward that mission?"

Sam smiled and nodded in agreement. "I was raised by devout Christian parents with Christian values. On Sunday mornings, we attended Church and always prayed before dinner. At dinner, my father, who is a professor of theology and an ordained priest, spoke about grace and forgiveness, redemption, and loving our neighbor as thyself as Christ taught us," said Sam.

Sam paused for a moment and then added, "But I'm a biologist, a scientist who believes in science and scientific inquiry. Therefore, my intellectual side always seeks evidence and critically analyzes everything before accepting it. So, in that regard, I am a skeptic as is necessary for the pursuit of truth."

The committee members were taken aback by that statement. There was a total silence for a moment. So, he continued...

"I understand my role and the mission of the College to help young men and women grow intellectually rooted in Christian values. I am totally committed to that mission and to ethical principles and moral integrity. My personal beliefs or ideas will never cloud or influence the training of our students," Sam assured them.

After the final interview, Sam's candidacy rose to the top. He became the leading candidate for the job, but they had an unanswered question about his Christian faith. They were concerned whether he was an agnostic or atheist.

The Principal called his friend, Johnnie, in confidence about the unresolved issue with his son that they had discussed. The Principal indicated to Johnnie that Sam's answer to the faith question was quite personal and that they did not know what that meant. Sam's father asked the Principal to speak to his son again. Johnnie asked his friend whether this would be an issue if the final candidate for the job was a Hindu or a Muslim.

Since Sam's father was a professor of theology at the seminary and had also been an ordained minister, and since he had been raised in a Christian family with Christian values, the Principal did not have any further questions. He recommended to the Governing Council that Sam be hired as a Junior Lecturer in Biology.

After a few days, Sam received the official letter from the College confirming his appointment as a Junior Lecturer in Biology. The letter further advised him to report to work in two weeks.

Sam was thrilled to have been selected for the teaching job. He accepted the job offer promptly and confirmed that he would be present on the scheduled reporting date. The College was located in Cochin, the largest city in Kerala, and was 100 miles from his home. So, he needed to find a place to live, furnish it, and get the essential kitchen utensils, linens, and silverware to prepare some of his meals.

His parents were thrilled that he landed the job, especially since it was at a college operated by their Church. The following week, the entire family set out on a journey to Cochin to find an apartment for Sam to rent. After a couple of days of looking around, they found an apartment on the second floor of an apartment complex overlooking the Arabian Sea. The complex was situated in a safe neighborhood, about four miles from the college campus.

After considerable thinking, the family decided that it would be convenient for Sam to buy a motorbike to commute to the campus. This would avoid waiting for the bus and fighting for a seat in rather congested local buses during rush hours. By using a motorbike, he could travel to the campus as needed and would not be late for teaching his classes and lab.

So, they shopped around and bought a Royal Enfield motorbike for Sam's commute to the college campus. The motorbike was scheduled to be delivered to the dealer five days before his moving into the apartment.

A week before Sam's scheduled reporting date, the apartment became ready to be occupied, and the furniture they ordered was delivered and set up. Johnnie and Elsy accompanied Sam and relocated him to his new dwelling place, where he could start a whole new, independent life in a busy city.

As assured by the dealer, the motorbike arrived at the dealership five days before Sam occupied the apartment. Sam picked up the motorbike and processed its registration and other necessary paperwork.

Sam went to the College on the scheduled date and reported to work. He was given charge of the Biology Laboratory and assigned three classes per day to teach first-year undergraduate students in biology. Before long, and within a few weeks, Sam became a popular teacher who was well-liked by his students.

Sam came home every other week. On his way home, he met Devi at the bus depot, and they had tea at the café. Devi eagerly awaited Sam's arrival and counted the days and hours until she could see him. Sam would have liked to pick her up from the depot and have her ride on his bike, proudly holding on to him, but he was worried sick that any of his parish members who might see them would raise hell for him and his family over the nerve-racking act of taking a woman on his bike, especially one not married to him, let alone a Dalit woman.

When he came home that Saturday morning from Cochin after a couple of months, his mother started a conversation about arranging a marriage for him. "Son, how is independent living in a big city away from home? Do you feel lonesome?" Elsy asked.

"*Amma*, I am so busy I don't even have time to think about it or feel lonesome. I come home just to sleep. I eat lunch at the college cafeteria and have dinner at a restaurant in town on my way back to my apartment," said Sam.

"So, don't you want to share your life with someone when you get home from work? Now you have a good job and can support a family. It's time for you to think about marrying a Christian girl, sharing your life, and starting a family. What do you think?" Elsy asked.

"*Amma*, I'm not ready to talk about marriage right now. I will be, in a few months, when the College Governing Board renews my contract and promotes me to Lecturer and when I'm more settled in my job. So, can we revisit this conversation after a few months?" Sam gently asked his mother to defer the matter, hoping for a little more time for Devi to fully come on board with him.

"Okay. But don't delay this matter any further. I want to remind you that it's time to start a family," said Elsy.

A fortnight later, when he came home for the weekend, he met Devi for tea at the café. One of the members of his Church, who lived in his village and worked as a staff nurse at Devi's hospital, saw Sam having tea at the café with Devi. Sam and Devi were unaware that the nurse had seen them together.

During Sam's meeting at the café, Devi mentioned, "I am coming to Cochin next week. My hospital is sending me for a one-day training session at Riverside Hospital in Cochin. As recommended, I plan to take the early morning train that reaches Cochin at 9:00 a.m., just in time for the training that starts at 10:00 a.m. After the training, which is scheduled to last until 4:00 p.m., I will return home on the train that departs at 5:30 p.m., reaching home by 7:00 p.m."

"Okay. I'm excited. I can probably meet you at the train station," said Sam.

"My training ends at 4:00 p.m. I hope they let us leave a bit early because I'm not sure if I'll have enough time to take an autorickshaw to reach the train station in time to catch the 5:30 p.m. train, especially with rush-hour traffic. Since you live there, you're more familiar with the traffic patterns. What do you think?" asked Devi.

"Don't you worry, dear? I'll pick you up on my motorbike right after your training at the hospital and drop you at the Railway Station in time for the 5:30 p.m. train. As you probably know, our trains are more often late than early," said Sam.

"But what if someone sees us riding the motorbike together? Though unlikely," Devi asked.

"There's always a chance of that happening, but I plan to marry you anyway. If someone sees us, so be it. It's none of their business. Don't even worry about it," said Sam.

As planned, Devi went to her training in Cochin. When she came out of the hospital after training, Sam was waiting on his motorbike to pick her up. She was visibly animated and overjoyed to see him. Impulsively, she rushed to hug him, a rare and socially impermissible act of public affection between unmarried individuals. For a moment, she forgot the societal taboos when she saw the love of her life.

Sam was surprised by Devi's embrace. "Devi, I'm so happy to see you. How was the training? Please hop onto the backseat. It's rush hour, so it'll take some time to reach the station, but I'll get you there in time," he said.

Devi climbed onto the motorbike and said, "The training went well. Sam, I've never ridden a motorbike before. I'm a little scared."

"Hold on to me, dear. I'll be extra cautious, especially because I have the most beautiful and precious passenger behind me," said Sam.

When they arrived at the station, the same staff nurse who had seen them at the café noticed them getting off the bike. She was also in Cochin for a training session and had her autorickshaw driver take her to the far end of the station to avoid being seen, although she continued to watch them.

Sam accompanied Devi to the platform and waited with her for the 5:30 p.m. train. Trains often ran late, sometimes by 15 minutes, other times by an hour. The station master announced that the 5:30 p.m. train would be delayed by an hour.

Devi grew anxious, knowing her parents would be worried. Their home had no phone connection, and there was no way to contact them.

After an hour, the station master announced that the train had broken down at Trichur station and that there were no spare parts or engines to continue the service. The train was canceled. It was the last one to Devi's hometown that day.

Devi began to panic. She had nowhere to go in the city. She had never stayed alone at a hotel and lacked the funds to do so, and it was dangerous for a young Dalit woman to be in a hotel unaccompanied by a male relative.

Sam quickly took her to the private and government-run bus stations to explore other options. They learned there was a direct state-operated bus to her town, but it required an advance reservation. Moreover, that bus was fully booked.

It was too risky for her to travel that night using connecting buses. She'd likely end up stranded in an unfamiliar town with no help. Sam refused to let that happen.

He asked Devi if she was willing to stay the night in the guest bedroom of his apartment. She agreed, seeing no safer option. Her greater concern was not being able to inform her parents.

Sam suggested that they go to dinner at a nice restaurant. Afterward, she could call his mother, Elsy, from a public phone booth and ask her to inform Devi's parents about the situation.

After dinner, they stopped at a phone booth. Devi called Elsy and asked her to pass on a message to her parents that the train was canceled and she was staying overnight with a friend. Elsy kindly agreed to help.

They reached Sam's apartment around 9 p.m. The security guard noticed Sam arriving with a woman late at night. Seeing that Sam was unmarried, the guard appeared curious, as such situations often raised suspicions of violations under the Immoral Traffic Act of 1956.

If someone reported them, both would have to prove their age and intent or face questioning by the police under suspicion of engaging in immoral activity. The Act, while aimed at preventing trafficking, was sometimes misused by police to harass innocent couples.

Sam calmly told the guard that Devi was his cousin, and her train was canceled, so she was staying over. The guard, reassured by Sam's reputation as a professor at a respected Christian college, raised no issue.

Devi was relieved and felt safe. Sam prepared the guest bedroom for her, and she thanked him for his protection. They hoped to catch the early train the next morning.

Devi hadn't brought a change of clothes or essentials. Sam gave her one of his *lungis* (a sort of men's skirt wrapped around the loins) and a T-shirt to wear. She changed and returned from the restroom, looking graceful and unexpectedly alluring in her lungi.

Before bed, Devi asked for a cup of water to drink. Sam asked if he could hug her. He gave her a casual hug, but they were then drawn into a tight embrace, overwhelmed by passion. They kissed deeply before pulling back, realizing the intensity of their feelings.

"Oh dear! I'll cherish this kiss forever. Let's save the rest for our wedding night," said Sam.

"Sam, I've promised my mother I won't have sex before marriage. It's too risky for a Dalit girl to get pregnant out of wedlock. It could ruin not only my life but also my family's good standing and reputation. I made that promise, and we'll have to wait," said Devi.

In the morning, Devi was surprised to find Sam had made coffee and a light breakfast. She had never felt such deep care and respect from anyone. She felt reborn in joy and affection.

After breakfast, Sam took Devi to the railway station. The staff nurse, who had stayed at a hotel, returned to the railway station and had already boarded the train. She saw Sam and Devi together again and assumed Devi had spent the night with him.

Outraged, she felt morally compelled to report this to the Church Vicar so that Sam could be "counseled." She was appalled that Sam, the son of a renowned Christian scholar and priest, would consort with a Dalit woman from an untouchable caste.

When she went to Church on Sunday, she informed the Vicar about seeing Sam and Devi in the Café and then riding on the motorbike to the Cochin train station twice.

CHAPTER 6

S am decided not to go home that weekend. After a busy week
filled with preparing lectures, teaching, and leading laboratory
demonstrations to help students learn about scientific inquiry and
proper techniques for using lab equipment, he was exhausted. Because
he was so tired, he preferred not to wake up early on Saturday morning.
So, he didn't expect any visitors that weekend.

However, around 10:00 a.m., he heard a loud knock on his apartment
door. He got up hastily, changed out of his sleepwear, and combed his
hair. Then he heard several louder bangs on his door and grew annoyed.

When he opened the door, he was so pleasantly surprised to find his
parents, Johnnie and Elsy, at the door. They both looked pretty angry
and not very pleasant. His parents seldom got upset with him, as he was
always steadfast and a high-achieving son who never got into trouble
during his upbringing, even as a teenager. He had a strong hunch that
this may have something to do with his love affair with Devi.

"Please come in, *Amma* and *Appa*. I'm so excited to see you. Please
come in and sit down. I am surprised to see you this early. Is everything
okay? Would you like some coffee?" Sam asked.

They did not say a word, and his father was sullen. His mother was on
the verge of tears. Her eyes were tearing up. He always made his mother
proud and happy, and so he had never seen her this sad and embittered.
She began to cry, and Sam hugged her and held her in his arms.

"*Amma*, what happened? Please tell me," asked Sam.

"Son, you have never disheartened or disappointed us before, but what we heard from our Vicar a couple of days ago was an earful of extremely embarrassing details of your consort with the Dalit girl, Devi. Your father and I are publicly disgraced and feel like outcasts in our own Church with the canards that are going around. We have never faced such public humiliation and shame in our entire lives. We want to believe this is all a misunderstanding and will disappear. Son, please tell us what is going on," said Elsy.

He could see his father's eyes brimmed with tears. He was hurt, rattled, and trying very hard to control his anger and not to explode in fury. Johnnie knew that he was no longer facing Sam, the teenager, but a mature, moral, and responsible adult who was also a learned professor and a well-read and respected man.

"Sam, would you be honest with your mother and me? I have always trusted you, respected your viewpoints, and believed you're morally responsible. Let me ask you, son, did the Dalit girl, Devi, come to visit you and stay in your apartment one night? Did you or did you not take her on your bike to the railway station?" Asked Johnnie in a tone of deep concern.

Sam was taken aback and needed a few minutes to absorb the new reality of his parents discovering the truth about his love affair with Devi. He regained his composure after being shocked.

"Yes, she was here in my apartment for one night. But let me be brutally honest with you both, I have not slept with her. She slept in my guest bedroom. She came to Cochin for training at the local hospital and, yes, I picked her up from the hospital and gave her a ride to the railway station, but the train's departure was delayed, and then later it was canceled; she did not have a place to go, and she was terrified of being stranded in the big city." Sam paused to contain his nervousness before telling the rest of the story. He was anxious about how his parents would accept that he had allowed her to stay in his apartment instead of a hotel.

"So, why didn't you take her to a hotel for her stay overnight," exclaimed Johnnie.

"Since she didn't have a reservation to go to a hotel and it was not safe for a Dalit girl to check in to a hotel by herself in a busy city like Cochin, I asked her whether she would like to spend the night at my place. She and I thought that was the best option available at the time. As you may have heard, Dalit women are assaulted and raped often by upper caste thugs. Still, even the government officials and police acted in collusion with them when they were attacked or raped. So, it is dangerous for Dalit girls in a busy city like Cochin, where they get gang-raped. She was panicking, and I invited her to stay with me. And that was when she called you, *Amma*, to pass on the message to her parents that she was staying with a friend," said Sam.

Sam's parents sighed in relief that he hadn't slept with her and was trying to help a poor, stranded Dalit girl. But then Sam choked up for a moment with emotions, and his throat tightened. He became conscious that what he was going to tell them next would make them really sad and upset. After a long pause, Sam recollected his thoughts and shared his love affair with confidence.

"*Amma* and *Appa*, I want to share something very consequential to me, and that might disturb you." Sam stopped and took a deep breath. This is the first time in his life he has encountered his parents with such disturbing news, now that the cat is out of the bag.

Johnnie and Elsy were perplexed by Sam's upfront warning. They were looking at each other anxiously, anticipating the disturbing surprise that awaited them.

"I have initially planned to share this matter with you during my trip next week. I didn't want you to find that news from anyone other than me. I was toiling with this matter for a while and was deeply concerned about how you would take it. I want you both to know that I have been in love with Devi for a while. To be precise, I have been in love with her since my late teenage years. This was not her fault. As a teenager and as an adult, she tried her best to talk me out of it because of the 'forbidden' nature of such a love relationship. Still, I persisted because I loved her deeply, and I couldn't help myself until she finally yielded. I would like to marry her now that I can support a family," Sam nervously told his parents.

Johnnie and Elsy looked stunned and out of their element as if lightning had struck them. They exchanged glances filled with shock and shame. Words failed them as they tried to process their son's most humiliating failure. They were in anguish, feeling bitter, sad, and disgruntled. Elsy began to sob, and Johnnie held her tightly, trying to comfort her.

Sam had somewhat expected such an agonizing reaction from his parents. The blatant and widespread prejudice and disapproval toward a love relationship with an untouchable was the reason he had waited so long to tell them about his relationship with Devi. He had anticipated and feared such a reaction from his mother, especially after she once explained the public shame and disgrace they would have to endure if a Syrian Christian boy entered into a love affair or exogamous relationship with an untouchable girl.

He believed that being honest and open about his love for Devi and his desire to marry her might ease his parents' concerns. So, he went on to share his feelings with hope and sincerity.

"I'm sure you want me to marry someone I like and deeply love. I strongly believe that love should be the foundation of a marriage and the primary reason for marrying someone. So, for me, what matters most is marrying someone I like, know intimately, and love deeply. I love Devi with all my heart. She is a beautiful woman, inside and out, with great moral character. She isn't just any Dalit girl—she is intelligent, college-educated, and a working professional. If you love me, won't you give me the freedom to choose the one I want to marry?" asked Sam.

"Sam, you have deeply hurt us with your choice and terribly disappointed us beyond belief. We believed in you and thought you would use good judgment and make better choices," said Johnnie with teary eyes while Elsy continued to sob.

"I'm sorry that I hurt and disappointed you with my choice and that you heard about my relationship with Devi from a third party, the Vicar. Please understand that it wasn't your fault that I fell in love with Devi. You raised me to be an upright individual with strong morals and Christian values. You taught me the teachings of Jesus, such as loving your neighbor as yourself and caring for the poor, the marginalized, and the oppressed. Devi is a good woman with great integrity and, above all, excellent moral character." Sam paused for a moment to collect his thoughts, then continued.

"I believe that character and moral integrity are not traits exclusive to the upper castes. There is so much good in all human beings, regardless of whether they belong to an upper or lower caste, have more or fewer material possessions, hold high or low social status, or are Christian, Hindu, or Muslim," said Sam.

"How can you do this to us, son? You didn't think about us? You weren't considerate of our feelings. You knew such an affair would bring us public disgrace, ignominy, and shame," Elsy blurted out sobbingly.

Sam choked up for a moment in sheer agony at seeing his mother in distress and then said, "I'm sorry to make you sad, *Amma*! Devi is a very special and decent human being. However, untouchability was assigned to her the moment she was born, and it was not her fault. This designation was predetermined for her even before her existence or birth by the religious exploiters of caste. Labeling individuals as 'untouchable' is an egregious social injustice and a violation of basic human rights. To me, she is very much a 'touchable' person. The practice of marking humans as 'impure,' 'polluting,' and 'untouchable' by birth, without any fault of their own, is a well-orchestrated, diabolical scheme by privileged castes. They stratify and oppress these individuals with the distinct intention of exploiting them for bonded labor," exclaimed Sam.

"I don't have anything against Devi. Yes, I agree that she has good moral character. But she is of untouchable origin and not a suitable girl for you to marry because of her caste status and socioeconomic background," exclaimed Elsy.

"*Amma*, it is unjust and immoral to keep people oppressed and subjugated by labeling them as untouchable. This situation is comparable to the institution of American slavery. However, unlike American slavery, there are no distinct racial differences between upper caste individuals and those considered lower caste or Untouchables. In other words, there are no significant phenotypic or genotypic distinctions between a brown Syrian Christian like me and a brown so-called 'Untouchable' like Devi. This is a grave injustice. I believe there are no 'Untouchables' for the Creator; all of God's creations are 'touchable.' As we all believe, the Creator delights in His creations since He continues to make them in His image!" Sam added.

Sam said all these profound truths to disarm his parents, who were profoundly hurt and rattled by his love affair with Devi. His parents were highly invested in their faith community. They lived their lives according to all its cultural and religious norms. The community and the Church respected them for their steadfastness, loyalty to their community, and adherence to its traditions and moral standards.

What their son said was rational and meaningful, and it made sense to Johnnie and Elsie. However, they lived in a community of believers where the Church played a central role in dictating the moral system and defining socially acceptable behavior. As a faith-based community, they were bound together by shared practices, rituals, and a worldview passed down from one generation to the next. Miscreants and iconoclasts were often rejected and ostracized.

Johnnie got up angrily, faced the window, and hid his somber face from his son. His eyes were filled with tears. His mother could not believe what she just heard, and so she sobbed, covering her face with the sleeves of her sari.

They were devastated, and their world was falling apart with their only son, whom they loved with all their heart, raised with enormous pride and joy and great expectations, and who they thought would do the right things, proposing to marry a Dalit girl from an untouchable caste.

Johnnie was an ordained priest and a professor at their Theological Seminary, where he trained students to become priests. He was respected statewide as a renowned biblical scholar and a de facto church historian.

Johnnie stood there gazing at the distant horizon to find an escape from the specter of this horrible, forbidden love that his beloved son was trapped in. He was aware of the reproach and ignominy they were going to face in Church and in his community if they allowed his son to marry a Hindu girl from an untouchable caste.

Their Syrian Christian tribe practiced endogamy and avoided marrying Hindus who worshiped God through images or idols (*murtis*) because idolatry violated the first and second commandments of the Ten Commandments, which they strictly observed. To make matters worse, Devi was from an "untouchable" and "polluted" Hindu caste, which caused them to worry about their progeny, knowing that their children would be born with the stigma of untouchability. Johnnie and Elsy knew their grandchildren would face no social acceptance if they married.

For the first time, Johnnie and Elsy find themselves trapped in a dilemma with no clear way out. They feared they were on a perilous collision course with both their beloved son and their faith community, caught in conflict with what was considered morally acceptable by the standards of their society.

After reining in on his emotions, Johnnie turned around and looked at Sam and said, "Thank you for your long-winded explanations. We gave birth to you; we raised and educated you; we loved you unconditionally and sustained you. So, please tell us what our role is in your life and in your marriage. Why did you get romantically involved with a girl who would cause us public humiliation and shame? We thought you knew how to make better decisions."

"*Amma* and *Appa*, I am sorry! Please know that I love you with all my heart, and I thank you for raising me to be a morally upright person with good Christian values. All I want to do is marry someone I love dearly, regardless of caste and socioeconomic status. So, your role is to bless and support us, conduct our marriage, and wish us well for an abundant life," said Sam.

"Why should we have any part in it after you have made a unilateral decision to marry her," said Elsy.

"May I ask you, if I marry Devi, how can that cause us public disgrace and shame? I'm not ashamed to marry her, and I don't recognize untouchability. She is a morally upright, intelligent, and college-educated professional girl. Marginalizing and despising her for her untouchability is immoral and so unchristian? Truly, she has no untouchability at all. Sadly, those who continue to categorize her as untouchable all have 'polluted' minds," exclaimed Sam.

"We are not questioning her moral character or intelligence," said Elsy with a feeling of guilt as Sam's rationalizations began to sink in.

"What does the Bible verse Matthew 25:40 mean to us as Christians?

It says, 'What you did for the least among us, you did it for me.' The Untouchables are the most impoverished, vulnerable, and marginalized in our society. They are the 'least among us.' When we love them as our brothers and sisters, we are serving our God," Sam paused and collected his thoughts.

"I did not do anything morally or ethically wrong. I did not have premarital sex with Devi. Yes, I fell in love with a beautiful, morally upright woman who is considered one of the 'least among us.' Devi is a far better person than most of the upper-caste hypocrites who label her as 'impure' and 'polluting.' So if she is the 'least among us,' then by proposing to marry her—and by marrying her—I am serving Him," exclaimed Sam indignantly.

Johnnie and Elsy seemed to have settled down after Sam's persuasive arguments like a skilled and articulate lawyer. His parents began to calm down a bit after they were made aware of society's "moral blindness"towards untouchability.

"I don't think the church will consecrate your wedding with a girl of 'impure' origin like a Dalit woman from an Untouchable caste. Even if she converts herself to our Christian faith, our Church won't conduct the wedding because we don't get into marriage relationships with Untouchable Christian converts. You have to arrange a civil wedding, and you are your own person for that," said Johnnie.

"I don't care, and I am not concerned about a church that colludes with untouchability." He paused and wanted to draw parallels from biblical history to convince his parents that the Church had been wrong many times in its stance in the past. So, he proceeded.

"The holy Church had been dead wrong many times over the centuries. We will readily choose a civil marriage simply because I despise their hypocrisy and the religious bigotry they practice! Remember *Appa*, the same Church, during Apostle Paul's time, didn't allow gentiles in the Church because they thought allowing the uncircumcised gentiles into the Christian church would make the Jewish Christians ceremoniously impure by their presence." He hesitated for a moment before citing more evidence of why the Church had been wrong many times and to convince them that the Church was not going to be right this time either.

"The same holy Church led by Pope Martin V ordered to dig out the mortal remains of John Wycliffe and put his remains on fire for translating the Bible into English; Cardinal Wolsey of the same holy Church was in cahoots with King Henry VIII to strangle and burn the highly respected theological scholar and linguist Rev. William Tyndale to death at stake also for translating the Bible into English; the same holy Church was supportive of executing believers for carrying unlicensed Bibles and for heresy and blasphemy; and, the same Church sold 'indulgences' for raising revenue for the papal office," said Sam.

"So, what? Why does Church's wrongdoing matter to you?" Elsy asked.

"Their prejudices against human beings of different ideas and opinions and their historical stance on slavery, gender issues, and 'untouchability' to me are so 'bigoted.' So, I believe the Church, by doing such unchristian things, is practicing unadulterated bigotry!" Sam exclaimed.

"You're correct, son! However, the Church has its canons to regulate conduct, belief, and practice, which are essential for governance. At any point in its history, the believers had to live by those rules and regulations for receiving sacraments," said Johnnie.

"*Appa*, you are a man I admire for standing up for what is right, especially for social justice. Please kindly stand with me, your only son, and don't be swayed by the bigotry of the Church and the upper caste," said Sam.

"Sam, the Church doesn't allow its members to marry Hindu women of Untouchable caste because they are of 'polluted' origin and, as Hindus, they worship God through idols. Worshipping God through images or *murtis* (idols) violates the first and second commandments of the Ten Commandments we adhere to," said Johnnie.

"But I don't have any problem with my wife worshipping the God or gods of her choice. No one has the exclusive understanding of which god is the right God," said Sam.

"Apostle Paul clearly said in 2 Corinthians 6:14, 'Do not be yoked together with unbelievers.' Our shared belief system is the foundation of our Christian marriages. The shared belief in Jesus Christ by a couple brings the 'oneness' necessary for a successful marriage and raising a family. You are proposing to marry a woman of a different culture who is non-Christian and who doesn't share your belief system and values. How will you raise your children? In what faith?" Johnnie asked.

"I'm sorry, I don't think I need a church to raise my children. There is so much 'good' in this world, with or without man-made religions and gods. I will raise them as decent human beings with morals and good values. I don't need a church to raise my children to be good people, especially when the Church is miserably failing in that very realm. In raising my children, one of my role models will be Jesus Christ, not just the religious figure, but also the philosopher and social revolutionary who taught us to 'love one another,' to 'love our neighbors,' and to care for 'the least among us,'" said Sam.

"I'm not disagreeing with you. You can raise your children to be decent human beings with or without the Church. But to be a Christian member of a Church, you have to respect their canons," said Johnnie.

"*Appa*, a Church that supports bigotry and gender bias, as seen in its deliberate exclusion of women from pastoral ministry and ecclesiastical hierarchy, is no longer relevant to me. This is also the same Church that doesn't accept converted Dalit Christians into its fold," said Sam.

"Son, let me repeat it. Devi believes in a different God or gods and worships through idols. That means she practices idolatry. You were raised as a Christian, and the Church will not consecrate your wedding," said Johnnie.

"*Appa*, may I ask you a question? What if Devi's God (or gods) is the true God and our God is the wrong God? If her God is the right God, and if we don't believe in that God, then you and I will go to hell. Who knows the truth?" Sam asked.

"Son, Jesus said, 'I am the way, the truth and the life. No one comes to my father except through me.' That is indeed the truth," said Johnnie.

"How do we know that is the truth, *Appa*? The truth to us is the 'phenomenal reality' we perceive through our sensory experiences. As humans, we don't even understand the 'noumenal reality,' which is a reality that exists independently of our sensory perception. We don't even know that Jesus is the way, truth, and life. That is a belief, and belief is a conviction or acceptance of something without proof. It is not something we can perceive through our sensory experiences and know with certainty," said Sam.

"Son, as a Christian, I believe Jesus is the way, the truth, and the life. I want you to give your proposal to marry Devi some serious thought before going through with it. The Church may excommunicate you, and possibly your mother and me as well, and we could face public disgrace. You might even lose your job at the college for what may be seen as a rebellious act: marrying an Untouchable," said Johnnie.

"If I lose my job for standing up for what is right, so be it. I am sorry!" Sam said.

"Although your mother and I are terribly disappointed and extremely sad that you made this shocking choice, I fully agree with your points about the social injustice of treating innocent humans as 'Untouchables.' I agree with you that there are no 'Untouchables' in the eyes of God, and we are all His creations, including the Untouchables," Johnnie continued.

A moral awakening overwhelmed Johnnie. As a loving father and a teacher, he could fully understand Sam's assertions and the injustice done to a large group of people due to the 'moral blindness' of society to such injustices.

"Thank you for concurring with me on that important issue of social justice," said Sam.

"As you probably are aware, when Dalit girls of untouchable origin fall in love with upper caste boys and marry them, that is sometimes followed by serious aggression and violence from the fringe elements in our community. Dalit women, particularly, are attacked and gang-raped with impunity, as you said earlier, as revenge for falling in love with upper caste boys, and their homes are sometimes set on fire with impunity to subvert and put them in their place," said Johnnie.

"Yes, *Appa*. You are right indeed," said Sam.

"Invariably, the police collude with the upper caste, and, in many cases, nothing happens to the criminals. I hope when our community finds out that you are in love with Devi, they will not show aggression against this poor family who depends on us for sustenance and burn their house down," said Johnnie.

Elsy regained her composure and got up and stepped up to Sam and said poignantly, "I'm your mother who carried you in my womb for 10 months and gave birth to you. I'll not allow you to unilaterally make that decision to marry an Untouchable woman. Your wife is going to be my daughter-in-law. I ought to have a say in this matter. I agree that Devi is a college-educated and intelligent professional woman with excellent moral character. However, she is still an "Untouchable" woman of impure origin from the lowest rung of our society," said Elsy.

Sam was not ready for a showdown with his mother. So he said, "I respect your sentiments and understand what you are saying. Yes, she is going to be your daughter-in-law, but I love her. I'm your only son. Don't you want me to choose the girl I want to spend the rest of my life with?" Sam asked.

"She isn't suited to be your wife and our daughter-in-law. If you're seeking freedom to choose, why did you choose the 'forbidden fruit'? Is that the only available fruit you like? I'm sorry I'm upset. When it comes to my only child, is it wrong to desire the very best for him rather than the forbidden one?" said Elsy, trying to mask her anger.

"*Amma*, using religion as the basis for classifying a class of people as of impure origin and hence as "Untouchables" was probably the diabolical contrivance of the dominant castes, who created the caste hierarchy for their own selfish and existential interest. The dominant caste seemed to have promulgated a religious falsehood that they came from the head of the Creator God Brahma, and the lowest castes came from the foot of such an apophatic and amorphous god. That is the greatest falsehood they were cleverly and successfully able to pass on from generation to generation," said Sam.

"But we have to live in this society and our community as respectable members. We cannot change those wrongs you are alluding to over-night," said Elsy.

"*Amma*, labeling humans as 'impure' and 'Untouchable' upon their birth is an abominable 'defilement' of human dignity. Suppose human beings are created by God in His own image. In that case, it is equal-ly true that God, in His ultimate wisdom, also endows every human with divine dignity and humanity. The Church, as a religious institution centered around God, should be an institution that must respect the God-given dignity in each human being and fight inequity and bigotry. But instead, they are the coconspirators in this crime of contriving 'un-touchability,'" said Sam.

"Son, there is one more thing. As you may already know, she is a *Manglik* born with a *Mangal Dosha* (Mars defect). The *Manglik* woman who enters into a marriage relationship with a man who is not also a *Manglik* may encounter widowhood or separation from the spouse, which, in other words, means the husband may even face death due to the malefic influences of *Mangal* (Mars). So, if you marry her, you may face either dissolution of marriage or even death, according to their Vedic astrology," said Elsy.

"*Amma*, do you truly believe that? Astrology is a pseudoscience, which is considered a woo-woo. *Mangal Dosha* is deeply rooted in *Mangal*, which is associated with Mars. Mars is a giant dead planet with absolutely no influence on the marital relationships of humans and their successes or failures. Think for a moment, who determines whether someone has a *Mangal Dosha* or not?" He paused for a moment and tried to rein in his emotions, but still, his face became flushed. He continued.

"The astrologer who writes the *Jathakam* is invariably a high school dropout who finds it hard to make a living. Interestingly, they allegedly have the power to know the fate of all others except their own. In our village, the person who writes everyone's *Jathakam* (horoscope) is the impoverished Keshavan Kaniyar, who lives in a dilapidated brick house. Why does he live in squalor if he has the power to predict the future?"

"He probably is not very successful at predicting the future of people," said Elsy.

"Yes, therein lies the truth. *Amma*, there is no scientific data to prove that the dead planet Mars, which is 225 million kilometers away from us, has any effect on humans and their fate. Mars isn't an Omnipotent, Omniscient, or Omnificent deity to control humans' behavior or fate! It is a dead red planet that is a massive round ball of dirt and minerals. I'm sorry, Devi being a *Manglik* doesn't change anything," said Sam.

"But Son, there are many things that we don't know in this world.

Some of the *Jathakams* are often found to be true by their bearers. Devi told me in no uncertain terms that the man, whom she was betrothed to before, died in a motorbike accident because of her *Mangal Dosha*. Otherwise, how many people drink and ride the motorbike, but very few only die in such a small accident. He was not a *Manglik*, and he married her because he was an atheist who didn't believe in anything irrational, such as *Mangal Dosha*. You know what happened to him! On the other hand, a *Manglik* can marry another *Manglik* without the ill effects of *Mangal Dosha*, as they say. If you were a *Manglik*, then at least the specter of such baneful effects of *Mangal Dosha* would not be there," said Elsy in a strategic way to dissuade her son from marrying Devi.

"Yes, *Amma*, I agree. There are many things we don't yet understand in this world. But through science, we know that the giant planet doesn't exert any malefic influence over humans. There's no evidence that Mars has any detrimental effect on us. So, *Amma*, did you have a *Jathakam* made when I was born?" asked Sam.

"No, Son. Our kind of Christians don't do *Jathakams*," said Elsy.

"Why?" Asked Sam.

"Because we don't have that custom or practice of writing *Jathakams* for our children. The Almighty God, the Father, determines the future or can change anyone's present and future or any curses or baneful effects if you ardently call upon him for his grace and mercy. However, many traditionalists and religious conservatives believe that if someone is born with a *Mangal Dosha*, that status can't be changed but can be alleviated. So, according to them, if a *Manglik* marries another *Manglik* with *Mangal Dosha*, they won't suffer the malefic effects," said Elsy.

"So, if I am a *Manglik* and marry Devi, then we will have a safer marriage, and I won't suffer the malefic effects of *Mangal*. Is that correct?" Asked Sam.

"Well, that is what the Hindus believe. Son, you are my only son, and I am scared about even superstitious threats to your life," said Elsy.

"Mother, I would like to show you something. Please wait here for a couple of minutes," said Sam.

He then went to his bedroom and retrieved the *Jathakam* he had recently created through Keshavan Kaniyar.

"*Amma*, here is my *Jathakam*. I paid Keshavan Kaniyar to write a *Jathakam* for me. He wrote a '*Sampurna Jathakam*,' and here it is." Sam handed the *Jathakam* over to his mother.

Elsy was blown away by her son producing his own *Jathakam*, which they had never written before. Elsy's hands were shaking when she took it out of the envelope as if she was encountering a ghost.

"As you can see in the *Jathakam*, I was born with a *Mangal Dosha*. I am a *Manglik* as well, so you don't have to be scared if I marry Devi. We will have a successful marriage, and I won't be harmed," said Sam.

Elsy was shocked that he had prepared his own *Jathakam* and was doubly determined to marry Devi. Elsy was lost for words to say anything further and realized that her strategy to scare him had not worked and that her son was ahead of the game. She handed the *Jathakam* back to his son after reviewing it.

Johnnie remained silent for the rest of the time and did not even want to see the *Jathakam* when Elsy handed it to him before.

"Okay, Son. As your father said, please give your proposal to marry Devi some serious thought. When we meet again next week, we will talk about your proposal further at that time.

We have to go now," said Elsy.

"Would you like to have some breakfast, *Appa* and *Amma*?" Asked Sam.

"No, thank you! Your father has a luncheon meeting in Kottayam on our way back. He needs to attend that meeting. Before it gets late, we need to head out, Son," said Elsy.

Elsy and Johnnie left after hugging their son.

CHAPTER 7

B y confessing the love that had blossomed between them, Sam and Devi transformed their vulnerabilities into strength and liberated the truth they had carried in their souls. Declaring their long-nurtured love was an act of courage that opened the gates of their inner universe, shattered self-imposed shackles, and empowered them to face the world fearlessly and live fully, no longer masquerading the truth. For them now, the stormy seas were navigable, and mountains of impediments ahead seemed conquerable.

When he went home that weekend, he planned his departure so that his estimated time of arrival (ETA) would coincide with Devi's arrival at the bus depot. During this trip, he felt emboldened to meet her because he had already made his parents fully aware of his love for Devi and his unrelenting desire to marry her soon. As a result, he no longer had to play the hide-and-seek game of wondering whether his parents would find out what they were doing. He was determined to face the world and make it known that he loved Devi.

Devi waited at the depot for Sam, her heart beating rapidly with anticipation. When the distinct *vroom* of the Royal Enfield motorbike's engine stirred the air in the distance, she became excited. As the deep, throaty hum sliced through the stillness of the surrounding areas of the bus depot and got louder and closer, that thunderous roar became a familiar melody for her ears. The roar that once echoed through empty roads now played like music tuned to the rhythm of her longing.

They were delighted to meet again and warmly embraced each other. Sam asked, "Devi, would you like to go to the café and have a cup of tea? I have a lot to fill you in on."

Then he leaned over to her and whispered in her ears, "My parents came to see me in Cochin. They found out that you stayed with me in my apartment and were upset. I had to confide in them that we are deeply in love, and I want to get married to you."

"Who told them?" Devi asked.

"The Vicar. One of the staff nurses from your hospital who came for training in Cochin saw us together twice at the train station," said Sam.

"I am petrified, dear," said Devi nervously.

"Don't you worry. Everything is going to be okay. Let us go to the café. We will have some tea and snacks, and after that, I will drop you off at your home on my bike. My parents know everything. We should now inform your parents as well, as soon as possible. You will have to ride home with me on the backseat of my bike," said Sam mischievously. He was not nervous or afraid of their love affair, and no longer wanted to keep it a secret. He was ready to face the world.

Devi was petrified at the idea of riding on his motorbike, clearly in public view. She became anxious and leaned closer to Sam in fear, totally unaware of the crowded bus depot full of people, some from her village and workplace.

At the café, they ordered tea and *vada* (deep-fried lentil patties) and tried to catch up on their news.

"Devi, my parents came to see me last Saturday morning. My mother and father were sorrowful and frustrated when they found out about our relationship from the Vicar. They were saddened that they had been disgraced at Church by the rumors circulating among the parishioners. My mother sobbed about us getting involved in a forbidden love affair.

They were so disappointed to find out from a third party, the Vicar of our Church, that you stayed with me in my apartment and that I took you to the railway station on my bike," said Sam.

"I am worried sick, dear," said Devi. She held her head down in fear but listened carefully.

"Apparently, that staff nurse from your Hospital, who is also a member of our parish, saw us together on both days at the Cochin railway station and complained to the Vicar that I was having an illicit consort with you. So, I have told my parents everything about our love affair and that I'm deeply in love with you and wanted to marry you," said Sam.

Devi was visibly scared and uneasy about the storm they were facing. She was worried that it would destroy her, just as many others in her situation had in the past. Sam was cautious not to reveal the details of his parents' reactions and their private conversations to safeguard their integrity.

After their tea at the café, Sam persuaded Devi to ride with him on his motorbike to her home so the world could see them together. He took her home on his motorbike with great pride and joy.

When Devi's parents heard the sound of the motorbike, they came outside and were shocked to see their daughter riding on the motorbike of their master's son. They could hardly believe their eyes. Devi was supposed to live in servitude, not ride on the back of her master's motorbike, holding onto him. As Untouchables, they knew they were not equals to their master's family. Sam dropped Devi off, greeted them, but left without speaking to her parents as he planned to return in a few days to ask for Devi's hand in marriage.

Devi's poor parents were stunned and had a million questions for her about riding in the backseat of the motorbike with their master's son. She briefly filled them in and deferred further details for a later time. Her parents were petrified of the consequences of such a relationship with an upper-caste man. They had often heard that such relationships invariably ended in tragedy, and they were terrified of the perilous path their daughter seemed to be on. Devi reassured them that she and they would be fine, calmed their nerves, and asked them to relax.

When Sam reached home, Elsy told him that the Vicar wanted to meet and counsel him as soon as possible as a parish member due to the canards going around in the Church about him. He told his mother that he was not interested in meeting with the Vicar, who had a bad reputation for womanizing. Still, his mother convinced him that the merciful God might have already forgiven him and encouraged Sam to see him and listen to what he had to say.

The Vicar was a judgmental guy with a broken marriage. Some of the parish members complained to the Diocesan Bishop that he spent too much time counseling women in their Church and wanted him to stop pursuing women. He was alleged to have had an affair with a woman at the previous Church where he was ministering. When the allegations became an embarrassment for the Church and affected his moral leadership, the only productive solution in front of the bishop was to transfer him from that location to Johnnie's Church, which was about 100 miles far to the south. So, Sam did not think this Vicar could offer him anything other than his usual judgmental pronouncements about his love affair with Devi, who was of an Untouchable caste.

That weekend, Sam's parents spent considerable time with him, talking about his desire to marry Devi. His father counseled him calmly about the pitfalls and dangers such an inter-caste marriage alliance could cause the family. Johnnie explained to him the sacredness of the Christian matrimony.

"Son, the institution of marriage is sacred. It is a sacred sacrament of a union between two individuals with similar faiths. Marriage is a contract or a covenant between two individuals that symbolizes the union of Christ and his Church. Therefore, a shared commitment to the Christian faith is sacred and central to a Christian marriage between two people," said Johnnie.

"Okay, I agree with you looking at it from a Christian perspective as a person brought up in the Christian faith," said Sam.

"When I think about it more, I'm even more concerned about your divergent faiths than I'm about Devi's untouchable status or her poor economic condition. I'm deeply concerned about the children who will grow up in such divergent faiths and the dichotomy of trying to function as a cohesive family unit while raising them to be morally and socially responsible individuals," said Johnnie.

"*Appa*, morals, and values are independent of religion. Religion is not a requirement for morals and values. I agree that codes of behavior based on morals are essential for a community of believers in a religion. Morals and values are the standards that guide a group's behavior in determining what is right and wrong," said Sam.

"I believe morality cannot prevail in the absence of religion. In other words, without God, any behavior is permitted. Therefore, religion is a precondition for morality, and the two are intertwined. Your mother and I worked very hard to raise you as a Christian with Christian values and morals, which are deeply based on the teachings of our living Christian God, Jesus Christ. But Devi worships an idol, and she doesn't have our Christian values. Religion is about affiliating with a community, adhering to its traditions, subscribing to its moral norms, and belonging to and identifying with it. Yes, religion plays a major role in the success of a marriage and raising children," said Johnnie.

"With your background and life's work as a Christian theologian, I know where you're coming from. I respect your stance on this topic. From a biological perspective, I can tell you that moral intuitions and behaviors predated religion and originated independently of it long before humans conceived of gods. Many evolutionary psychologists and biologists believe that morals have biological and social roots. Therefore, I believe morals can exist independent of any religion and God," said Sam.

"Son, for Christian morality—specifically the kind rooted in the teachings of Jesus—to truly prevail, it must be grounded in God and anchored in religious faith. That said, I do believe that non-Christians, non-believers, and secular humanists are also capable of living moral lives," said Johnnie.

"You see, 'reason' is the root of all morals and values, not God or religion. I am not convinced that there is objective morality. Morality is subjective. Immanuel Kant argued that morality is a 'categorical imperative.' According to him, it is our duty. So, we must treat others as we would want to be treated. As Kant says, we must respect the dignity and inherent value of all humans, not merely as means but as ends in themselves. We absolutely must respect the dignity of all humans, including 'Untouchables,' regardless of their skin color, race, caste, ethnicity, religion, or nationality," said Sam.

"Son, as a Christian theologian, I can tell you that the Christian religion has played a powerful role in codifying and transmitting moral values widely in Western countries and worldwide. In other words, Christian ethics have provided the framework for many of our ethical and moral practices and Western rule of law," said Johnnie.

"Yes, I agree that Christianity has powerfully influenced codifying and transmitting morals. But my contention is that morality preexisted religion and will continue to remain independent of God and religion," said Sam.

"I agree that morality may have preexisted religion. My point is that religion is necessary for codifying and transmitting morality," said Johnnie.

"*Appa*, I don't know whether religion is necessary for that. We have over 200 professional sports, and they all have standards and codes of behavior that determine right and wrong. None of those sports are based on religion, but humans have developed such codes of behavior or conduct. We can raise our children based on the standards of what is right or wrong rather than basing them on any religion. With the fully developed and advanced cognitive abilities gained through evolutionary adaptations over millions of years, Homo Sapiens evolved to develop morals and codes of behavior and have learned to live by them. For that, we don't need a religion or a God," asserted Sam.

"Sam, I'm a Christian, and you were raised a Christian. I can only see those things through that lens, and I don't have a wider secular world-view as yours," said Johnnie.

"My dearest *Appa* and *Amma*, I have been analyzing and thinking about marrying Devi for many years. As you asked last week, I have given my decision to marry her some more serious thought in light of the social consequences we face as a family. With all my love for you both, I remain resolute in my decision to marry Devi. If you and *Amma* support me in marrying the one I deeply love and being with her for the rest of my life, I beg for your approval. All the bigoted reasons that would be articulated by the upper caste that we represent are just attacks on an innocent human being's dignity and humanity. She did nothing wrong in her life to be treated with this much contempt for no fault of hers," said Sam.

"Son, we respect your decision. We support your 'moral imperative' to honor Devi's dignity and humanity," said Johnnie with a deep moral conviction and renewed understanding and awakening from the discussions.

Johnnie seemed resolved, and his face was flickering with joy now that a significant burden was removed from his shoulders by Sam's edification. The moral awakening he underwent helped him achieve moral clarity, and he wholeheartedly supported his son's choice.

"If we can't stand up against that kind of bigotry and social injustice, what kind of values and morals do we have as the followers of Jesus Christ, who taught us to 'love thy neighbor as thyself.' Jesus also instilled in us another profound idea that 'whatever you did for one of the least of these brothers and sisters of mine, you did for me,'" said Sam.

"Son, we counseled you and asked you to give your proposal to marry Devi some serious thought. If you still decide to marry her, your mother and I will fully support you. You are our only son, and we want you to be happy and live with the consequences of the choices you make in your life. You are a highly educated man, a professor and scholar, and a well-read man in philosophy and theology. You have been a good son who lived a moral life, but if you want to marry the woman who is the love of your life, then we are behind you. No matter how forbidden that love is based on our Christian customs and regional cultural practices, we will support you regardless of the consequences," said Johnnie, and he paused.

"Thank you, *Appa* and *Amma*! I love you with all my heart!" said Sam.

"However, I can assure you that our Church will not permit a Christian wedding ceremony to be held in our Church, but you can have a civil wedding and live your life as husband and wife. We're both okay with your civil marriage, so you can both live happily ever after in your place of residence. We'll take whatever negative social consequences that may come our way, and we'll face those together as a family," said Johnnie.

"Thanks again, *Appa* and *Amma*, from the bottom of my heart," said Sam.

Elsy remained silent, appearing sad and disappointed. But finally said, "Please meet with the Vicar at his office around 3:00 pm tomorrow." She was holding out hope that the Vicar might change Sam's mind.

"Okay, I'll give it a chance, although I don't expect anything to come out of it," said Sam.

When Sam met with the Vicar, he said, "Sam, some of the members of our Church are upset and disappointed that you, as the son of a priest and the most prominent theologian, have a consort with a Dalit girl of untouchable origin. The members are deeply concerned about the fallout and ill will that could cause the Church and its members in the community. Several of our members wanted me to counsel you and ask you to stop your consort with the Untouchable girl."

"Vicar, I don't have a consort with an 'Untouchable girl' as they pejoratively characterize. I am deeply in love with a woman named Devi, who is a college-educated professional with an exemplary moral character and integrity. She is a stunningly beautiful woman both inside and out with great values and less material possessions. I love her exemplary moral character along with her poor economic condition," said Sam defensively.

"Sam, Christian marriage is a sacred covenant between a man and woman that makes them one in Christ. The covenant of marriage metaphorically represents Christ's relationship with the Church. A Christian marriage and family life are centered around Christ. When the man and woman belong to divergent faiths, their morals and values are often misaligned. The partners in such a marriage become unequally yoked in faith. In such marriages, the 'oneness' of a union of two different individuals in Christ is not going to be possible if they have divergent beliefs, and raising children in such an environment is going to be very challenging and unhealthy for children," said the Vicar.

"Vicar, I don't have any concerns or objections about her personal faith or her God. She can believe in any God that her forefathers worshipped, just as we do. That is her personal choice. It is utterly bigoted for us to assume that her religion and God of ages are not good enough and that the children growing up in such families are unhealthy," exclaimed Sam.

"I want you to know that there are many rumors in our Church about your love affair with Devi. I spoke to your parents a few times about this development. As Syrian Christians, we are strictly endogamous and don't marry Hindus, much less Untouchables of impure origin. Untouchables are historically from the lowest rung of our society. The untouchable Dalits are like the slaves in the Old Testament times. They are somewhat similar to the African slaves who were traded to work in America. The Brahmins placed the Untouchable Dalits at the lowest among all castes. They were stratified into such roles to perform menial jobs. The upper caste and the Syrian Christians, therefore, don't enter into a marriage covenant with their untouchable slave servants," added the Vicar.

"Vicar, that is a disgusting, immoral, and un-Christian characterization of a group of hard-working humans who have the same humanity as us as 'slaves' because they are Black or as "Untouchables" because they do menial jobs! Let me ask you, in your opinion, are all humans created by God? If they are, are they all created in the image of God?" Asked Sam.

"Yes, Sam, all humans are created by God in his own image," the Vicar answered.

"If all humans are created by God in His own image, then there is no doubt that the so-called 'slaves' and 'untouchable humans' are also created in His image by the Creator, God. In that case, God also endowed them with the same 'human dignity' as any other member of the upper caste. Classifying humans as 'Untouchables' just because they were born into a family that is affixed with a label of untouchability is an abominable 'defilement' of their 'human dignity' granted by God." Sam exclaimed, visibly annoyed.

"Hey, take it easy, Sam!" said the Vicar.

"As a Biologist, I can tell you that there are no significant racial differences between the brown Brahmins, the brown Syrian Christians, and the brown Dalits. They're all brown-skinned human beings endowed with the same kind of 'human dignity' by God. In other words, no remarkable genotypic and phenotypic differences exist between the brown Brahmins and the brown untouchable Dalits of Kerala. Vicar, how do you feel if someone classifies you as an Untouchable for no fault of yours? Will that make you an Untouchable? What is the untouchability of Devi?" Asked Sam with his face flushed. He seemed incensed by the Vicar's derogatory remarks.

"Relax. Take a deep breath," said the Vicar.

"Why is she Untouchable? She is a college-educated, intelligent, and professional woman who is even more attractive than many of the more conventionally attractive women from the Brahmin and Syrian Christian communities. Then why is she Untouchable?" Asked Sam.

"Sam, she was born into a family of untouchable parents as per our regional customs, cultural traditions, and practices. That makes her an Untouchable," the Vicar said.

"Vicar, you certainly represent the hypocrisy and bigotry of many of the upper caste. Just because casteism has been practiced for centuries doesn't make it right. How can anybody be born a slave or an Untouchable? Of course, they are made 'slaves' and 'Untouchables' by the diabolical contrivance of the clever and powerful exploiters who exploit them for their self-interest and convenience. They use religion to sanctify and give it legitimacy," Sam exclaimed.

"What I'm saying is that your love affair and decision to marry a Hindu untouchable girl violates the code of conduct and practices of our church, which you are a member of," said the Vicar.

"So what? You alluded earlier that the Untouchables are like the slaves in Biblical times, and they are from the lowest rung of our society, and Syrian Christians do not marry their slave servants. I'm sure you implied that Devi being an untouchable woman is beneath us. So, please tell me, if Abraham the Patriarch had slept with his wife's slave, Hagar, and had a son, Ishmael, what is wrong with Sam taking on a wife legitimately from among the Untouchables? It is a shame and a disgrace that Abraham slept with his wife Sarah's slave, Hagar, and committed adultery and broke God's commandments," said Sam.

"Hagar the slave also was his wife. In that culture and time, men could have multiple wives," said the Vicar.

"How do you know that Hagar was his wife, Vicar? There is no biblical reference to Hagar being Abraham's wife. She was indeed a slave. If Abraham had taken Hagar, the slave of his wife Sarah, as his wife, then what would be the problem with Sam marrying an Untouchable? It is such a shame that in that culture, men could have multiple wives. Why can't we follow that tradition of having multiple wives literally today like in Biblical times? How hypocritical and self-righteous are all these meaningless practices?" Asked Sam.

"Sarah could not bear a child despite them trying hard to have one. So, God blessed them to have a child through Hagar," said the Vicar.

"That's so ridiculous, Vicar! God couldn't bless Sarah to have a child with Abraham—but had no problem with Abraham breaking His commandments, sleeping with a slave, Hagar, and committing adultery, only to bless that union with a child? According to your story, God couldn't bless Sarah, but He blessed Abraham for committing adultery with a slave and fathering a son, Ishmael! This just proves it's a very human story full of contradictions and falsehoods," Sam continued.

The Vicar was shocked by Sam's profound analysis and counterarguments. Members of the parish don't usually cross the Vicar or have the knowledge to debate him. The Vicar got up from his seat in frustration and wanted to end the conversation.

"Vicar, I'm disappointed and concerned that you and the Church you represent support such religious bigotry perpetuated to subjugate and subvert innocent human beings like Devi. She is a college-educated working woman of excellent moral character and a stunningly beautiful lady inside and out. She is many times better than the hypocrites who want to see her as untouchable and impure by birth for no fault of hers. My decision to marry her is nobody's business but mine. I'm unrelenting in my decision to marry Devi," exclaimed Sam. He got up from his seat.

"Wishing you good luck with it," said the Vicar, patronizingly.

"I need to go. I will get back to you regarding our wedding at a later date. Goodbye, Vicar!"   Sam walked out of his office, shaking his head in discontent. Sam was not very happy with the Vicar's religious arrogance and his righteous justification of the prevailing bigotry and injustice. Sam was much more incensed about the Vicar being so patronizing to him.

After meeting with the Vicar, he went straight to Devi's house to meet her parents and knocked on the door. Since it was a late Sunday afternoon, Devi and her parents were home. Devi was overjoyed to see Sam. He said he wanted to speak with her and her parents about an important matter. Devi's parents were taken aback by the unexpected visit from their master's son, who was the heir apparent to all of Johnnie's wealth. They stood back in servitude and deep reverence, hesitant to sit in Sam's presence.

Devi brought the only three available seats in their hut: one wooden round stool and two wooden chairs. Sam asked Devi's parents, Sarasu and Balan, to sit on the chairs, but they were wonderstruck when Sam asked them to sit in front of him. Since sitting down in his presence was irreverent of them as Untouchables living in servitude, both Balan and Sarasu refused to sit down.

Sam went and politely snatched their hands, then gently and affectionately dragged them to the two chairs and made them sit down. Next, he politely asked Devi to sit on the wooden stool as well. She reluctantly sat down because Sam was still standing. But he told them he did not have to sit down and proceeded to inform them of something important.

"Balan and Sarasu, I'll tell you something that will probably overwhelm and shock you and make you feel uneasy and insecure because of its impermissible social overtones. Please listen to me carefully for a few minutes, and please don't get up until I'm finished," said Sam, addressing all three of them.

Sarasu sensed that Sam was probably going to tell them about his love for their daughter, as she had been suspicious ever since Sam dropped Devi off on his motorbike the previous evening, something that was absolutely beyond the pale. When her mother asked Devi in astonishment why she had come home with Sam on his motorbike, Devi explained that when she arrived at the depot, the bus had already left. Her story, that Sam saw her walking home and offered her a ride, was unusual in their culture and hard for Sarasu to accept. Devi didn't want to elaborate further, fearing that her parents would become angry at the foolishness of her being seen with their master's son.

Sam amassed courage and began to speak with confidence and great excitement.

"I have been in love with your beautiful daughter for many years. She tried to talk some sense into me and persuade me out of it for fear of the forbidden nature of such a relationship and the possible eviction of your family from our property and aggression and violence from the fringe elements in our community. But my love for her grew daily, and I pursued her until she finally fell in love with me. We're in love, and nothing can separate us from our love and commitment for each other," Sam momentarily paused to gather his thoughts.

Balan and Sarasu couldn't believe what they had just heard. They looked at each other in astonishment, trying to grasp the gravity of such a relationship in light of the cultural taboos surrounding it.

Sam proceeded. "Now, I have a full-time job at a college as a lecturer, and I can support her. I'm ready to raise a family. I love your daughter with all my heart and would like to marry her as soon as possible. I spoke to my parents about this, and they were initially concerned about your family, your daughter, and how the members of the Church and our community would react to such an impermissible marriage alliance. Since I was steadfast in my desire to marry Devi, my parents finally gave in. They offered me their permission and support in marrying Devi. Then I asked Devi for her consent to marry me, and she agreed, with one condition: only if her parents agreed."

Sam took a step closer to Devi's parents, bent down politely, looked casually into the eyes of both Balan and Sarasu and then asked confidently: "So, may I ask you, would you please kindly give me your daughter's hand in marriage? I'll be forever grateful to you and assure you that I'll take good care of Devi with everything I've got."

Sam was beaming with joy, lighting up the entire room. He anxiously waited for a reply from Devi's parents. Devi looked nervous and locked eyes with her parents.

Sarasu and Balan began to shed tears of joy. They remained silent for a few minutes. They were overjoyed, yet tried hard to cope with the overwhelming reality of Devi's marriage to their master's only son, a college professor. Their hearts were filled with immense joy, awe, and gratitude, and they looked exuberant at the news of an incredible fortune that had come their way. Finally, Balan collected his thoughts, broke the silence, and said,

"Yes! That's an incredible honor for us as Dalits, one that we could never have dreamed of or ever deserved. We can hardly dream of a relationship like this, even in our wildest dreams. If Devi and her mother are okay with it, I give you my full consent, Sam *Kunju*. Thank you, son."

"Sam *Kunju*, this is an incredible alliance that my daughter could never dream of in her wildest dreams. We're blessed by God, and that blessing is now manifested through you. This is God's doing. Yes, son, you have my consent to marry my only daughter if she has consented to marry you!" said Sarasu.

Devi got up and gave Sam a big hug, followed by a kiss on his cheek. "Yes, I love Sam with all my heart. He is the love of my life," said Devi.

Sam hugged both her parents, said thank you, and proceeded to say, "I will discuss this further with Devi, and we will plan the details of the wedding. We will run those details by you and then decide on a date for our wedding. Since our Church is unlikely to officiate a wedding ceremony, it will be a civil wedding at the Registrar's Office," said Sam.

The Vicar was disappointed and annoyed that Sam didn't succumb to his coercion to end his love affair with the Untouchable woman, which would have saved the Church from disrepute. He was also upset that a Dalit untouchable woman had dared to entice an upper caste Christian man into a love affair with her.

The Vicar represented a community that collectively believed an Untouchable woman should never be empowered either socially or economically to entice an upper-caste Christian man into a love affair. He believed that if such relationships were not discouraged and dealt with firmly, they would set a dangerous precedent. If Sam and Devi succeeded, it could inspire other Untouchables and upper-caste men and women to fall in love, thereby undermining the sacred institution of marriage and the traditional practice of endogamy.

So, the Vicar agreed with the other members of the parish that such love affairs between a parish member and an Untouchable individual should not be tolerated. The couple must suffer some consequences to deter others from attempting similar affairs.

The Vicar was advised to discuss this matter with one of his parish's wealthy and influential members. As a successful businessman in the community, he had served for several years on the Governing Board of the Christian Hospital, where Devi worked as a part-time physiotherapy assistant.

The Vicar decided to consult him about the possibility of terminating the Untouchable Dalit woman, Devi, from her job so that she would not continue to have the financial independence that empowered her to ignore her servitude and dare to marry an upper caste man.

The Vicar gained the support of the other parish members in leadership positions of the Church and then met with the Hospital Board Member. The Board Member informed the Vicar that the Hospital could not terminate Devi without cause, even as a half-time employee, since she was hired under the state-mandated Scheduled Caste/Dalit quota. However, he told the Vicar that he would consult with the Hospital's president about her termination and explore a legal loophole to terminate her.

When the Board Member met with the Hospital's president, he informed him that the Physical Therapy Department had already proposed, in its short-term plan, abolishing the existing half-time Physiotherapist Assistant position and converting it into a full-time job. Therefore, the Hospital could abolish the position at any time without incurring any adverse legal consequences. When the full-time job opened, Devi could also apply for it. However, it was unlikely that she would get the job because a full-time job required more qualifications and experience.

As planned by the PT Department and as per the president's advice, the Department proposed to the Human Resources Office that the half-time physiotherapy assistant position be phased out to create a full-time position and then terminate the incumbent, effective immediately.

The Human Resources Office contacted Devi and gave her the letter of termination as requested by the PT Department. The HR Department informed Devi that when the full-time position became available, she was welcome to apply and would receive concessions for her prior experience at the PT Department.

CHAPTER 8

S am was preoccupied with his students' semester exams that week and his days consumed by grading papers and proctoring. Yet, like every other Friday afternoon, he was making plans to stop by the bus depot, their quiet refuge, where he and Devi had shared many tender moments sipping tea in the safe corner of the café, trading stories over steam, sweetness, and savory lentil patties.

But a shadow had crept over their once-innocent meetings, and he had become intensely aware of its pangs. Whispers had grown into rumors, and love had turned into danger. It dawned on him, slowly and painfully, that being seen with Devi in public was no longer safe. Their bond, now a target of gossip, risked drawing the wrath of lurking fringe voices, ready to turn words or worse into weapons.

So, Sam called her office to let her know he would not meet her that Friday afternoon at the bus depot. This was only the second time he had ever called Devi's office during her entire tenure at the hospital.

Someone who answered the phone told Sam that Devi no longer worked in the PT Department. Sam was momentarily confused and stunned by the news. When he collected his thoughts, he began to suspect something was wrong. He strongly suspected that Devi had likely been unfairly let go. Before hanging up, he asked the person on the phone again whether she was sure Devi was no longer with the hospital. She confirmed it.

Sam rode directly to Devi's home that evening and knocked on her door without stopping by his own house first. She was home with her parents. Seeing Sam, she was overcome with sadness.

"Sam, I…" Devi choked up. She was trembling with fear and sorrow. After regaining her composure, she said, "I was terminated unfairly—without any reason or prior warning."

She knew this was probably the first of many consequences they would face for their forbidden love. Sam held her close, consoled her, and said, "Don't worry. We'll find a better job. You're not alone. I'm here for you and your family."

"Thank you, dear," said Devi. She clung to him, looking both sad and anxious.

"Devi, I called your office to let you know I wouldn't be meeting you at the bus depot to protect us from public insults or violence. I was shocked to hear from your office that you no longer worked there, and that is why I came here directly. The rumors have only grown worse. But please tell me, did they give you any reason for the termination?" asked Sam.

Devi pulled out her termination letter and handed it to him. The letter stated: "Effective immediately, the hospital is phasing out the half-time Physiotherapy Assistant classification to create a full-time position in the PT Department and hire a full-time employee as soon as possible." It also mentioned that the current half-time employee was eligible to apply for the full-time position.

Sam suspected that the Vicar and the wealthy member of their parish who was on the Hospital Board were behind the dismissal. Unfortunately, they had orchestrated the termination cleverly and legally, leaving no grounds for complaint. Their true intent was to financially disempower Devi and send a clear message to her and to other Dalits about the consequences of defying social norms, especially by falling in love with or marrying someone from an upper caste or Christian background.

Devi's father was distraught that she had lost her only livelihood, and, with it, their only chance to escape poverty. Balan expressed his anguish and asked Sam why Devi had been dismissed.

"Sam *Kunju*," Balan began, "we are poor Untouchables who live in servitude, subject to the whims of the upper caste. We often fall into traps laid by the powerful and wealthy. We fear the consequences your love affair may bring upon us. Only *Bhagwan* can save us from their malice. We get no justice from the authorities, the police even collude with the upper caste without shame."

Sam reassured Devi and her parents that everything would be all right. He then voiced his own sense of moral outrage.

"If there is a God who is omnibenevolent, omnipotent, omniscient, and omnificent, who governs the universe and cherishes human beings as His creations, He would never sanction such cruelty by the upper caste, regardless of their power or numbers. To marginalize and oppress impoverished Dalits for selfish purposes under the guise of religion is evil by any standard of morality. Just because it's practiced collectively doesn't make it right," Sam declared.

Balan seemed distraught and flustered. "May *Bhagawan* save us from this evil," said Balan

"Devi and I are considering officiating our marriage at the Registrar's Office in the next few weeks. I would like to host a grand reception at our home for our friends and family who support us. But I need my *Appa's* and *Amma's* full support to hold the reception there. Many relatives are opposed to my marrying a Dalit woman. While I don't care about their opinions, my parents do. They value the cultural and religious customs of our community and want to stay in good standing with them." Sam added.

He looked to Devi's parents for their affirmation of what was proposed. Balan and Sarasu nodded in agreement. Devi remained quiet and shaken, clinging to Sam for comfort.

"Sadly, my love for Devi and our proposed marriage contradict their beliefs. In their eyes, an inter-caste marriage is a violation of tradition. That's why my parents may be hesitant to hold the reception at our home. If they feel too much pressure, I'll hold the wedding reception at a public venue for both our families and friends who support our marriage to my beautiful bride, Devi. Or we may decide not to have such a public event at all out of caution against potential reprisals," said Sam.

Sam calmed their nerves and returned home in time for dinner. His parents noticed that he seemed unusually silent and pensive. So, Johnnie asked, "Sam, what's up? Is everything okay?"

"I'm a bit disappointed. Devi was terminated from her half-time physiotherapist job at the hospital earlier this week. *Appa*, have you heard anything about her dismissal, perhaps from the Vicar or someone else in our church or community who's connected to the hospital?" asked Sam.

"No, I haven't heard anything. Son, I'm not surprised she was terminated. Given the rumors about your relationship with Devi, her dismissal, likely orchestrated by the bigots, is probably a retaliatory act for falling in love with a Syrian Christian man with a good education, high status, and wealth. I'm sure they didn't want a love story like yours to succeed because it could set a precedent and inspire other economically empowered Dalits to dream of marrying into upper-caste families. They clearly wanted to nip this in the bud," said Johnnie.

"Yes, *Appa*. You're absolutely right," said Sam.

"Although I privately condemn such social injustice, I still hesitate to swim against the powerful current of casteism that has existed for generations. That's why I was initially disappointed in your 'forbidden love,' as we're now witnessing its consequences. Eventually, they will ostracize us for defying cultural and religious traditions," Johnnie added.

"I'm sorry for causing you heartache, dishonor, and potential ostracization. But I've never felt more motivated than I am now, driven by the moral imperative to marry Devi because of the sheer hypocrisy and bigotry shown toward her. All I ask is that you stand with me in doing what is right and Christian. It is morally repugnant to despise the dignity of a human being simply because she was born into a man-made category called 'untouchability,'" exclaimed Sam.

"Son, trust me, I'm with you all the way," said Johnnie.

"It's grossly immoral and un-Christian, even if the majority practices this bigotry. Discriminating against someone just for being born into a family branded as untouchable is a desecration of human dignity. Such discrimination is profoundly unholy and ungodly. I believe Jesus would have fought against it," Sam said, trembling with emotion.

"As a family, your *Amma* and I have decided to stand by you and do what is right. You made this choice because you believed it was the right thing to do. You did nothing immoral or illegal—only fell in love with a beautiful, dignified woman born into poverty. We're already in the stormy seas, but we'll face them together. I'll stand for what is right, regardless of religious or social backlash. As you once told me, there are no untouchables in the eyes of the Creator who created them in love. Thank you for opening my eyes to the evil of casteism," Johnnie said gently, trying to soothe Sam.

"Thank you, *Appa!*" said Sam.

"Son, I don't dislike Devi. I've known her since she was born. As a teen and adult, she would come to me for counsel whenever she was distressed. She's intelligent and wise beyond her years. Now, she's a college-educated professional. Though she lost her job, she'll find another soon. As you said, she is beautiful inside and out. And yes, we were initially unhappy because of her untouchable label and the social taboos surrounding it," Elsy added to comfort Sam.

"Thank you for your affirmation, *Amma*!" said Sam.

"But we can't fight this centuries-old evil of untouchability alone. It's a monstrous, immoral institution that violates human dignity. That's why we initially resisted your love for Devi. But now you are deeply in love with her and want to marry her, we'll stand by you, no matter the consequences," said Elsy.

Sam felt deeply satisfied and elated by his parents' support and change of heart.

"Son, go ahead with your plan to marry Devi at the Registrar's Office. Your *Amma* and I will be there to support and cheer you on. Make sure Balan and Sarasu are also present. They are dignified human beings with the same dreams and shared humanity as any other members of the upper caste. As you said, they have God-given human dignity, a gift from our Creator. They work hard and live honestly. They deserve respect, not condemnation," said Johnnie.

Johnnie looked to Elsy for affirmation, then continued, "Your *Amma* and I will host a wedding reception for you and Devi at our home after the official ceremony. We'll serve a lavish meal for guests who support this union, free of prejudice and hypocrisy. Also, be sure to arrange for two witnesses to sign the marriage registry."

"Thank you, *Appa* and *Amma*, from the bottom of my heart. *Appa*, you are my beacon of hope in this fight against bigotry," said Sam.

"Son, I want to tell you something in confidence. Balan's family has lived in the shack we built for them as vassals for many years, serving our family loyally. They don't have a home of their own because the wages they earn from us aren't enough to make ends meet or save to buy a house." Johnnie paused, then went and sat beside Elsy and held her hand. Then he continued:

"We've been praying and thinking about building a small home for their family. Now, since you're marrying Devi, your *Amma* and I feel this is the right time to make that dream a reality."

"Thank you, *Appa*," Sam was overjoyed.

"You're welcome! We've decided to give them a gift of 20 cents of land and build a modest, comfortable house with three bedrooms, two bathrooms, a kitchen, and a family room. We'd like to start the process as soon as possible and cover the full cost. This will also be a home where you and Devi will occasionally stay. So, we'll ensure it has running water and electricity," said Johnnie.

Sam was overwhelmed by his parents' compassion and generosity. His eyes filled with tears of joy. He felt this was the beginning of a new reality—a turning point in which they, as a family, could change the life of at least one Dalit family.

"*Appa* and *Amma*, I can't thank you enough for your unconditional love. More than anything, thank you for your compassion toward this impoverished family, condemned to live on the margins through no fault of their own. This generous act will change their lives forever. You're my heroes. I love you with all my heart," Sam said.

"You're welcome, son," said Johnnie.

"We can wait a few weeks to get married. During that time, we'll transfer the land and build the house. I'll help draw up the plans and coordinate with contractors to expedite the process," said Sam.

"Tomorrow, your mother and I will meet with Balan, Sarasu, and Devi to share our plans. We'll give them 20 cents of land at the farthest corner of our sugarcane fields, with direct access to the street. After living as vassals on our land for years, they deserve this. The plot will be large enough to grow cassava, coconut palms, mango trees, banana plants, and vegetables," said Johnnie.

"*Appa,* that's so thoughtful. Isn't it one of the core messages of Jesus and central to Christian theology? As Matthew 25:40 says, 'Truly I tell you, whatever you did for one of the least of these brothers of mine, you did for me.' You're walking the talk, and you touched my heart today. I'm sure they'll be deeply moved," said Sam.

"Let's not tell them yet. *Amma* and I'll meet with them tomorrow. We want this to stay quiet until the house is complete and they've moved in. No one else needs to know. God has blessed us abundantly—this is our way of expressing gratitude. Yes, son, we are trying to practice what we preach, as Jesus taught: 'Since ye have done it unto one of the least of these, my brethren, ye have done it unto me,'" said Johnnie.

On Sunday afternoon, Johnnie and Elsy walked over to visit Balan, Sarasu, and Devi. They had sent word of their visit through their maidservant, so the family was expecting them. The hut had been tidied, and everything was in its proper place in preparation for the visit of their esteemed guests.

As advised by Johnnie, Sam accompanied his parents. Balan, Sarasu, and Devi were immeasurably happy to see them. Johnnie and his family had never made a personal visit like this before. But today's visit felt different. Balan's family was no longer viewed as mere Untouchables living in servitude. They were now the family from which the bride of their highly educated son would come.

They welcomed Johnnie, Elsy, and Sam, treating them like honored guests. Meanwhile, Balan, Sarasu, and Devi remained standing out of respect. Balan and Sarasu were eager to hear what Johnnie and Elsy had to say, while Devi stood nervously, worried they might try to persuade her against marrying Sam.

"Balan and Sarasu," Johnnie began, "our children have fallen in love and have decided to spend their lives together. Elsy and I want you to know that we fully support our son, Sam, in marrying Devi. He loves her with all his heart, and we believe he should marry the one he truly loves."

He paused for a moment, noticing Elsy's eagerness to add something.

"Yes," Elsy said, smiling, "we love our son and support him. Johnnie and I have been praying about Sam's deep desire to marry Devi. He has known her since childhood, and his love for her is genuine. We accept his choice and are happy for them both."

"The coming weeks may not be easy for either of our families," Johnnie continued. "We may face opposition from our extended relatives and community members. There's also the possibility of violence against your family from extremist elements. But we will face it together. I plan to inform my friends in law enforcement, including the District Superintendent of Police (DSP) and the Circle Inspector, about our concerns. I'll request increased surveillance around your home. Please report any threats, abuse, or harassment to me immediately. I'll personally speak to the DSP and Circle Inspector to ensure you are protected."

"Thank you, sir," Balan and Sarasu said in unison.

Tears of gratitude welled up in their eyes. They could hardly believe that their daughter's marriage to a highly educated and well-placed Syrian Christian man was not only being blessed but also defended by the family. They offered their heartfelt thanks and reverence to Johnnie, Elsy, and Sam.

Johnnie then turned to Balan and Sarasu and asked gently, "How is your house doing? Does it need any repairs before the rainy season? Are you comfortable living here in this hut?"

"Sir, we're managing," Balan replied humbly. "We're happy with what we have. As Untouchables, we never dreamed of anything better. The only issue is the roof; it leaks a lot during the rains because it's thatched with coconut leaves. Devi wanted to use some of her savings to help rethatch it, but I told her to save that money for later. When she gets married, she may need it to buy jewelry. We are fine, sir. We don't want to burden you. We're grateful just to stay here rent-free."

Johnnie smiled and looked into the eyes of Balan, Sarasu, and Devi with affection and said, "We bring great news. I want to share something very exciting and life-changing with the three of you. Please keep this proposal confidential until it is finalized. As a family, we've been thinking about building a house for you for some time now. After careful consideration, we have decided to provide you with 20 cents of land and build a modern home featuring three bedrooms, a kitchen, a family room, and two bathrooms at no cost to you. The house will be connected to public water and electric systems, so you'll have running water, electrical connections, lights, and fans."

Johnnie paused for a moment to take in their stunned expressions and the joy beaming from their faces. Balan, Sarasu, and Devi were breathless with joy and looked at each other in disbelief, trying to verify whether what they had just heard was real or a hallucination. They couldn't believe their ears. Tears of deep gratitude welled up in their eyes and began to overflow. They were speechless, wiping away their tears.

Elsy, filled with emotion, rose from her seat and hugged Balan, Sarasu, and Devi—an unprecedented act that shocked them even more.

Sam smiled as he watched them enjoy this moment of pure happiness and joy. He got up, hugged Devi, and sat back down. The room fell into a peaceful silence, filled with an abundance of joy.

"We are forever grateful to you for changing our lives. Thank you," said Balan, filled with emotions of immense joy and gratitude.

"We are so incredibly grateful to you," said Sarasu.

"You are most welcome. May God bless each of you," Johnnie replied. He hugged Balan, Sarasu, and Devi for the first time ever, then returned to his seat.

"We've chosen a location at the corner of the sugarcane fields near the street for your house, giving you direct access to the road. You won't have to pay anything for the land or construction. We'll also fully furnish the home, including fans for the bedrooms and the family room, and purchase a refrigerator for you. The 20 cents of land and the house will be deeded to you, and the property will be placed in your name. You'll even have enough space to plant cassava, grow a vegetable garden, and raise fruit trees," said Johnnie.

Overwhelmed with joy, Balan and Sarasu instinctively knelt at Johnnie's and Elsy's feet, a traditional sign of reverence Untouchables often showed to upper castes. Both Johnnie and Elsy immediately stood up, gently lifted them up, and embraced them warmly—another extraordinary act rarely seen between upper castes and those considered "polluted."

Devi was stunned by what she had just heard and witnessed. Gratitude and admiration filled her heart for Johnnie, Elsy, and Sam. She could hardly believe such a gesture of love and dignity was being shown to Untouchables like her, something she had never dreamed possible, no matter how beautiful or deserving one might be.

Sam, too, was beaming with pride and respect for his parents. He was awed by their compassion in making one Untouchable family feel dignified and loved. Despite his parents' initial concerns about his choice of a bride from a "polluted" caste, their love and support remained steadfast.

Sam suggested to Devi that they postpone their wedding until the new house was completed and the Balan family had moved in. Devi fully supported Sam's suggestion to postpone their wedding until the house was completed.

Meanwhile, Elsy and Johnnie began planning a grand wedding reception. Sam took the lead in helping his father partition the 20 cents of farmland and transfer ownership to Balan and Sarasu. He also hired a contractor to begin drafting plans for the house.

At Johnnie's and Elsy's official request, the Taluk Office partitioned the land, prepared the deed, and transferred ownership of the 20 cents to Balan and Sarasu. Johnnie's residential contractor then created an architectural plan for a three-bedroom, two-bathroom house with a kitchen and family room. The plan was submitted to the Village Office (*Panchayat*) for approval, along with an application for a construction permit.

Once the permit was granted, the contractor erected a small thatched shed on-site to store materials. His crew began laying the foundation and delivering construction supplies: timber, bricks, stones, pebbles, rebar, cement, doors, and windows. Work progressed steadily, and the workers built the walls and roof and installed plumbing and electrical wiring.

As the walls began to rise, rumors started spreading throughout the community, especially among the members of Johnnie and Elsy's church. They whispered that Johnnie and Elsy were building a house for their son's Untouchable lover, who was also afflicted with *Mangal Dosha* (Mars defect).

Because Devi was a *Manglik* and from a "polluted" caste, some in their community gossiped that Sam would be cursed with an ill-fated marriage and possible death. Many claimed the *Mangal Dosha* would bring ruin upon the Johnnie family and that Devi's presence was a bad omen.

The rumors spread like wildfire. Soon, the entire village knew that Johnnie and Elsy were building a modern house for the destitute family of Balan, whose daughter was about to marry Sam, and that an impending curse would befall their family because of Devi's *Mangal Dosha*. Envy and anger began to grow toward the Balan family, especially toward Devi.

As workers began fitting the windows and door frames, a group of extremist thugs launched a surprise attack. They vandalized the structure, toppling the newly installed windows and causing damage to the building.

Johnnie and Sam assisted Balan and Sarasu in filing a complaint with the Office of the District Superintendent of Police (DSP). The DSP opened an investigation into the unlawful entry and vandalism of their property and assigned the case to the Circle Inspector in charge of the area.

Construction was halted for a week to allow for the investigation. Since the vandalism occurred in the early morning hours, there were no witnesses, and the perpetrators left no material evidence behind.

After a week of investigation, the police remained tight-lipped about the outcome. Johnnie was advised to resume construction once the investigation concluded. The vandals had caused several thousand rupees' worth of damage to the structure, which required repair.

This act of vandalism was the first material and symbolic expression of violence against Devi for engaging in a romantic relationship with an upper-caste Syrian Christian boy. In response, the police began patrolling the area at night to demonstrate to the miscreants and upper-caste thugs that such violence against a Dalit family would not be tolerated. This sent a clear message that any future acts of vandalism or violence against the Balan family would result in arrest and criminal prosecution. The vandalism stopped.

The house for the Balan family was completed nearly on schedule, with only a one-week delay. Johnnie encouraged Devi to visit the furniture store with her parents to select the items they needed for their new home. They were provided a generous budget to furnish the house with essential items, including household utensils, linens, and furniture.

Sam also asked Devi to choose a refrigerator for the kitchen with his help. After their selections were delivered, the house was ready for occupation. Together with the Balan family, they set a date for the house-warming.

The Balan family requested Johnnie to perform a Christian house-warming ceremony, which included a prayer service. Fifteen days before the Onam Festival, the Johnnie and Balan families gathered at the new house without fanfare for a private prayer service. After Sarasu and Balan boiled milk and drank a ceremonial cup, Johnnie led a Christian prayer, completing the housewarming ceremony.

The Balan family expressed heartfelt thanks to Johnnie, Elsy, and Sam. They felt undeserving of the unprecedented compassion, mercy, and care they had received, something no one else had ever shown them. They thanked Johnnie and Elsy's Christian God, Jesus Christ, for the kindness shown through them. They believed the love of Jesus was working through Sam, Johnnie, and Elsy and expressed their desire to learn more about Him.

After the ceremony, as both families conversed casually at the new house, Devi humbly asked for a moment to speak. She turned to Johnnie, and with a smile she said:

"After much reflection on the events of the past several years and experiencing the redemptive love and affection shown by my love, Sam, and your family, I've developed a deeper conviction for the teachings of Jesus Christ and decided to convert to the Christian faith before our marriage. I wish to be married at Sam's church. Until I fell in love with Sam, neither my family nor I had experienced such profound love. I believe the selfless love taught by Jesus throughout His ministry and on the cross inspired your family to love me and my family, despite our poverty and untouchability."

Johnnie, Elsy, and Sam were deeply moved by Devi's declaration of faith. The unconditional love she had received from Sam over the years, along with the extraordinary compassion shown by his parents, had been redemptive for her and her family. The kindness shown by Johnnie's family toward their impoverished neighbors seemed to reflect the love of Christ, something Devi believed was born from their deep religious convictions. This experience ultimately led her to embrace the Christian faith.

"Are you sure, dear?" Sam asked. "I never asked you to convert. I love you just the way you are, with whatever faith you follow. Whether you're a Dalit, Hindu, or Christian, I love you unconditionally. But if you're choosing Christianity because of your new convictions and your experience of Christ's love through my family, I fully respect that," said Sam.

"You are an adult and free to choose your faith," Johnnie said.

"If your decision is based on your belief in Christ's love, then as an ordained priest and teacher of the Bible, I believe the Holy Spirit is working through me and my family to bring you this message of love, salvation, and eternal life. That love is the manifestation of God's redemptive work in your life. All praise and glory be to Almighty God, the Father, and His Son, Jesus Christ," Johnnie added.

"Sir, please say a word of prayer for Sam and me, your family, and especially my parents," Devi replied.

"The love of Christ, the salvation through Him, and the transformation I see in your lives are what I seek for spiritual peace," Devi said.

Sam stood in awe, witnessing their lives transform. Johnnie placed his hand on Devi's head and prayed in the name of Jesus Christ, asking for her and her family's redemption.

During the prayer, Johnnie asked Devi if she wholeheartedly accepted Jesus Christ as her Savior and Redeemer. She confirmed her faith. Johnnie then declared that, since she had accepted Jesus publicly, she was, from then on, a child of Christ and a Christian.

Johnnie said he would speak with the Diocesan Bishop and the parish Vicar regarding Devi's conversion and her wish to be married in their church. However, he cautioned that simply converting to Christianity did not guarantee her the right to a wedding ceremony at their church. In the eyes of the endogamous Syrian Christian community, Devi would still be seen as a converted Dalit, an untouchable by birth.

The Saint Thomas Christians, who were the modern-day Syrian Christians, maintained strict caste boundaries and did not allow marriages with Untouchables who converted to the Christian faith. They believed they were evangelized by Apostle Thomas and upheld cultural practices of caste purity similar to upper-caste Hindus. As a result, they did not accept converts from untouchable backgrounds into their community or churches.

Johnnie explained that while the church might not make an exception, he would still request the Bishop to consider allowing a wedding ceremony for Sam and Devi. Without any fanfare, Johnnie and Elsy then handed over the house's title and keys to Balan and Sarasu, congratulated them, and gave them a heartfelt hug.

Before leaving, Johnnie asked Balan to seek help from other domestic workers to demolish their old thatched hut and dispose of the materials and debris. He also advised Balan to build a fence around the new property for privacy and safety. Balan agreed to carry out the work.

After his parents left, Sam stayed at Devi's home to discuss alternative wedding plans in case the Bishop and parish Vicar allowed a ceremony at their church. Once the discussion concluded, Sam returned home.

CHAPTER 9

The following week, Johnnie and Sam met with the Diocesan Bishop and the Secretary, a clergyman, of the Church of Malabar Coast. As well-respected professors and scholars in the institutions of their Church, Johnnie and Sam were respectfully welcomed by the Bishop and the Diocesan Secretary.

The Bishop's Secretary had Johnnie and Sam sit on a conference table across from the Bishop after both Johnnie and Sam ceremonially kissed the ring of the Bishop. With great reverence, Johnnie smiled and asked the Bishop, "How are you doing, *Thirumeni* (Your Grace)."

"I am doing well, Johnnie. How is your work at our theological school going? May God bless you on your dedication to train generations of our young men for ministry," said the Bishop.

"Thank you for asking, *Thirumeni*! My work is going well. Your support and confidence in my work matters the world to me," said Johnnie.

"My son, Sam, and I are here to share great news with you. It is his marriage proposal, along with the background and circumstances surrounding it." He leaned forward and smiled.

Then Johnnie continued, "My son has fallen in love with his childhood playmate, Devi, the daughter of our neighbors, Balan and Sarasu, after knowing her well for over two decades. Devi is a college-educated, beautiful young woman with exemplary moral character and integrity. Devi was born into the Dalit family of Balan and Sarasu and is, therefore, a member of the Dalit community. As a child, she attended our Church's Vacation Bible School for several seasons. According to her, she was redeemed with Sam's unconditional love and due to our family's influence. By her own convictions, she has recently professed her faith in Christ in front of our families. As a family, we love her and pray for her. She now seeks to join our Church before their marriage and requested a wedding to be held at our Church," said Johnnie with some level of tension on his face.

"Congratulations on finding the love of your life, Sam," said the Bishop, although his voice and demeanor reflected his disappointment in this marriage proposal. He became silent momentarily as he was facing two highly respected teachers of remarkable scholarship from the two premier Christian teaching institutions of his own Church.

Johnnie and Sam looked anxious about the unpleasant conversations awaiting them. They eagerly leaned forward to listen more from the Bishop.

"I have already heard about this matter from the Vicar of your parish. But more than anyone else in our Church, you know, Johnnie, that our canon prohibits such exogamous marriage alliances between our Syrian Christians with Dalits of untouchable origin. With the changing demographics, we could make an exception. However, the canons of our Church, our Governing Board, along with the Presiding Bishop, and, more importantly, the laity are the ones opposed to such changes to our traditions and practices," the Bishop paused and proceeded.

"That aside, what troubles us is that it is your son of all young men, a highly educated and learned professor of highly respected lineage, who didn't use good judgment and made an unwise choice to fall in love and then propose to marry someone from such an undesirable family. I am sorry to say it reflects poorly on you and your son and our faith community," said the Bishop bluntly.

"*Thirumeni*, I understand your position and the canons of our Church. However, the times have changed, and we must acknowledge this. As a highly educated individual, my son has the right to fall in love with anyone he deems suitable for him, given that we live in changed times and an evolved secular world. So, what we are requesting is an exception to the general practice respecting the changing times and demographics," Johnnie replied.

"Allowing such exogamous marriages in our Church is recognizing that such inter-caste marriages are sanctionable for our Church. That will embolden other young men and women of our Church to fall in love with Dalits of untouchable origin and marry them. Moreover, it will gradually erode our practice of endogamy and dilute the purity of our community. We are the descendants of Brahmins converted by the Apostle of Jesus Christ, Thomas, in 52 AD, and hold a high place and status among all other castes. Therefore, if we allow such exogamous alliances, it would undermine our cultural heritage and elite status, even if they were converted to the Christian faith," the Bishop reiterated.

"She is a Christian, and Jesus loves her regardless of her caste or economic status. Don't you think? Won't we love her as Jesus taught us as one of 'the least among us?' That is also 'loving thy neighbor as thyself,'" quibbled Johnnie gently and pleasantly with reverence.

Unflinching and firmly, the Bishop reaffirmed, "It is still the position of the Church not to allow even those Dalits who were converted to the Christian faith to join or get married in our Church because it would dilute its purity and upper caste standing. Those are the reasons the Church would not make any exceptions to our traditional practices and allow holding a wedding ceremony of a Syrian Christian marrying an Untouchable."

The Bishop's words were not comforting or conciliatory; instead, they were words of condemnation. For such matters, the laity in the Church, mostly unschooled farmers and peasants, want the bishops and the Governing Board, which represent them, to stand tall and enforce its canons.

Sam was offended by the religious arrogance of the Bishop and how he denigrated his falling in love with a beautiful human being just because she was labeled Untouchable by no fault of hers. As a highly educated biology teacher and scholar of philosophy and theology, Sam decided it was not appropriate to remain silent and wanted to speak up on a matter of great significance to him and the community, whether he was addressing the Diocesan Bishop or the Presiding Bishop.

"With all my great respect for you, *Thirumeni*, may I point out that there was a time in history when the uncircumcised gentile converts were not admitted into the Early Christian Church because the Jews at the time held the view that mixing the uncircumcised gentiles with the Christian Jews would make them ceremoniously impure. As you know, gentile converts were not allowed in Christianity until the successful mission of Paul and Barnabas at the Jerusalem Council, held in 50 AD, which corrected that wrong. When we consider such historical mistakes, it is time that our Church takes the leadership and recognizes the dignity of every human being who is created in the image of God, regardless of whether that person is a Christian, Brahmin, or Untouchable. I'm sure there are no Untouchables in the eyes of the Creator who created them. All humans He created are "touchable" creations. Therefore, it's high time that our Church would reconsider its bigoted position," said Sam confidently and respectfully.

"I respect your long-winded historical perspective, reasoning, and insights. But it is not up to me. I am only explaining the current position of the Church. The Church has a Presiding Bishop, who works with a policy-making Governing Board. It is up to the Board to make such changes and new policies. Moreover, even if the Presiding Bishop and the Members of the Governing Board want to change the position of our Church, it is truly the laity who are against such changes. They certainly do not want their sons and daughters to marry the sons and daughters of Untouchables of polluted origin. It takes time, possibly decades, to make such changes," said the Bishop.

"May I humbly point out that the ecclesiastical leaders have a moral obligation to educate the laity about what is religiously and morally right and wrong, especially given changing times and the need for policy changes. You have a bully pulpit and tremendous influence to shape the thinking of the laity," said Sam.

"Maybe. What you are proposing is a radical overhaul of our traditions and practices. I can assure you that it will take many decades for that to happen," retorted the Bishop.

Sam was really incensed at the Bishop's and the Church's position and insensitivity to respect the humanity and dignity of the 'least among them.' He became mildly belligerent and proceeded to speak...

"If you recall, holding an unlicensed Bible was a crime centuries ago, and believers were executed for possessing unlicensed Bibles. The great Biblical scholar and linguist William Tyndale was strangled and burned at the stake for translating the Bible into English. Do the Church and its ecclesiastical authorities still support the execution of scholars for translating the Bible into another language today? The greatest contribution of John Wycliffe and William Tyndale to Christianity was the translation of the Bible into the English language. The Church was wrong to be complicit in digging up and burning Wycliffe's remains 44 years after his death, killing Tyndale, and placing Galileo under house arrest for upholding the heliocentric view of the solar system, which opposed the widely held but false geocentric view of the medieval Church."

The Bishop took his pen and wrote some notes on his notepad and then began to show impatience with Sam's tirade. He clenched firmly on the arms of his chair and leaned back. Sam was not ready to give in to the hypocrisy and the self-righteousness of his own Church in justifying bigotry.

"We, as a church, are repeating similar mistakes when it comes to 'untouchability' and Untouchable Christians. The Untouchables are humans with the same God-given dignity as you and me. Every converted Dalit to Christianity is redeemed by the Holy Spirit, as Scripture teaches." Sam added.

"I heard you, and I understand your point, but it is up to the Governing Board and the Presiding Bishop to initiate any changes," said the Bishop impatiently.

"I'm absolutely sorry for speaking up about this matter. May I also point out that it is unadulterated 'bigotry' to treat thousands of humans, who are created in the same image of God, as less than human and without dignity! I apologize for being unrelenting in my decision to marry the beautiful Untouchable woman, who is a moral exemplar and a quite 'touchable' dignified human in my eyes and in the eyes of the Creator, who loves His creations. I would rather have our wedding at the Registrar's Office than in the bigoted environment of our Church," said Sam indignantly.

Johnnie was alarmed by Sam's arguments and looked concerned, wondering whether his son had gone beyond the boundaries of polite discourse. But he kept silent in support of his son.

"Sam, I understand your sentiments, frustrations, and where you're coming from, and you have made a rational case for why we need change. However, I don't have the power to change the status quo. Let me tell you this: although you have the freedom to choose whom you like as a citizen of our free country, please understand that there will be religious consequences for your actions if you violate the canons and traditional practices of our Church. Your father knows this, as he is part of the same ecclesiastical group you alluded to, and he is our Biblical scholar and church historian. Please note that you may be subject to excommunication for your actions. I wish you good luck, God's grace, and Godspeed in your marriage," said the Bishop.

"Thank you for listening and for your patience, Thirumeni," said Sam.

"Thirumeni, I fully endorse my son's views regarding this particular issue of untouchability and Untouchable Christians. The practice of not accepting those Untouchables who converted to Christian faith as our brothers and sisters in Christ and not as equal to us is religious bigotry and just sheer arrogance. The time has come to stand up collectively against this religious bigotry and speak up and accept the converted Dalit Christians as our brothers and sisters and our equals in Christ. It is time that the Church stop being party to this bigotry of treating a section of our population as polluted and Untouchables. It is so unchristian and inhumane to subvert them, and it is a violation of human rights and social justice. They are clearly "touchable" creations in the eyes of our Creator," said Johnnie.

"We have heard and noted your valid concerns, and I'll convey them to the presiding Bishop. This issue must be addressed at a future Board meeting. Thank you for visiting me and bringing these concerns to my attention. We'll inform the Vicar of your parish that you're not allowed to conduct the wedding ceremony in our Church. May God bless you abundantly," said the Bishop gently.

"Thank you for meeting with us and hearing our concerns," said Johnnie.

After thanking the Bishop, they left the meeting and headed home, with Johnnie riding in the backseat of Sam's motorbike. They were disappointed and frustrated by the rejection from their own Church, based on its age-old bigoted practices and traditions. Both Sam and Johnnie concurred that this was the same Church with a long history of misogyny and gender discrimination, as evidenced by its long-standing prohibition against ordaining women as priests and bishops since its formation in 52 AD.

When they reached home, Johnnie and Sam sat down for tea and light refreshments. Elsy joined them and wanted to know how their meeting with the Bishop had gone. Johnnie updated Elsy about the Bishop rejecting their request with the same old religious bigotry and arrogance.

"It's unchristian to hold the view that Syrian Christians are of a higher status than all other castes because of their legendary pride in their so-called Brahminic origin. Moreover, it's shameful and contemptuous for a reformed modern church to follow the rules of casteism and its manifestations. It's time for the Church to stand up against this bigotry. There is absolutely no 'love of thy neighbor' in this position of the Church," said Sam.

"Yes, I agree, son," said Johnnie.

"*Appa*, what baffles me is that even nearly 2,000 years after the formation of the Christian Church, it hasn't made any significant changes in its misogynistic attitude towards women, as we discussed earlier today. I can understand the social and cultural status and role of women during Jesus' time, which might explain why Jesus didn't choose even one woman as an apostle. Those very social and cultural reasons might also have contributed to the decisions of the founding fathers of the early Church and its leaders not to attribute even one book in the New Testament to a woman. However, we can't ignore the fact that many of the books were considered by scholars as pseudepigrapha," Sam continued.

"When considering the Biblical evidence in the Gospel of Luke, Chapter 8:2-3, Jesus' ministry was financially supported exclusively by women, namely Mary Magdalene, Joanna, Susanna, and others. It was also evident from the scriptures that Jesus' closest confidant among all his disciples was Mary Magdalene, to whom he appeared first after the resurrection. But yet the founding fathers and leaders of the Church corrupted this truth and over the centuries perpetuated an abiding gender discrimination which is still prevalent within our Church," said Sam.

"You're absolutely right in understanding the Biblical truths! I'm a scholar and professor who taught the Bible to theological students for 25 years. As an ordained minister and a devout Christian, I categorically believe in the divine messages in the Bible. In other words, when I read the Holy Bible with devotion rather than a critical eye, I'm spiritually at peace with it," replied Johnnie.

"Biblical exegesis is a critical explanation or interpretation of the text. And, critical explanation of the text is a valuable tool for understanding the Bible," said Sam.

"But in my disinterested search for truth as an intellectual and scholar, when I do research and study the Bible critically, there are obvious contradictions in the way the 'Son of Man' was portrayed in the various books of the Bible, especially when we compare those with the now evident truths from the Gnostic Gospels. If you study the non-canonical Gnostic Gospels discovered in Nag Hammadi—those intentionally left out of the official canons—a different image and persona of Jesus Christ becomes apparent," Johnnie continued.

"*Appa*, thank you for being intellectually honest about it," said Sam.

"For example, in the 'Coptic Gospel of Thomas,' there are 114 'secret teachings' of Jesus Christ. In the 114th secret teaching, when Simon Peter said, 'Women are not worthy of life,' Jesus replied, 'I myself shall lead her in order to make her male so that she too may become a living spirit resembling you males. For every woman who will make herself male will enter the kingdom of heaven.' This gospel presents a different persona of Jesus Christ in his private teachings, as intimately known and portrayed by the Gnostics. These findings made me wonder who Jesus Christ truly was and what concerted efforts were behind the scenes in selecting the canons to characterize an altogether different Jesus to the world. I'm glad I'll be retiring soon and won't have to deal with conflicting truths undermining my faith. I can tell you, truth is stranger than fiction. But my simple faith gives me spiritual peace," said Johnnie.

"Thank you for sharing such scholarly details concerning the contradictions in how Son of Man was portrayed," said Sam.

Sam was awestruck by his father's admission regarding the contradictory accounts of Jesus Christ in the Church's canons and the detailed, recorded accounts of the Gnostics, as portrayed in the "lost scriptures" discovered in Nag Hammadi in the 20th century, which were not included in the New Testament. Johnnie could no longer deny those contradictory accounts and chose to be brutally honest with his adult son, a well-read scholar.

Since Johnnie was turning 55 by the end of the academic year, he was required to retire from his services as mandated by the University to which his Theological Seminary was affiliated. So, he applied for retirement from employment after 25 years of teaching theological students, which he dearly loved. Hundreds of his students became priests in various churches around the state, country, and in some foreign countries.

His application for retirement from service was approved by the Governing Council of the Seminary and the University. Johnnie was scheduled to retire within four weeks. He would then start earning a decent pension from the University. However, Johnnie was independently wealthy and could live comfortably without the retirement income, thanks to the generational wealth he had inherited from his parents.

Johnnie and Sam were fully aware of the religious consequences they would face if they challenged the prevailing sacraments and rites of the Church or condemned its traditions and practices, as reminded by the Diocesan Bishop. They began focusing on coordinating the official wedding at the Registrar's Office, rather than holding it in their Church, and making arrangements for a grand reception at their home for their guests.

Sam, Elsy, and Johnnie met with Balan, Sarasu, and Devi again at their new home. This meeting also allowed them to discover how Balan, Sarasu, and Devi were getting used to their new home. Sarasu and Devi were thrilled to have running water, electric lights, and refrigeration in their house. Most Dalits seldom had such luxuries because they lived hand to mouth and, in many cases, as vassals in their masters' properties or in squalor.

Balan told them that he was so relieved that Devi did not have to go to the river any longer to take a bath and wash her clothes while being objectified by naughty ogling men. He was deeply grateful to Johnnie's family for these luxuries. Even the bare necessities of life, like a bathroom and toilet with or without running water, were luxuries for the impoverished Dalits.

Johnnie and Sam told them that after the wedding, they would help Devi find a full-time job as a physiotherapy assistant in one of the hospitals in the City of Cochin, where Sam and Devi would be residing. Sam told them that they need not worry about their water and electric bills; he would take care of those expenses from there on.

"When Devi starts working again after our marriage, we'll pay all your expenses. Balan no longer needs to do the risky job of climbing coconut trees. Sarasu can stay home and no longer needs to work as a housemaid for my mother. If she wants to help my mother occasionally, Sarasu is welcome to do that. Whatever the case, we'll meet all your financial needs," said Sam.

"Thank you, son," said Balan.

"Yes, I agree with my son. Balan can now stop the hazardous task of climbing the tall coconut trees. Today, I ask that Balan serve as an Overseer for our coconut farming and seasonal sugar cane cultivation. That means he doesn't have to do the hard labor himself but only needs to hire workers and coordinate their activities for us. In other words, you need to coordinate only the labor and other activities related to farming and oversee these activities as per my direction. As I'll be retiring in four weeks, I'll be available full-time to work with you. Rather than your usual hourly wages, I'll now pay you a monthly salary for serving as the Overseer. We'll work out the specific terms of your work soon. This will also allow you to earn a steady income," said Johnnie.

"Thank you, Sam's *Appa* and *Amma*," said Balan.

"I would like to propose the Saturday after *Appa* retires from his job as our official wedding date. We will schedule our official wedding ceremony at the Registrar's Office at 9:00 a.m. on that Saturday. After the wedding, *Appa* and *Amma* will host a grand luncheon and celebrations at our house if that date is okay with Devi, my parents, and Balan and Sarasu. If we agree on that date, we will have four weeks to plan the wedding reception and invite all our guests. As I have already mentioned, *Appa* will serve as the officiant of an informal vows ceremony and lead a brief, meaningful prayer service, not in any official capacity of the Church, but as my father. What do you think?" Asked Sam.

Both families accepted Sam's proposed schedule of activities, especially the official wedding date and the reception at Sam's house. Johnnie and Elsy thought it was a great idea to wait until after his father retired from service to hold the wedding so that he could officiate a private vows-taking ceremony as a retired minister.

"My summer holidays will begin two weeks before our wedding date, so I'll have two weeks before the wedding to finalize all arrangements and the reception. After the wedding, we plan to go to Ooty for our honeymoon and spend two weeks at a private resort," said Sam.

Sam contacted the Registrar's Office the next day and scheduled his official wedding date and time, as agreed upon by both families. He also arranged for two of his trusted college friends to join him to witness their wedding at the Registrar's Office and later attend the reception.

All arrangements for the wedding and reception were made as proposed. Sam and Devi were traditionally expected to return to the bridegroom's home after the wedding and reception to spend the first night and, after a couple of days, go to the bride's home to spend a few days with her family. Accordingly, they decided to sleep at Sam's house on the night of the wedding and go to Devi's home the next day. On the third day, they were scheduled to go to Ooty by train to celebrate their honeymoon there for two weeks.

Devi and her parents looked forward to receiving Sam, their son-in-law, in their new home. They made plans to ensure that they provided a comfortable home for their master's son, now their beloved son-in-law, on the second night after their wedding, with them at their new home before they left for their honeymoon.

Balan cleaned the house and paid extra attention to doing minor landscaping, then cleaned up the front and backyard of his property so Devi and Sam could spend the day and night together at their home. Devi bought new towels, wall mirrors, and other bathroom accessories, as well as bedspreads and comforters for their queen bed, using the funds she had saved from her job.

As expected, the Vicar and several of Johnnie and Elsy's friends and fellow church members declined their invitation to the wedding reception in protest of Sam marrying a Dalit. Some of Johnnie and Elsy's close relatives were also angered by Sam's marriage alliance with a Dalit and declined their invitation. The Johnnie family disregarded the baseless rumors and gossip circulating in the community, focusing instead on the reception.

Meanwhile, Balan's and Sarasu's relatives and friends were ecstatic that she was marrying an upper-caste Syrian Christian man. They were proud that the groom was a highly educated college lecturer and the wealthy son of a famous professor and highly respected clergyman in the state. All the guests invited by Balan, Sarasu, and Devi had agreed to attend the wedding reception.

The only issue was that many of Devi's guests were impoverished Dalits who didn't have proper attire to wear to the wedding reception.

Sam offered Devi a generous amount of funds to buy clothing for her family and some of their immediate relatives so that they could all present themselves as respectable guests on that day rather than as impoverished Untouchables. Sam and his parents were very generous in assisting Devi and her parents with all their financial needs related to the wedding. They gave Devi substantial funds to purchase authentic gold jewelry, allowing her to present herself elegantly, like a princess, in a trendy and opulent Banarasi silk sari, complete with a neck full of authentic gold jewelry.

Johnnie had requested a limited police presence at the reception as a precaution against any miscreants who might express their anger over the marriage of an upper-caste Syrian Christian man to an untouchable Dalit woman since they had previously directed their anger at this Untouchable family and vandalized their house, which was under construction. He had also invited the District Superintendent of Police (DSP), the Circle Inspector, and his staff, who had occasionally surveilled Balan's house after it was vandalized, to the wedding reception. All of them had expressed their desire to attend.

CHAPTER 10

There are few feelings more exciting and profound for the human soul than the anticipation of being joined for life through a legal vow or sacred sacrament. Holy matrimony feels like both the culmination of two lovers' intense passion and the beginning of a shared destiny for their once-wandering hearts. Love lingered in the air; the scent of a wedding stirred all things tender and awakened in Sam a deep, aching yearning for Devi.

Almost a week had passed since Johnnie's retirement reception at the seminary, and two weeks since Sam's college had closed for summer break. That morning, he awoke with thoughts of Devi and a quiet, overwhelming joy—an unprecedented excitement—for today was the day they would be bound as one.

His parents were already awake; his father was on the phone discussing the arrangements while enjoying his morning coffee. Men were working on setting up the round tables and chairs and draping them in white covers under a lily-white wedding tent they had erected and decorated the previous day for the reception. They decorated the tent, the stage, and the podium with real red roses and jasmine flowers, as directed by Sam's mother.

The stage was set up at the farthest end of the rectangular tent, facing the audience, who will be seated on draped chairs around large round tables. A decorated podium was placed on one side of the stage, accompanied by three microphones. In the center of the stage were two decorated chairs reserved for the bride and bridegroom, with another chair positioned near the podium for the officiant of the ceremony, Johnnie.

On a large piece of white cloth that hung at the back of the stage, just behind the chairs of the bride and bridegroom, there was a large inscription in glittering gold Darleston font that read: "Welcome to the Wedding Celebrations of Sam & Devi." That inscription set the tone for the day.

The appetizing aroma of sautéed shallots, curry leaves, ginger, garlic, red pepper, turmeric, and coriander, along with the freshly ground garam masala—comprising cardamom, cinnamon, cloves, and fennel seeds—filled the air. One group of workers was making the *appams* (pancakes) and chicken curry, which would be the first course of the elaborate lunch, while others were sautéing onions, masala, and chevon (goat meat) in extra-large stockpots to make mutton *biryani* for the main course. Another group was preparing traditional Kerala desserts: *adapradhaman* (a sweet pudding made with pasta, coconut milk, and jaggery) and *parippu payasam* (a sweet lentil pudding).

The guests were expected to arrive around 12:30 pm. The eldest brother of Elsy, or Sam's uncle, oversaw the caterers as they prepared and served lunch. Johnnie was in charge of conducting a brief nondenominational Vows and Ring Ceremony, which would not follow the liturgy or format of any formal wedding ceremony of a Syrian Christian church in Kerala.

The religious part of the Vows and Ring Ceremony, which included "taking the vows" and "exchanging the rings," would be led by Johnnie by reading out a set of specially designed wedding vows, developed by Sam with input from Devi under the guidance of his father. The bride and the bridegroom would follow the officiant, Johnnie, as they took the vows in front of their family and friends. Then, they would exchange the rings to declare their commitment to each other before God and the community. After this brief ceremony, the bride and bridegroom could exchange a kiss on the cheek. Johnnie would speak for a few minutes and then conclude the ceremony with a prayer.

Upon the conclusion of the ceremony, the bride and groom were expected to take a break for a photo session. During this time, a couple of entertainment programs would be presented to engage the guests for about 40 minutes. Lunch was expected to be served at 1:30 p.m. That was the order of events for the wedding reception that day. Elsy had arranged for a beautician to apply makeup and a hairstylist to style Devi's hair before they went for the official wedding at the Registrar's Office.

After the hairstylist set Devi's hair and the beautician applied makeup, they fitted her in an elegant silk sari, which made her look so gorgeous like a princess. Sam looked elegant and dapper in his off-white, embroidered Nehru jacket and kurta pajamas, resembling a Royal Figure. The off-white Nehru suit beautifully accentuated his skin tone and usual masculine demeanor.

As planned, their driver took Sam, Elsy, and Johnnie to the Registrar's Office at 8:15 a.m. for the official wedding. Devi, Balan, and Sarasu arrived in another car around the same time. Sam's college friends, the designated witnesses, arrived at the Registrar's Office around 8:30 a.m.

At 9:00 a.m., the Registrar officiated the wedding in his office, followed by the bride and bridegroom signing the Wedding Registry and the two witnesses affixing their signatures. After the marriage registration, all of them returned home around 10:00 a.m. and took pictures with the bride and bridegroom.

Upon their return from the Registrar's Office and after the photo session, Elsy took Devi to her master bedroom, where the beautician was waiting to dress her in a beautiful Banarasi white silk sari, chosen by Devi and Elsy for the religious vows and ring ceremony. Draped in the white silk sari, Devi looked radiant and absolutely stunning. Sam looked confident, handsome, and well-poised in his elegant Nehru-style wedding suit. After Sam and Devi dressed in their gorgeous wedding attire, they looked like the Raja and Rani, the monarchs from an old East Indian fairy tale.

It had been an arduous journey, and now, an impossible dream had come true for Sam and Devi. They were euphoric to be legally husband and wife, and nothing could separate them, not caste, not untouchability, not even the church hierarchy could stand in the way of their union. After the well-planned, brief religious ceremony at the reception, followed by their parents' blessings and lunch, they were finally going to be in each other's arms until death. An overwhelming sense of elation had taken hold of Sam and Devi, making it difficult for them to contain their emotions.

Since they were expecting only 400 guests, including Johnnie's and Balan's immediate family members, the wedding tent was built to seat exactly 400 guests. However, as a precaution, they had added eight extra seats to accommodate any unexpected overflow. They set up 51 large round tables, each with 8 chairs. The caterers prepared food to serve 410 guests.

As the guests arrived, they were all served various non-alcoholic soft drinks and an assortment of light refreshments. When all the seats were filled by 12:30 p.m., Johnnie, representing both the Balan family and his own, introduced himself from the podium.

"Friends, relatives, and immediate family members and distinguished guests, my name is Reverend Johnnie Jacob, the bridegroom's father and your host for the event. A couple of weeks ago, I retired from my position as Professor of Theology at the Theological Seminary. I have also relinquished my duties as an ordained priest upon retiring from my job at the Seminary. Therefore, I want you to know that I am not standing here in any official capacity of the Church of Malabar Coast but was serving in the private interest of both families and as the father of the bridegroom, Sam Jacob, and father-in-law of Devi," announced Johnnie using the microphone.

"I cordially welcome everyone who accepted our invitation and joined us in this auspicious celebration of our children's wedding. I would like to inform you that Sam and Devi were married this morning at 9:00 a.m. at the District Registrar's Office. Let us congratulate Mr. and Mrs. Sam Jacob by giving them a round of applause," said Johnnie.

Sam and Devi, who were already seated in the front of the hall on two separate ornate chairs, rose and waved to the guests, who greeted them with thunderous applause. When the applause waned, they got up and bowed to the audience.

"Today's celebrations include four parts: an unofficial brief Vows and Ring Ceremony, prayer, light entertainment, and lunch."

"Now, I invite Sam and Devi to please come to the stage and stand here facing the audience." When Sam and Devi stepped onto the stage and stood facing the audience, Johnnie positioned himself in front of them with his back to the audience, facing both Sam and Devi.

"Sam and Devi have prepared a few wedding vows together, working with me. Now, I'm going to ask them to repeat the vows after me."

Johnnie then handed both Sam and Devi a microphone and began reading the vows using his own. After each vow was read, Sam and Devi repeated it in unison, as instructed by Johnnie, using their individual microphones. After the vows were completed, Johnnie took out two gold rings from a tiny jewelry box.

"Sam and Devi, you may please stand facing each other," instructed Johnnie.

Sam and Devi stood facing each other while Johnnie faced both of them.

"Now I ask that Sam take a ring from the box and insert it onto Devi's ring finger on her left hand," instructed Johnnie. As directed, Sam took a ring and put it on Devi's left ring finger.

"Devi, now you may please take a ring from this box and insert it onto Sam's ring finger on his left hand." Devi did the same as directed by Johnnie.

Johnnie then asked them to continue facing each other while holding each other's hands.

Then Johnnie requested Sam to repeat after him: "I, Sam, take you, Devi, as my wife, to have and to hold till death do us part." Sam took his vow.

After Sam took his final vow, Johnnie then asked Devi to repeat after him: "I, Devi, take you, Sam, as my husband, to have and to hold till death do us part." Devi took her vow as well.

"I congratulate you both for entering the Christian matrimony, which is an unbreakable covenant. Ladies and gentlemen, I present to you Mr. Sam and Mrs. Devi Jacob, husband and wife." He then told Sam, "You may kiss your wife, Devi, on her cheek." When Sam kissed his wife on the cheek, the audience broke into thunderous applause.

Johnnie thanked and congratulated them individually. Then, he blessed them by putting his hands on both Sam and Devi's foreheads and prayed for them. Next, Johnnie thanked the audience.

"Again, Mr. Sam and Mrs. Devi Jacob were officially married at the District Registrar's office this morning at 9:00 a.m. The unofficial and symbolic religious ceremony I have just conducted merely reinforced the legal commitment they had made to each other earlier today before the government official. This religious ceremony was a pledge of their love, devotion, trust, and faithfulness to each other as they united their separate lives into one before their families, friends, and, above all, God," announced Johnnie.

"I want to remind you once more that I have conducted this prayer ceremony not as an officiant of any religious denomination or Church but only as requested by both the bride and bridegroom and our families," Johnnie reminded the audience.

"At this time, I invite everyone to sit back, relax, and enjoy the entertainment. Lunch would be served after the entertainment. Please enjoy."

As everyone enjoyed a delicious lunch and conversation, two motorbikes passed by. They stopped on the street right in front of the wedding tent, with two riders on each, their helmets covering their faces and masking their identities. Then they revved up their motorbike engines with a loud 'vroom' sound, shouted "To hell with the Untouchables," and left the scene immediately.

The policemen on duty rushed out to accost them, but by the time they arrived at the scene, they had left. Although the thugs disturbed the luncheon for a moment, they knew as well as the police that they could not be apprehended for revving up their engines on a public street or for shouting, "To hell with the Untouchables." The reception continued without disruption.

When the reception was over, the guests began to leave, but before they left, some of them stayed on and took photos with Sam and Devi, as was customary.

When the last guests disappeared, Sam wrapped his arms around Devi and walked her to his house. He whispered in her ear, "Devi, you are like a princess in that beautiful dress. My princess, indeed," said Sam.

Holding Devi's right hand, he led her to his home's front doorstep. Sam's mother, Elsy, who was already waiting at the doorway for this moment, warmly received Devi with open arms and a welcoming hug, which made her feel at home and comfortable.

"Welcome to our home, Devi. From here on, you are our daughter, too. Please come and have a seat on the special seat we set up for you," said Elsy. Elsy and Johnnie led Devi, now rightfully their daughter-in-law, to an ornate chair that had been made ready for the bride.

"Devi, you look stunningly beautiful in your silk sari with your make-up and styled hair," said Elsy.

She did not look like an Untouchable, but she was better looking than the most beautiful Syrian Christian or Brahmin lady. She was well-endowed with a sharp nose and curvaceous physical features, her skin shimmering in a rich, brown hue. Above all, she was poised and walked around with an elegant demeanor, exuding confidence and maturity.

Elsy and Johnnie then went together to receive their very special guests, Balan and Sarasu. They invited them into their house with a broad smile and after a tight embrace.

"Welcome to our home, Balan and Sarasu." Johnnie took Balan's hand, and Elsy took Sarasu's hand and walked them to their sofa. "Please sit down," Johnnie asked politely and gently to Devi's parents. They both hesitated to sit down and then moved to the corner of the room, diffidently avoiding the sofa. They let them take their time before sitting down.

This was a sea change and an unprecedented moment for the Untouchable family, and they acted like fish out of water. As Untouchables, they had never been invited to a wedding reception as special guests where they mingled with the upper caste, much less sat on the sofa with them. In almost all instances, the Dalits were not welcomed inside the formal part of the homes of the Syrian Christians or other upper-caste people during auspicious occasions during that era. They mostly were helpers in the kitchen or outside. Despite the glorious and joyful occasion of being there as very special guests at their master's house—this time as their son's in-laws—Balan and Sarasu began to feel anxious and nervous.

As expected, Balan and Sarasu felt out of place, although, for the first time, they were dressed in fancy and expensive upper-caste clothes and jewelry, especially wearing new cowhide shoes, well-groomed hair, and clean nails. Johnnie held them by their hands and said,

"Balan and Sarasu, you're here as our son's father-in-law and mother-in-law. From here on, you will be an important part of our lives. This is a new reality for you and the beginning of an exciting journey for us. Please come and sit down with me and Elsy on our Sofa."

Balan and Sarasu sat down on the sofa, reluctantly yet nervously. Johnnie and Elsy knew it would take time for them to adjust to a life they had never dreamed of or envisioned.

"May I have your attention, please!" announced Johnnie. "Syrian Christians have a custom called '*Kacha* (a sari) *Koduppu* or 'presentation of a sari," when the bride and groom come to the groom's home along with the bride's parents and immediate family members. It is customary for the groom to present the bride's mother, who is now a new mother to him, with a *Kacha* (sari). So, at this time, I ask Sam to come forward and give the gift of sari to his mother-in-law, Sarasu," announced Johnnie.

As advised by his father, Sam presented Sarasu with a beautiful sari. She accepted the gift with gratitude from her son-in-law and, in turn, gifted him a gold ring, as Elsy had arranged in advance.

"The '*kacha koduppu*' concluded all the ceremonies for the day," said Johnnie, and sat down with pride and joy.

The two families and their immediate family members, Sam and Devi, sat in Johnnie's family room, mingled, and enjoyed each other's company. They all complimented Sam and Devi on what a beautiful couple they were together. Balan and Sarasu expressed their gratitude, telling everyone that they were incredibly fortunate and that Devi was exceptionally blessed to have Sam as her husband.

Elsy and her female servants continued to serve the guests tea, coffee, and a variety of refreshments until dinnertime. She instructed her housemaids to prepare dinner for all the guests. In the meantime, everyone discussed the day's events and how well the religious ceremony and reception had gone. They chatted about their visitors and the day's comings and goings.

When dinner was served, Elsy said, "Devi and Sam, you have special seats here on the table," she seated the bride and the bridegroom.

"Now, Balan and Sarasu, please come and sit by us for dinner. Balan, you sit by Johnnie, and Sarasu can sit by me," directed Elsy.

Johnnie and Elsy had to firmly persuade Balan and Sarasu to sit with them for dinner, along with Sam and Devi. This was another awkward moment for Balan and Sarasu, as they had never dined with the upper caste on the same dinner table, especially during a ceremonial meal in such an extravagant home, where the Syrian Christian relatives were eating a formal dinner together.

The Dalits usually sat on the floor and ate meals with other impoverished Untouchables. Sarasu tried to bail out, sitting with Johnnie's family under the pretext that she wanted to help the maids serve dinner to the guests. Elsy knew what Sarasu was trying to do, so she insisted that Sarasu sit down with Balan next to Johnnie and her, and they would all eat dinner together. Balan hesitantly and bashfully sat with them and had dinner while Sarasu helped serve the meal.

After dinner, Devi's parents hugged their new son-in-law and their daughter and said, "We will see you tomorrow at our house, Sam and Devi. Good night!"

"Thank you, Sam's *Appa* and *Amma*, for your kind hospitality and for welcoming us warmly to your home." Balan and Sarasu addressed Johnnie and Elsy as "Sam's *Appa* and *Amma*" to show respect, as they didn't feel equal to call them by their first names. After thanking Johnnie and

Elsy, they left with an inner joy they had never felt before.

When all the guests left, Sam's parents wished Sam and Devi an exciting first night and told them they were exhausted and wanted to retire for the evening. Before going to bed, Elsy told Devi that she had just kept two cups of warm milk for both of them on the dinner table, and she should take the milk and serve one cup to Sam before they went to bed, as was customary.

"Good night, Devi and Sam," Johnnie and Elsy said in unison. Sam's parents left Sam and Devi alone in their family room. His parents were exhausted after a long day and happy to go to bed.

Sam put his hand around Devi's bare waist and led her slowly to his bedroom with a small tray of two cups of milk in her hands. As he walked to his bedroom with his hand around her waist, he could feel for the first time the warmth of her body under her sari, the rapidness of her heartbeat, and the heaviness of his breathing. Sam and Devi were exuberant and sensual! They had been waiting for this moment for years.

Sam felt immense joy at finally reaching the finish line after a long and arduous journey. That finish line happened to be in his bedroom, which he had been preparing for his princess for many years.

After she placed the tray on the nightstand and affectionately handed him a cup of milk, Sam knew this was the moment he had been waiting for his entire life. He felt that Devi was nothing but a heap of affection, wrapped in an exuberance of love, beaming with excitement to reciprocate his unconditional love, which had led to this moment of truth.

The love that had sprouted in forbidden soil grew into a strong, verdant green tree despite the adverse conditions it faced, and its "Untouchable" flower, seldom smelled or tasted for fear of its 'polluting' nature and untouchability, now belonged to him—to explore, cherish, and admire, for he had made it his own "pure" and "touchable" one with the light of their mutual love.

Sam drank the cup of milk, the first-ever drink served by Devi. He could not remember what happened next or where he placed his cup. He knew one of them had turned off the lights, and before long, they were in a tight embrace, remaining there in contentment for a while. But that long embrace was deeply intimate, with the fire of love burning wildly.

They felt highly vulnerable, anticipating the melting of themselves in the pleasure of love, yet equally nervous about losing control. That night was too short for them, and many more nights would not be enough for them to explore and satiate their uncontrollable desire for each other.

Sam was awakened from his deep sleep in the morning with a gentle caressing touch on his face by someone. It was Devi with a cup of coffee caressing his face gracefully and gratefully for the exciting and fulfilling night they had enjoyed together in uncontrollable sensual pleasure.

He loved her natural scent, the alluring pheromones emitted by her body that first drew him in and ignited his passionate love for her. It was the most captivating fragrance of "love hormones," and he wished to savor it repeatedly with every moment of his life. She tasted sweet and salty, like the cleanest person he had ever encountered, free from any hint of "untouchability" or "pollution."

Her perfectly curvy body sparked a fire in his eyes, and he recognized that she was unfathomably more beautiful than anyone of the opposite sex he had ever seen. Her touch unleashed an inferno of sensual pleasure that melted him in its intensity.

"Sam, good morning, dear! Please have a cup of coffee. *Amma* made this for you. Please wake up. It is already 8:00 a.m. *Amma* is making breakfast for us now. Please have coffee and take a shower," said Devi.

Devi then bent down and whispered in his ear with naughty humor, "You must be tired from last night, but you will need a shower after all. I have enjoyed every moment of our intimacy. Thank you for such a pleasurable night."

He gave her a wet kiss and sat on the side of his bed, beginning to sip the coffee. Even the coffee had an enticing smell and taste that he had never experienced before. For a moment, he was lost in a moral awakening, the epiphany of which felt ethereal and profound.

Devi's so-called "untouchability" was elusive beyond any sensory and observable experiences of objective reality. So, the notion of untouchability vanished from his world into thin air without any meaning or rationale. He knew well that those social elites, the purveyors of untouchability, who imposed "untouchability" on innocent humans like Devi, were the ones seemingly "corrupted" and "polluted" by their diabolical dark nature. They adapted their gods and religion to fit their narratives and attributed religious legitimacy to it. They exploited the vulnerabilities and credulity of innocent humans, such as Devi and her family, for their own economic benefits and social advantages. Yes, they were the ones who had corrupted and subverted those precious creations of God!

After their first night in his parents' house, Devi and Sam went to her house in the evening to spend the night. Sarasu and Balan were thrilled that Sam would be spending the night at their house. Sarasu made a sumptuous dinner for her new son-in-law.

"Sam, we have made your favorite fish curry and fish fry, chevon curry, spinach, and okra 'thoran.' Please come and eat dinner," said Sarasu with excitement.

"Thank you very much, Amma," said Sam. Sarasu was overjoyed to hear Sam calling her Amma. To her, it was music to the ears—an unprecedented privilege, seldom granted to a Dalit by an upper-caste Syrian Christian man.

"Devi, please serve Sam his favorite dishes, baby! Then, you also sit down and eat your dinner. We will eat after you both finish eating," said Sarasu.

"Please come and have dinner with us, *Appa* and *Amma*," Sam called out to Devi's parents, also addressing them as *Appa* and *Amma*, and insisted that they join them for dinner. They were all deeply touched by Sam calling Devi's parents *Appa* and *Amma*.

Balan and Sarasu sat down with them for dinner. After dinner, they all gathered to talk before going to bed. Despite Sam's repeated requests, Balan and Sarasu sat on the floor rather than on the sofa with them the entire time they were having a conversation. After some time, Sam then got up and sat on the floor with Devi's parents, who refused to sit with Devi and Sam on the couch.

Their second night was even more exciting than the first. They spent a lot of time lying on the bed, talking and reminiscing about their past while caressing each other. Then, they made love again and again. When morning broke, Devi hurriedly began packing her bags for their honeymoon trip to Ooty until Sam woke up.

Sarasu and Devi prepared Sam's favorite breakfast: *idli, sambar,* and English tea with cream and sugar. After breakfast, they spent some more time with Devi's parents, and around noon, they returned to Sam's house for lunch and to prepare for their trip to Ooty.

While they were having lunch at Sam's house, the driver began to get the car ready and load the bags to take them to the train station, where they would catch the afternoon train to Ooty. They had already reserved two first-class seats on the train.

The two weeks they spent in a resort in Ooty was the most memorable time of their life. Sam learned more and more about the most affectionate and caring nature of Devi. He became more aware of her sense of moral integrity and honesty, unlike any Christians he came to know in the community. He learned she was very protective of him, precisely like the Devi of his younger days, who protected him while playing in the lagoon.

Sam's love for her had grown like the roots of a giant tree, deeper and stronger. Remarkably, Sam's unconditional love boosted her confidence and made her more resilient every day, helping her overcome her deeply ingrained and insidious attitudes of servitude and the 'untouchability complex' that had been instilled in her psyche by society and had eroded her self-esteem.

When they returned home from their honeymoon, Sam and Devi were two transformed adults joined together in the unbreakable bond of love who were willing to face any challenges of the world as one.

Elsy and Johnnie greeted and welcomed them home after a long day's rail travel from Ooty.

They were tired and famished. Elsy told them that dinner was ready and that they had both been waiting for them to return home and have dinner together.

While they were eating dinner, Elsy casually said, "Sam, I have accepted a registered letter on your behalf. I will give it to you after dinner."

After their dinner, Elsy handed the letter over to Sam. He was shocked by the letter stating that his employment contract would not be renewed. He was visibly disturbed by the unexpected news. Sam, his colleagues, and the campus community all knew he was the most popular and highest-performing junior lecturer at his college. His evaluations were excellent, and he never had even one complaint against him on file.

The message was unmistakable! Sam was indignant and furious!

"May I know what is in the letter, Sam? Please talk to us. Why are you looking agitated and upset," asked Johnnie.

"What happened, Sam? Please tell us," Elsy chimed in.

Devi had never seen him this upset and was perturbed by his demeanor, which made her nervous.

"The letter was to inform me that they have decided to discontinue my contract and not to recommend me for a promotion from Junior Lecturer to Lecturer. The termination of my contract will be effective the last day of April," said Sam in an indignant tone.

"My goodness! They told me before your marriage that you were the shining star among all junior lecturers in terms of research and publication and the most popular teacher among students at the college. Then what happened?" Asked Johnnie.

Johnnie knew what was obvious and did not want to say it in front of Devi, which might sadden her. Elsy was stunned and filled with moral indignation for the bigoted decision of the Christian College's Governing Board. Johnnie restored his composure, fearing he would upset Devi and make her feel guilty.

Devi began to feel the tension in the room, stemming from the wrongdoing and the misfortune that had befallen them. Sam went over to her, held her, and said, "Don't worry. Everything is okay. I am not sad or worried. I am only indignant. I will easily find another job. So, everything is going to be alright, my love." But Devi felt responsible for Sam losing his job.

The defenders of endogamy, along with caste separatists and segregationists, tried to send an early warning by terminating Devi from her half-time job as a physiotherapy assistant at the hospital. Their message was subtle but clear: one should not cross caste boundaries. However, Sam remained unrelenting in his decision to marry Devi, the Dalit girl.

Now, they wanted to send an even stronger message about the consequences of breaking their long-standing cultural traditions and the practice of endogamy. Although Devi was a Christian by faith, they cared little for Dalits who converted to Christianity. The Syrian Christians did not consider converted Dalit Christians equal in status, as they believed themselves to be the elites.

Devi began to cry and said, "It's all my fault and not Sam's. I'm a *Manglik* with *Mangal Dosha*, which is currently being played out. This is the malefic effect of my *Mangal Dosha*. It was written in my *Jathakam* that, because of the Mars defect, I would not ever enjoy peace and harmony in my married life. I'm terribly sorry," said Devi in a trembling voice.

"Devi, my love, it is absolutely not your fault! Come on, to think that the giant dead planet made of dirt and minerals sends baneful effects to punish humans who are nearly 225 million kilometers away is so irrational, to say the least. Trust me, dear, *Mangal Dosha* is a lie, and your horoscope is irrelevant now in our lives. What some of the Syrian Christians are practicing with their discrimination against the Untouchables is bigotry, plain and simple. We're not going to accept their bigotry and hatred. I'm not upset about losing my job. I'm upset that they continue to play these games to justify their hatred. They want to punish anyone who is iconoclastic and challenge their bigotry." Sam continued.

"You see, in America, there was a civil war between the Confederate states that supported slavery and the states that opposed it. The Confederate states, which wanted to continue the slave trade, justified its morality and legitimacy with the imprimatur of scripture," Sam added.

"In all this, there is a 'right,' which is much more powerful than the 'wrong.' But the masses are afraid of the 'right' because it is the truth, and the truth shall set them free. So, they're afraid to let go of the wrong. I'm not afraid or worried about losing my job. I'm confident I can find five other, better ones. So, please don't feel sad, my love. You didn't do anything wrong. I love you with all my heart, no matter what happens around us. We must stand up against such social evils; it is our responsibility as decent and moral individuals. We can't remain silent about it," said Sam.

"Devi, Sam is our only son; he doesn't have to work to make a living. All he needs to do is take care of our coconut farming and sugar cane cultivation. Farming can be highly lucrative, allowing you to lead an extravagant lifestyle without relying on a salaried job. However, he is a highly educated scholar who wants to fully realize his potential. He can easily get a public university teaching job with the kind of credentials he holds," said Johnnie.

"They will not stop Sam and you from living your life to the fullest. I'll call my uncle, who is a university official in Bangalore, and inquire about any open positions in their affiliated colleges so that you both can leave and lead your lives in another state; not that I want my only son to leave town and live in another state. But their bigotry and inequity are becoming loudly clear. We are not going to be defeated or be on the side of moral depravity," said Elsy.

With their reassurances, Johnnie and Elsy calmed Devi's nerves and made her feel at home and relaxed. After dinner, they spoke for a while about their trip to Ooty and enjoyed spending time with the new member of their family, their daughter-in-law. They all went to bed after their time together as a family without any worries about the troubled world they were part of.

Sam and Devi's plan was to stay home for a few more days and then move into his existing apartment in Cochin to explore new opportunities. This would enable him to explore other teaching opportunities at public universities in Cochin. Moving to Cochin would also allow Devi to look for a full- or part-time physiotherapy assistant job at any major hospital there. She was also interested in earning a four-year degree in physical therapy.

They discovered that two professional colleges in Cochin offer four-year degree programs in Physical Therapy in collaboration with the hospitals there. She hoped to work and take classes concurrently to complete her degree in physical therapy.

They spent the rest of their vacation between Sam and Devi's houses. They loved roaming around their familiar sugarcane fields. Now that they didn't have to fear the world, they spent a lot of private time together by the lagoon and in their usual secret meeting place under the jackfruit tree, regardless of the worries of the inequitable termination of Sam's employment.

To complicate matters, the bigoted members of his parish, who opposed Sam marrying an Untouchable girl, whipped up a controversy involving Johnnie, which went public. The Johnnie family tried to shield Devi from learning about this dark controversy.

That morning, Johnnie received a call from the presiding Bishop of his Church, who wanted to meet with him immediately. The charge against Johnnie was that he conducted his son's official wedding at home as an ordained minister of the Church of Malabar Coast, which was initially rejected by the Diocesan Bishop of the Church and the Vicar of his parish. The members of his parish were so upset that they wanted to excommunicate and defrock Johnnie.

So, they filed a complaint against Johnnie, a retired Professor of Theology at their Seminary. Although an ordained priest, Johnnie never served as a pastor in any of the parishes of the Church of Malabar Coast because he was a full-time professor at the Seminary. However, some parish members wanted him excommunicated and defrocked for violating the Church's rules and, more importantly, for insubordination.

Johnnie was not worried or concerned about the complaint. He decided to stand up for what was morally right and support his son in fighting the bigotry of the Church and its meaningless traditions. He had asked Sam to take Devi from that environment, move her into his apartment in Cochin as soon as possible, and live there.

Sam and Devi changed their plans and left for Cochin earlier than they had initially planned. They both moved into Sam's apartment. Devi set up their kitchen and fully furnished the two bedrooms—the master bedroom for them and the other for Johnnie and Elsy, in case they came to visit. Balan and Sarasu never liked to travel to big cities because the big cities and their people made them nervous and uneasy.

When they started living in Cochin, Devi found a full-time job as a physiotherapy assistant at the Riverside Hospital, the largest corporate hospital in the City of Cochin. The hospital offered a joint bachelor's degree program in physical therapy with the University of Cochin. She was selected for the program and enrolled in PT classes, with her employer covering 50% of her tuition. The lessons and clinics were conveniently held at the hospital facility, and the employer provided her with time off to attend the classes and clinics while also paying her a decent salary.

Although Devi was living an extravagant life that she or another Dalit could not ever dream of in a large city with the love of her life, she desperately missed seeing her parents and her conversations with Elsy. So, they made trips to their homes every fortnight.

Devi's life became very busy with keeping a home in Cochin, working full-time, and taking classes for her undergraduate degree in physical therapy. She did not have any personal time to keep track of the religious controversies surrounding Johnnie and the threat of his defrocking and excommunication at home. Sam and Johnnie deliberately protected Devi from learning more about it, fearing she would feel guilty, hurt, and sad.

Around that same time, Sam was admitted to the University of Cochin for his doctoral studies in Evolutionary Biology with a unique research focus on Evolutionary Genetics. After six months into his postgraduate studies and research, he successfully published two scholarly articles in professional journals. The two scholarly articles he published enabled him to secure a job as a Lecturer in Biology at the University of Cochin's University Center for Biological Sciences in Fort Kochi, which was five miles away from their residence.

CHAPTER 11

Although Johnnie had led an unblemished career and an exemplary life, he seemed to have been bruised and tarnished by religiously arrogant, vindictive, and self-righteous bigots who had misconstrued his righteous and well-intentioned act of conducting a prayer service for his son and daughter-in-law after their legal marriage at the District Registrar's Office. In the end, the forces of diabolical evil had caught up with him, determined not to let his good deeds go unpunished.

He realized that even the most well-intentioned deeds could have negative consequences when pride was bruised and egos were scorched. Johnnie's moral integrity and intellectual honesty were at stake. He was not willing to compromise his integrity or honesty in the face of evil-doers.

As scheduled by the Presiding Bishop of the Church of Malabar Coast, Johnnie went to meet with him at the Church's headquarters in Kottayam. The bishop welcomed him and invited him to his private office, where he had him sit down across from him at his desk, as Johnnie was a highly respected former professor and biblical scholar at the Church's Theological Seminary.

He was often consulted on matters related to Biblical scholarship, Church schisms, early Church history, and internal controversies. He also served as the de facto Church historian and was often referred to as the modern-day Eusebius of Church history. However, this time, the controversy centered on his alleged officiation of his son's wedding to a Dalit woman, a union that had been rejected by the Church.

After some initial small talk, the Presiding Bishop said, "Johnnie, I'm concerned about the complaint filed by a few members of your Church. I spoke to the Diocesan Bishop and the Vicar of your parish to gather some background on the issue. Their complaint was that you officiated your son's marriage to a Dalit woman, which was banned by our Church, at a private ceremony held at your home. Please tell me what happened. I would like to hear your story directly before making any judgment."

"*Thirumeni*, it is true that my son, Sam, a lecturer at our Christian College, fell in love with a college-educated, working woman of untouchable origin. She is a beautiful woman with great moral integrity and exemplary character. Since our Church had refused to consecrate their wedding, they got married at the District Registrar's office. Before their marriage, Devi accepted Jesus Christ as her Savior and became a Christian of her own volition. So yes, she is a Christian by faith, and that is good enough for my son and for our family," said Johnnie.

"Okay! I'm disappointed that Sam married a Dalit girl, but I'm glad that she became a Christian," said the bishop.

"When my son and I initially approached the Diocesan Bishop and our Vicar to conduct the wedding at our Church, they rejected our request based on the prevailing endogamous traditions of our Church. Since they denied us the opportunity to hold the ceremony in our Church, my son and his bride had a civil marriage at the District Registrar's Office. After their legal marriage at the Registrar's Office, my wife, Elsy, and I hosted a wedding reception for our guests at our home. As requested by my son, my daughter-in-law, and our families, I conducted a brief, secular, non-denominational, and unofficial ceremony for the exchange of vows and rings. Since Christian marriage is ordained by God, Sam and Devi asked me to officiate them taking their vows after their legal marriage at the reception, in front of their families, relatives, and friends, and more importantly, before God," said Johnnie.

"Then what happened?" asked the bishop.

"Together, the bridegroom and bride wrote a few meaningful Christian marriage vows to pledge before God and in front of our families and guests. They also wanted to exchange rings as a symbol of their commitment to each other. So, I helped them take their vows in front of everyone. Then Sam and Devi exchanged rings, as the circle in the ring symbolized their everlasting love and devotion to one another," Johnnie paused and smiled.

"Okay," said the bishop.

"After they exchanged their rings, I prayed for God's blessings upon their marriage. Before the Vows and Ring Ceremony, I informed the guests that I was not acting in any official capacity of the Church since I had retired from all formal duties. That was what happened. The bride and groom wanted to commit to each other before God, and I was simply there to assist them. It was a non-denominational, private Christian prayer ceremony that did not follow any official liturgy or format of any Syrian Christian denominations," Johnnie explained with reverence and humility.

"But the congregants are upset that you conducted a typical Church of Malabar Coast wedding ceremony at your home and had them officially exchange wedding vows and rings. Specifically, they claim that, as an ordained priest of our Church, you defied the Church's decision by conducting a wedding that had been rejected by the Diocesan Bishop and the Vicar. They filed a complaint with me and the Governing Board, calling for your excommunication, defrocking, and complete removal of your priestly rights and privileges. The Board is outraged that an ordained minister of our Church conducted what they viewed as an official Church wedding at his residence," said the bishop.

"But the truth is that I did not conduct any official wedding ceremony on behalf of the Church. I wasn't wearing a cassock under a cope, which is officially worn by our priest when conducting a wedding. I didn't perform the 'Blessing of the Crown' ritual and the 'tying of the knot' (*minnukettu*) using a '*minnu*' (a pendant with a cross), which are the most significant rituals in our Syrian Christian wedding. Moreover, in our Church's liturgy, the priest is the one who places the ring on the fingers of the bride and groom. At our reception, it was Sam who placed the ring on Devi's finger and Devi who placed it on Sam's. As you know better than anyone, that is not how we perform an official wedding ceremony in our Church," said Johnnie.

"But Johnnie, the congregants don't see it that way. They don't seem to understand the nuances in our liturgy or the symbolism of your actions. A few who attended your reception saw the couple exchanging rings and concluded that you had officiated the wedding. It's hard to reason with people who don't understand the distinctions. They saw an ordained priest conducting what looked like a wedding ceremony that the Church had already rejected, although I am surprised that they didn't notice that you were not wearing a cassock and a cope," the bishop said.

"I'm sorry they misconstrued the private prayer ceremony we held at our home. The fact is, it was not an official wedding and did not follow the liturgy of our Church. Sam and Devi wanted to take their vows and exchange rings, and I was merely there to help," Johnnie explained calmly, with a smile.

"So, before this issue escalates further, I proposed to the Governing Board that we resolve it by asking for a public apology from you—to protect you and in respect of the concerns raised by the congregation. Therefore, I am requesting that you issue a written public apology. I will personally handle any other consequences," said the bishop.

"With all my reverence and love for you, I do not want to make your role more difficult. But I must categorically reject the baseless accusations of these unreasonable critics. They are angry because I allowed my son to marry a Dalit woman of so-called untouchable origin. These are the same people who fail to respect the God-given dignity of those wrongly labeled as Dalits.

The Dalits are also God's children and deserve equal dignity," Johnnie said, pausing for a breath.

"Issuing a public apology is one easy way to calm them down," said the bishop.

"The religious arrogance of these complaining congregants makes them feel superior and elitist. They know I did not conduct an official wedding, but they are upset that my son married a Dalit woman. That is the real reason behind their outrage, not because I officiated any ceremony. With all my love and respect for you, I cannot issue a public apology for something I did not do," Johnnie concluded.

"Johnnie, in that case, the Board will likely recommend that I take disciplinary action by defrocking and excommunicating you for disobeying Church orders and refusing to issue a public apology," said the bishop.

"What I respectfully request from the Church under your leadership is due process. An investigation should be initiated to establish the facts. Even if wrongdoing is found, I still will not issue an apology because I did nothing wrong, other than allow my son and his wife to exchange vows after their legal civil marriage at the Registrar's Office. I don't consider that a violation. Thank you for listening and for discussing this issue openly. Regardless of the outcome, you will always have my loyalty and friendship, as you have for the past 25 years," said Johnnie.

"Given my deep respect for you and the long-standing friendship we share, I will initiate an investigation within the next few days. I will assign our Church's Rector, another respected servant of God like you, to lead the inquiry and report back to us," said the bishop.

"Thank you," said Johnnie, who then left the residence of the Presiding Bishop after paying his respects by kissing his ring.

Two weeks after their meeting, the bishop called Johnnie again. "Johnnie, I've received the report of the investigating committee. They interviewed the Diocesan Bishop, the parish Vicar, a few guests who attended Sam's wedding reception, and the members who filed the complaint," the Bishop said.

"Okay, what did you find out?" asked Johnnie.

"Johnnie, I'm sorry! The report indicated wrongdoing on your part as the officiant of the religious wedding ceremony held at the reception. Their finding was that the exchange of rings and the declaration of Sam and Devi as husband and wife symbolized an official act by you as an ordained priest of the Church. Unfortunately, the complainants do not understand the nuances, such as who placed the rings on their fingers. They only saw that the rings were exchanged and that the couple took wedding vows, which they interpreted as symbolic of a formal church wedding. I am deeply sorry about the report, Johnnie," informed the bishop.

"Wow, that is a complete misrepresentation, misinterpretation, and manipulation of the facts by the Vicar and the bigoted rabble-rousers in our Church, who are trying to accuse me of wrongdoing. It is retribution, and it is deeply unchristian," said Johnnie.

"Johnnie, for your information, the investigating committee, in its report, recommended taking disciplinary action against you. The resolution they proposed included two parts: (1) the presiding Bishop would issue a formal warning letter against you, and (2) you would appear in person at a public meeting of the Governing Board to publicly apologize and seek reprieve. If you need time, I'll give you two days to think about it and get back to me," the bishop informed him.

"Okay, I will get back to you in two days," said Johnnie.

Johnnie called his son and updated him on the situation. Sam felt deeply saddened that his father had to endure public humiliation and disgrace simply because he had married a Dalit woman.

"Sam, what do you think? I haven't done anything wrong. I was well within my rights as a father to hold a prayer ceremony after your legal wedding at the Registrar's Office. I didn't conduct an official wedding wearing an official cassock and a cope on behalf of the Church. I didn't follow the wedding liturgy of our Church, and there was no 'blessing of the crown' and no 'tying of the knot' (or *'minnu kettu)*.' I did not place the wedding ring on your finger or Devi's finger, as is customary in our Church's wedding liturgy," Johnnie explained.

"That is diabolical. This is a coordinated effort to disgrace you and our family," said Sam.

"I'm not worried about their nefarious efforts to shame us. I know I didn't do anything wrong," replied Johnnie.

"I am sorry they are dragging you through the mud," said Sam.

"I stand firmly by my actions. If they want to excommunicate and de-frock me, so be it. But I will not issue a written apology or appear before the Governing Board to make a public apology. Please make sure Devi doesn't find out about this. She will feel sad and guilty, even though it's the actions of a few malicious people trying to disgrace us," said Johnnie.

"*Appa*, it's your call. Whatever you decide, I am with you one hundred percent. I've got your back, no matter what. Thank you for standing up to the bullies and arrogant religious bigots," said Sam.

Two days later, Johnnie called the Bishop and politely but firmly informed him that he would not apologize, as he had done nothing wrong and would not accept any responsibility or guilt.

"Johnnie, are you sure you don't want to apologize and appear before the Board? If you don't, they will ask me to excommunicate and defrock you. I feel deeply saddened that I may have to take such severe action against you, especially considering your exemplary service and unblemished record," said the bishop.

"*Thirumeni*, yes, that is my final decision. I did not do anything wrong to warrant an apology. It is now up to you to decide what action the Church must take. If excommunicating and defrocking me will satisfy them, and if the Church believes that is the right course of action, please proceed. I won't love you any less for doing your duty. I understand that you must address the grievances of those who are ignorant and misled," said Johnnie.

"Okay, Johnnie, my friend. I have no other choice. You will soon receive a decree officially excommunicating you and removing your clerical authority, rights, and privileges. I truly regret having to do this. May God bless you," said the bishop.

"Go right ahead. May God bless you, too. Goodbye," said Johnnie.

One week after his phone conversation with the Bishop, Johnnie received a registered letter containing the formal decree of his excommunication and defrocking. The decree detailed his laicization from the clerical state, including the loss of all clerical rights, privileges, vestments, and authority to perform ceremonies or sacraments. Johnnie was disappointed, but he did not feel defeated. He remained confident that he had done nothing wrong.

Johnnie called his son. "Sam, the Church has officially removed me from the priesthood. I could no longer perform any religious rites, ceremonies, or sacraments. I have also been officially excommunicated from the Church. That is the final resolution," said Johnnie calmly.

Sam was devastated and angry. He felt responsible for his father's fall from grace and the public humiliation he had endured because of his marriage to a woman of untouchable origin.

"*Appa*, I'm sorry I'm the reason for your public disgrace. I'm deeply sorry for your fall from grace. Please kindly forgive me for my selfishness that led to this. I was trying to do the morally right thing for me," said Sam.

"Son, I don't want you to worry about this. I love you! You did nothing wrong, and neither did I. They have sold their souls to the devil, and I want no part in that. Strangely, I feel relieved," said Johnnie.

Elsy was unhappy that the Church had publicly humiliated Johnnie after his lifelong and dedicated service to it. However, she was not entirely sad, as their parish had become a financial burden and drain on their resources. The parish needed Johnnie and Elsy more than they needed the bigoted rabble-rousers.

A sizable portion of the parish's financial support came from Johnnie's family, and whenever the Church needed additional funds, they always turned to his family, yet they were rarely grateful. Many newer members were unaware of the extent of Johnnie's family's contributions and took them for granted. The parish members were divided over the issue of Sam marrying a Dalit woman and over the Vows and Ring Ceremony conducted by Johnnie at the wedding reception.

A week after his excommunication and defrocking, Johnnie and Elsy met with the pastor of the Episcopal Church of South India (ECSI) parish in town, which was located about four miles from their home.

The Episcopal Church of South India was one of the reformed united Protestant churches in India and was part of the Anglican Communion. Johnnie informed the pastor of the reasons and events that had led to his excommunication and defrocking, as well as other issues. They expressed interest in joining the ECSI church and inquired about the process. The pastor was pleased to welcome them with open arms but explained that he needed to consult the Church's lay leadership regarding their admission.

A few days later, the pastor of the ECSI parish visited Johnnie and Elsy's home and informed them that the Church's leadership was willing and happy to receive them as members. Johnnie and Elsy told the pastor that they had decided to join his Church and would begin attending services the following Sunday.

That Sunday, the pastor announced Johnnie and Elsy's membership during the public announcements before the sermon and welcomed them to the Church. The entire congregation rose to its feet and embraced them wholeheartedly. Johnnie and Elsy had no regrets about losing their membership in the Church of Malabar Coast, which Johnnie and his forefathers had cherished for Decades, especially in light of the false allegations and, above all, the bigotry they had experienced.

A few months later, Johnnie's former parish began to suffer a significant loss of income and struggled to make ends meet, including paying the Vicar's salary. Johnnie's wealthy family had previously contributed generous offerings and additional funds to cover parish expenses, but that source of income was now gone. Members of the parish who had supported Johnnie began to blame those who had filed the grievances that led to his excommunication and defrocking.

In the following months, the church's deficit worsened, and they had to seek financial assistance and guidance from the Presiding Bishop. Supporters of Johnnie threatened to leave the church and join the ECSI parish, as Johnnie had done.

Eventually, a few supporters, disillusioned by the persistent complaints from bigoted members, left the parish and joined the ECSI parish. This led to further conflict and division in the local Church of Malabar Coast. The Presiding Bishop had to make a notable trip to a general body meeting of the parish to help resolve the tensions.

However, the local parish continued to struggle to raise its share of the Church's funds. Over the next couple of years, several more affluent members of the Church of Malabar Coast left to join the local ECSI parish. Johnnie's former church eventually reached a financial crisis it could not avert due to the loss of multiple members and their monetary contributions. Those who had initially complained about Johnnie and his family, and who had triggered his excommunication, began to blame Devi, the Dalit woman, for the church's financial and membership decline. Their anger was misdirected at the empowerment of lower-caste Dalits.

They were also angry at liberal-minded academics like Sam, whom they saw as a corrupting influence on upper-caste society and a bad example for the younger Christian generation. They feared that people like Sam and converted Dalit Christians like his wife, Devi, might radicalize the youth and lead them toward secularism. For Syrian Christian conservatives who believed they were of Brahminic origin, exogamy and inter-caste marriages posed existential threats to their notions of purity. They thought it was their duty to keep Dalits in servitude to preserve their own sense of superiority.

After three years of rigorous education while working full-time at the hospital, Devi successfully completed her four-year professional degree in physical therapy. Sam accompanied her to the commencement ceremony. On that auspicious occasion, she walked proudly to the podium with a broad smile and received her diploma. It was one of the few days in her life when she was not reminded of her caste or her horoscope. She held the diploma tightly in her hands, her eyes shimmering with a mix of disbelief and pride.

When she got home, she jumped, danced, and sang with sheer joy at having completed her degree. She held the diploma close to her heart and held on to the tassel from her commencement dress as another symbol of her achievement. No other Dalit from her village has achieved such a professional degree in physical therapy.

It took her three hectic years of juggling full-time work and heavy coursework that finally led to this moment. Sam couldn't believe her transformation from the torment of her untouchability to earning a professional degree.

He stood beside her, beaming with enormous pride and contentment. "You did it, my love," he whispered, his voice loaded with emotions. She looked into his eyes and gave him a long, lingering kiss, and they both melted.

"We did it together," Devi said.

While others like her spent their weekends relaxing, Devi buried herself in textbooks after her eight-hour workday and the classes, as well as some days' clinical rotations. The hospital became her second home, where she spent a lot of time attending lectures, clinics, and reading. She came home to sleep. Sam and Devi saw each other before going to bed. Her kitchen table was piled high with books, scribbled notes, and half-eaten snacks, which bore silent witness to her struggle. There were days she fell asleep on the dining table chair with a pen in her hand, still wearing her hospital scrubs. Sam had to wake her up and take her to the bedroom.

Meanwhile, Sam barely saw the light of day himself. His clothes were not washed, and his lab coats bore stains from lab work; his hair was overgrown and needed a hair-cut; his motorbike had not been cleaned for months, and he had puffed up eyes and perpetual bags under his eyes from staying late and doing research, which all told their own story. He was holed up in the lab for many weeks to complete his study and revise the final chapters of his doctoral dissertation.

The day they took a break was on the day of Devi's commencement.

Returning from her graduation, the two didn't want to go anywhere other than spend some private time celebrating Devi's well-earned- diploma—that too with honors. They stopped to pick up food on their way back and had a sumptuous meal at their apartment. Then they went to sleep till morning with no deadlines or exams looming in the future.

They planned to spend two whole weeks of their break doing absolutely nothing. However, they were reminded of how long it had been since they last saw their families. Devi was missing her *Appa* and *Amma*. After a few days of taking it easy and dining out at restaurants, they were preparing to leave for home to visit their parents.

That morning, as they were packing their bags to go home, Devi was nauseous and feeling unusually sick. Her face was pale, and she was sprinting to the bathroom often and trying to throw up frequently. He held her, rubbed her back, and comforted her. Her condition worsened.

Sam was distraught and immediately caught a taxi and took her to the doctor. The lady doctor listened to her symptoms and mischievously smiled at her. Sam felt incensed by her smile when her wife was sick. The physician took Devi's urine sample, ran a test, and returned with the same mischievous smile, showing the results of the test.

"Congratulations, Devi and Sam," she said softly. "You're seven weeks pregnant, and that explains your symptoms and sickness. Don't you worry, it will go away. The morning sickness will continue for a while," said the physician.

"Thank you, doctor," said Sam excitedly.

Sam and Devi looked at each other in disbelief and joy. Devi's eyes filled with tears. Sam kissed her forehead, barely blurting out the words, "We're having a baby! Congratulations, dear!"

"Now be careful, the next few weeks are critical. Most miscarriages happen during the first three months of pregnancy. So, please avoid riding on a motorbike, Devi," warned the physician.

Despite the morning sickness, they were eager to share the news with everyone back home. The next morning, they took a cab to the railway station in Cochin and boarded a train to their hometown. Even the comfortable journey through the enchanting, verdant landscape and stunning countryside of Kerala seemed too much for Devi; she leaned against Sam's shoulder, a paper bag in hand, eyes half-closed from nausea.

Johnnie was waiting at the train station. He waved from the car, his smile stretching ear to ear. When they reached home, Elsy's eyes brimmed with tears as she hugged Devi. "A grandchild!" She whispered. "Congratulations, Devi and Sam," wished Elsy.

Balan and Sarasu, glowing with pride, brought a pot of creamy *payasam*. Sarasu had stayed up late to season the *payasam* and make it the way Devi liked it—just enough cardamom, not too sweet. But still, Devi turned her face away from the bowl, her stomach churning.

The days passed with Devi curled under blankets, suffering from morning sickness, her cheeks losing color, becoming very pale, and her clothes hanging looser. Sarasu hovered with trays of soft rice, stewed lentils, and masala tea, her brow furrowed in quiet worry. Elsy joined in, the two women cooking and praying in hushed voices.

Sam, torn between his research and her well-being, kissed her forehead before boarding the train back to Cochin. He promised to return by the weekend. Devi watched him go, her body drained but her heart holding onto the excitement of seeing him again.

Two weeks later, Devi stood by the window, feeling sunlight on her face for the first time in days. The nausea had begun to fade. She was ready to return. When Sam arrived that weekend, she met him at the gate. She gave him a hug and kiss and said, "My bags are packed, and I am ready to get back to work, dear."

"I am happy for you, my love," Sam was so relieved and happy that she was okay. After the weekend, they boarded the train, hand in hand—heading back to the life they had paused but were ready to embrace, this time with a heartbeat growing quietly between them.

It was a time of political turmoil in the country. Nearly two years earlier, the Prime Minister, Mrs. Indira Gandhi, had declared a state of emergency and began enforcing stringent regulations across the nation. She initially imposed temporary restrictions that curtailed the freedoms of many, but later expanded them, suspending freedom of speech, expression, assembly, and other civil rights.

The police were granted special powers to arrest anyone without providing a reason. Those apprehended were denied their fundamental right to know the charges against them under the new restrictions imposed during the Emergency by Prime Minister Indira Gandhi. Her government maintained that even judges had no authority to demand an explanation for the arrests. The police exercised their powers arbitrarily under these restrictions, leading to many "no-cause" arrests.

Young couples who were lovers were oftentimes arrested for violations of the Immoral Traffic Act. The Police abused their newfound powers and reined the street with impunity and arrested who they wanted without giving them any reasons for arrest and jailed them because the sections of the constitution that guaranteed "equality" under the law and "due process" of law had been suspended under emergency. There were complaints of sexual crimes, such as rape and fondling, reported against the Police.

The upper-caste thugs, toadies, and gangsters of the ruling political party used the Emergency powers to persecute the marginalized groups and the untouchable Dalits. Often, when their women were raped by these gangsters and thugs with impunity, the police either looked the other way or actively colluded with the perpetrators. Despite their violent crimes, no charges were filed against these upper-caste political operatives if the victims were Dalits. In some cases, the police themselves committed such crimes under the cover of the Emergency Rule.

When Sam and Devi returned to Cochin, his father reminded him of the newfound powers granted to the Police under the State of Emergency, which were corrupting their conduct. Johnnie alerted Sam how innocent people were being arrested without rhyme or reason and thrown in jail. He urged Sam to protect Devi and use a cab to avoid encounters with both thugs and Police.

So, they went out only when necessary, either for work or to take Devi to the doctor. Sam handled the grocery shopping and ran all errands by himself. Since Devi had completed her degree, she no longer had to attend night classes. As a result, they mostly stayed in their apartment during the evenings and weekends, avoiding going out together at night. When they visited their hometown, they usually took the train.

Devi began gaining weight again during the fourth month of her pregnancy and looked radiant, anticipating the arrival of their first child. Her evenings and weekends were free, and she used the time to cook at the apartment and prepare special dishes for Sam when he returned home from work.

Then she received the news she had been waiting for weeks from her employer. After completing her degree in Physical Therapy, she was promoted to a full-fledged Physical Therapist position, accompanied by a significant salary increase. Devi and Sam were jubilant about their successes and the fruits of their hard work.

With handsome salaries from their well-paying jobs, their income and purchasing power grew significantly. Out of necessity, for commuting to work and making fortnightly trips to their hometown, they felt the need to buy a car. After shopping around Cochin for a new four-door sedan, they finally purchased a beautiful, fuel-efficient white Fiat.

Since Devi didn't know how to drive, Sam dropped her off at her workplace every morning and picked her up in the evening on his way back from work. Owning a car allowed them to avoid the risk of Devi riding in the backseat of the motorbike, especially since she was expecting a baby.

CHAPTER 12

S am and Devi looked forward to their weekend trip to home in their brand-new Fiat. The anticipation buzzed between them, not just for the drive but for the joy of surprising their parents with exciting news. Devi had just been promoted to a full-fledged physical therapist with a higher salary. Sam had completed his doctoral dissertation, which was now awaiting final review. Seeing their parents' eyes twinkle with pride was the most exciting reward for their achievements.

Sam's doctoral dissertation defense, scheduled for the following week, would fulfill the final requirement for his Ph.D. in Evolutionary Biology, with a special focus in Evolutionary Genetics. Upon successfully defending his research and dissertation, he would receive his diploma at the university's annual commencement ceremony and officially become Dr. Sam Jacob.

His research was of interest to many scholars in the field of Evolutionary Biology. His recent publications in two professional journals gained attention from scholars abroad. They have begun to reach out to him, inviting him to speak at professional conferences. The scholarly community was taking notice.

That Saturday morning, Devi woke up with unprecedented enthusiasm because they were going to visit their parents, and she had so much to share with their families. Her morning sickness had vanished, and a healthy glow had returned to her cheeks. After having breakfast together, they packed for the trip. It had been nearly a month since they had last visited their families, owing to Sam's relentless work on his dissertation, followed by car shopping and getting the paperwork for the new vehicle in order. Now, with everything finally in place, they were free to enjoy a moment of peace.

As they drove along the coastal highway, the salty breeze from the Arabian Sea filtered in through the open windows, cool and refreshing. The clean air tasted like freedom, so different from the city's smog. For the first time in months, life felt light. The chaos of cultural expectations and social judgment faded into the rearview mirror. At that moment, it felt like they were finally living the life they had fought so hard to build.

But serenity on the highway was deceptive. With the State of Emergency still in force, traffic checkpoints were scattered along the route. The police had broad, unchecked powers. They stopped vehicles for flimsy reasons, such as burned-out tail lights and expired documents. The police took cash bribes to let drivers go. Corruption thrived under the guise of law and order.

More insidious, though, was the misuse of the Immoral Traffic Act. Police targeted young couples, accusing them of trafficking women or engaging in immoral conduct. The Act became a pretext, especially when the couple was poor and the woman was a Dalit. Bribes could buy release; silence could be coerced with threats or worse. For Dalit women, justice was often a mirage. Sexual assault by officers went unpunished, swept under the rug by complicit superiors, or ignored entirely.

When Sam and Devi neared the city of Alleppey, about 40 miles from their hometown, they encountered one such checkpoint. A local report had claimed a woman was being trafficked. The police were stopping every car with couples inside. Sam's car was flagged down. A Circle Inspector, Sub-Inspector, two Head Constables, and three junior officers manned the stop.

185

The moment they stepped out of the car, questions began: "Are you married? Where are you headed? Names of your parents? Proof of age?" The interrogation was sharp and invasive. The Circle Inspector was an infamous predator in uniform with a long history of sexually abusing women. Investigations against him always seemed to disappear, thanks to his loyal Sub-Inspector, who helped cover up the evidence.

It didn't take long for the officers to discover that Sam was a Syrian Christian and that Devi, though now Christian, was of Dalit origin. Her honesty in answering their questions only seemed to fuel their curiosity and contempt.

The Sub-Inspector connected the dots and recognized Sam. Memories fell into place as he recalled the story of Sam's inter-caste marriage, which had scandalized his father's parish and led to financial ruin and public disgrace. The Sub-Inspector's own father had once shared the story with him. And now, here was Sam, vulnerable and alone on the road.

The Sub-Inspector pulled the Circle Inspector aside. "I want to book them for drug possession, just to make a point," said the Sub-Inspector. The Inspector agreed. "It is a fair sport, after all, humiliating a man who had disrupted the caste order."

While Sam waited anxiously, the Sub-Inspector "searched" the car and discreetly planted a small packet of marijuana, which was confiscated earlier that day from a drug bust, in the backseat.

When he returned from his search, he declared flatly: "We found cannabis in your car."

Sam froze in fear, not for himself, but for Devi. Despair gripped him. His mind raced through the implications. The trap had been laid, and it was personal. Sam asked for their names. From the names they gave him, he knew both were Syrian Christians. That stunned him more. He couldn't understand why men from his own community would target him so ruthlessly until he remembered the price of breaking caste.

But Sam did not understand why they were framing him now or how these officers were connected to the ongoing drama of his family and the public humiliation they suffered with his father's excommunication and defrocking.

"Officers," Sam said firmly, his voice steady despite the fear, "I'm a teetotaler and publicly advocate against drugs. You wouldn't find marijuana in my car unless you planted it. My wife doesn't even know what marijuana looks like. I'm a professor at the State Government's university, and my wife is a Physical Therapist at the hospital. Neither of us uses marijuana or deals drugs. We're highly educated and well-paid individuals. We don't need to sell drugs to make a living or survive," said Sam.

"But we found this packet of marijuana in your car that you own. You're under arrest and have a right to remain silent," said the Sub-Inspector.

Sam's voice sharpened. "There's something very wrong with this finding. You're making a terrible mistake, one you'll regret."

"We don't think so," said the Circle Inspector.

Sam's fists clenched. "Officer, do you know that I'm a Class A Officer of the State Government and that you both do not have the necessary official rank to arrest me? It's up to the District Superintendent of Police (DSP) to arrest me, and I would like you to call him right now," said Sam with firmness in his voice as a state government officer himself.

The Sub-Inspector sneered. "Under the restrictions of the 'State of Emergency,' such rights are suspended now, and we have the right to arrest you anyway without the DSP," said the Inspector.

As this drama was unfolding on the shoulders of the national highway and while the officers were getting ready to put the handcuffs on Sam, one of Sam's first cousins (the son of his uncle) happened to be riding his motorbike that way and immediately noticed the police activity and recognized the victims as Sam and Devi. He was shocked and immediately stopped his bike to ask what was going on.

Sam's mother hailed from Alleppey, and her family and relatives lived there. The District Superintendent of Police (DSP) in charge of the State Police in the Alleppey District was his mother's first cousin and a great friend of Johnnie. His mother's cousin, the DSP, and his family were in attendance at Sam's and Devi's wedding reception.

The officers told Sam's cousin not to interfere or stop there. They warned him that, otherwise, he would also be arrested.

Before the police could put the handcuffs on Sam, he pulled his hands away and called out to his cousin, "Please go immediately to the nearby shop, call Phil *Achayan*, and ask him to come to this site immediately. Do it now, please," Sam cried out.

"Will do it right away, Sam," said his cousin. Even if the police officers had understood what he said, they wouldn't have known who Phil *Achayan* was. Besides, they were so foolhardy and arrogant, they didn't even care.

His cousin rushed to the nearby department store, offered them cash, and made an urgent call to their other cousin, Philip (Phil), the District Superintendent of Police (DSP) in charge of that district. Philip's office was in the City of Alleppey, less than three miles away. These two officers, who were arresting Sam, reported to Philip's Assistant, the Deputy District Superintendent of Police.

When Sam's cousin called Philip's office, he was out in the field. Still, his office radioed him about the family emergency, and the office requested that he go to the site where the arrest was in progress.

After making the urgent phone call to the DSP's office, Sam's cousin returned to the site and stayed clear of the police activity, maintaining a safe distance while having a clear view of what was happening.

When the officer was about to put the handcuffs on Sam, Devi became agitated about the unlawful arrest and impulsively rushed to stop him. She knew the police were making an atrocious mistake in arresting her innocent husband. It was a visceral reaction to protect the one she loved with all her heart. She held Sam's hand tightly and was unwilling to let go. Her grip was so firm that the officer could not free Sam's hand from hers to put on the handcuffs.

Even more humiliating for the officer was that an Untouchable was standing up against him, shielding Sam from arrest. He was infuriated and indignant that an Untouchable had dared to resist her husband's arrest. The ruthless Sub-Inspector tried to push her away. Still, when he realized she was not going to release her hold on Sam's hand, his frustration turned to rage. He kicked her. Devi tried to evade it, but the kick landed on her groin. She fell and hit the police jeep and was seemingly in trauma.

They placed the handcuff on Sam and were about to arrest Devi next but noticed she was bleeding profusely from her groin area and grew concerned. She was in a pool of blood and was moaning with intense pain.

Devi was injured from the kick of the officer in her groin. Sam began to scream in fear that Devi might bleed to death and lose their baby too. He begged the officers to release him from the handcuff and rushed toward the Sub-Inspector. But the officer took him and tied him to the side railing of the police jeep so he would not interfere.

As Devi bled and Sam was handcuffed to the police jeep, another police jeep with its piercing siren on, followed by a second distinct jeep with a different insignia, rushed to the scene. Sam's uncle, Phil *Achayan,* the DSP, was in the second car just behind the 'pilot jeep.'

Sam cried out, "Phil *Achayan,* please save Devi. She is bleeding to death."

DSP Philip immediately ordered an ambulance and called the Alleppey Medical College Hospital, which was only a couple of miles away, to prepare for a trauma patient. The ambulance rushed to the scene and provided life-saving aid to Devi before taking her to the hospital.

In the meantime, the DSP asked his assistant to release Sam from both of his handcuffs and advised Sam to sit in the air-conditioned police car. He then went to speak with him.

The Circle Inspector and Sub Inspector were shocked and petrified and remained with their hands on their forehead, frozen in a fixed posture of police salute. They were stunned and knew they were in deep trouble, and their boss's boss, a highly reputable and high-ranking DSP of the Indian Police Services (IPS), was in charge of this tragic incident.

The DSP and his assistant officer interviewed each of the policemen present. One of the Head Constables, a trustworthy officer of good standing, witnessed the sub-inspector's wicked actions. Under duress, he confessed what he had seen. The Constable told the DSP that the marijuana had come from the contraband they had seized earlier and did not belong to Sam.

When the DSP verified the other packets, he was convinced that they had the same type of packaging and weight as the other packets, which were still in their custody in the police jeep. Additionally, DSP Phil was confident that neither Sam nor Devi would ever use or traffic 'cannabis.'

The DSP immediately placed the Circle Inspector and the Sub-Inspector on suspension and advised their office to prepare written suspension orders for both.

The DSP then contacted the Office of the State's Inspector General (IG) of Police, who is the supreme head of all the police departments in the State of Kerala, and informed him of their suspension and requested to open a disciplinary inquiry for unlawfully arresting Sam, his false imprisonment, and for assaulting and critically injuring a pregnant Dalit woman, humiliating and intimidating her, and for maliciously trying to kidnap both Sam and Devi. DSP Philip asked his Deputy and his assistants to hold Sam's car in their custody.

The DSP took Sam to the hospital, where Devi was admitted. When they reached the hospital, they found out that Devi was in surgery. As they were waiting in the lobby, Devi was then moved to the surgical ICU unit for further observation and care. Initially, a highly specialized surgeon had to be called in to remove the dead fetus and surgically repair Devi's uterus.

Sam was told that Devi was in serious condition and that she lost her baby from the injury, and the bleeding was the result of the injury she sustained from the Sub Inspector's forceful kick in her groin area.

Sam could not control his grief for losing their precious unborn child and the injury Devi suffered, for no fault of hers, while trying to save him from arrest. Sam was traumatized, and he cried in agony, an agony brought by others because of their wickedness and no fault of his or Devi's. DSP Philip held Sam in his arms, but he could not control his sorrow for Devi getting injured and for the death of his five-month-old unborn child.

He could not see Devi because she had just come out of surgery and was recovering from her anesthesia. One hour past their arrival at the hospital, the surgeon came out, asked for Sam, and told him the surgery went well and she was out of danger. But he also told Sam that the injury to her uterus caused irreparable damage, and he was not sure whether Devi could ever bear a child again because of the severity of her injury. However, he assured Sam that she would make a full recovery, although she lost a lot of blood. The injury she sustained to her head from hitting the jeep was only minor and did not need any stitches.

After a few hours, Johnnie, Elsy, Balan, and Sarasu arrived. Elsy was crying and was trying hard to remain calm. Balan and Sarasu were traumatized by the news and were petrified. They were always paranoid about the police throughout their life because they all knew as Untouchables they did not get justice, and this incident was a self-fulfilling prophecy for both of them.

Johnnie was sad and angry but remained calm and collected.

When Johnnie and Elsy came to the hospital, DSP Phil had a long conversation with them, and then he left. Phil had experienced enough of the police abuse after witnessing with his own eyes the wrongdoing done to an innocent married couple by his police. Before Phil left, he told Sam that his assistants were almost done with collecting evidence and searching his car. After their investigation, they would bring it to the hospital, park it there, and return his car keys to him.

Devi had asked for Sam immediately after she woke up from her anesthesia. The surgeon had ordered staff to keep Devi in the Surgical Intensive Care Unit for observation until further notice. Sam was allowed to see her and be with her for a short while.

After an hour of waiting, they were all allowed to visit her. She was recovering from anesthesia and in a moderate level of pain from the injury and surgery. Still, she was alert and fully responsive to their inquiries.

At around 7:00 p.m., they brought her dinner, and she ate it with some water. Devi was so relieved to see her parents and her in-laws. She asked them how they were all doing and assured them she was okay. Sam stayed by her side, and Devi asked her in-laws and parents to go and have dinner at the hospital canteen. Sam wanted to stay with her and insisted they all go and have dinner.

They were all extremely sad about losing their unborn grandchild and the violence that had befallen their children. They agreed that it was unforgivable because the violence came from those who were paid to protect and enforce peace. They were mostly silent during dinner, but they all thanked God for saving Devi, who had been on the verge of death.

The Sub Inspector seemed to have attacked Devi without hesitation because he knew she was a Dalit woman of untouchable origin. Otherwise, he would not have assaulted her for protecting her husband from wrongful arrest. Dalits were easy targets for the police because they never got in trouble for attacking the marginalized and impoverished. This time, it would be different because she was the wife of a highly placed and well-to-do Syrian Christian man. It was apparent that the officers were going to lose their jobs for serious felony crimes done to a respectable Dalit woman.

Sam stayed with Devi throughout the night and convinced Johnnie and Elsy to leave, taking Balan and Sarasu with them. They were to get some rest and return the next day if they wanted to.

By the next day, Devi's condition improved, and she was moved to a private room for recovery. Most often, tears welled up in her eyes as she thought about the unfortunate incident that led to her losing the unborn baby. But she was thankful that she survived the injury and did not bleed to death because of the intervention of DSP Phil at that critical moment.

Occasionally, she wondered why she had to endure such tragedies and misfortunes in her life. In her weakest moments, she asked Sam whether she was still afflicted by the malefic effects of her *Mangala Dosha*. After grieving three more days for the loss of her baby, Devi asked, "Sam, if *Mangal Dosha* is not the reason for losing our precious child, how else can you explain such a heart-wrenching tragedy and the devastating misery that we are going through? That too for no fault of ours."

"Devi, my love, these things happen to humans due to their wickedness. If you analyze it profoundly, Mars has nothing to do with it. If Mars had a heart of its own, I'm sure it wouldn't allow the violent death of an unborn baby and serious injury to its innocent mother like you for no fault of yours. It was the Sub-Inspector's wickedness; it was the wickedness of some of those religious Syrian Christians who think they are superior to others because of their Brahminic origin; and, because they want to maintain the status quo was also why they are collectively fighting change," replied Sam.

Sam paused momentarily to regain his composure, having been overcome by the agony, and then continued. "They consider any change to the status quo to be an existential threat to them. They think their God and religion are better than the gods and religions of others. 'Loving thy neighbor' doesn't seem to be attainable in practice, but they preach it and want others to follow this ideal, not themselves; in fact, some of them simply hate their neighbors, especially if they belong to a lower caste, class, or have a different skin color. I am disillusioned with their self-righteousness, their god narratives, and their hateful religious fervor," said Sam.

Devi was discharged from the hospital on the fifth day after arrival. She was healed and physically feeling much better, but a little bit sore here and there. She needed a few more days of rest.

While she was in the hospital, there was news coverage of their police attack in the radio and newspapers. Many of her colleagues were resentful of the police violence and came to visit her after reading the news in the newspaper. They were in shock and could not believe such atrocities done by the police.

Devi and Sam returned from the hospital and rested for a week. Sam had to reschedule his doctoral dissertation defense and his seminar presentation. Everyone at their respective workplaces was very thoughtful and considerate of their situation, and they were ready to help them.

When she went to see the doctor after a week, he gave her a clean bill of health and suggested that she might want to return to work. Fortunately, she did not sustain any serious injury to her head. The physician asked her to take pain medications if she had persistent pain. The occasional minor bleeding she had also completely stopped. Devi miraculously recovered entirely from her injury.

Devi and Sam returned to their apartment after recovering physically and mentally from the trauma they suffered from police violence. On Monday morning, Sam drove her to work and then went to his office at the University. Sam picked her up from work in the evening and took her home.

Devi often became sad and was in a depressed mood as a result of losing her unborn baby.

The guilt of losing her child kept bothering her at times. She could not fathom the atrociousness of the wicked people and the extent they go to inflict pain on others. Sam suggested that they go for some counseling to ease her pain if her sadness continued to persist.

After a month, the report of the police investigation summoned by the Office of the Inspector General of the State of Kerala was submitted to the Inspector General of Police. The criminal investigation of the police violence by the experts provided incontrovertible evidence for the criminal indictments of the two officers who attacked Sam and Devi.

The Circle Inspector and the Sub-Inspector were arrested and sent to jail, awaiting trial. After their arrest, they both were dismissed from their police jobs for criminal felony charges, including false arrest, false imprisonment, kidnapping, planting and tampering with evidence, and assaulting a pregnant Dalit woman.

The public uproar against police abuse and lack of confidence in law enforcement became significant issues for the State Government. Sam and Devi felt that justice was finally served, but they could never replace the lost life of their unborn baby. They continued to grieve the loss of their baby; however, the inner pain became so challenging to get over.

The Senior Head Constable who told the truth about the Sub-Inspector planting evidence in Sam's car was promoted to Sub-Inspector. DSP Philip initiated his promotion for standing up against his superior officer and telling the truth, which made all the difference on that day. He felt the need to reward such a courageous policeman who had the integrity and strength of character to rise to the occasion.

As Devi began to recover from the pain of losing her unborn baby, the troubling thoughts about the baneful effects of her *Mangal Dosha* continued to haunt her, and she became preoccupied with her curse of being a *Manglik*. She could not help but rationalize and attribute her miseries and the public humiliation and ignominy that Sam's family had been going through, on the one hand, to her *Mangal Dosha* and, on the other, to her status as an untouchable Dalit. She readily found causation and reasons to connect the tragedies to the baneful effects of *Mangal Dosha*, although they were not based on objective reality.

Knowing deeply about her self-affliction and for offering some relief for her pain from her superstitious doubts, Sam clandestinely devised a plan that he thought might eradicate the source of her pain.

When they went home the following week, Sam went to see Keshavan Kaniyar alone and asked for his assistance again. Keshavan was going through rainy days and was short of sufficient income to meet both ends despite occasionally receiving orders for writing *Jathakams*. It was feast or famine for him; lately, it had been famine, as people were slowly growing disenchanted with his charlatanry.

Sam told Keshavan that he would pay him 2,000 rupees if he could rewrite the existing *Jathakam* of his wife. The money Sam offered was sweet enough for him not to decline the request. Sam wanted Keshavan to inform his wife that the horoscope chart he had used in developing her *Jathakam* many years ago contained a printing error when it was written. But that horoscope chart was corrected about 20 years ago, and a new one was issued. So, he wanted Keshavan to tell Devi that, based on his corrected natal chart, there was no *Mangal Dosha* for Devi.

Keshavan agreed to do it on one condition: no one should come to know about making up this story to rewrite the *Jathakam*. Sam assured Keshvan that he would keep the promise. He told him he would pay the fee later when he came to pick up the revised *Jathakam*.

The next day, Sam convinced Devi to go with him to Keshavan to consult with him about the status of her *Mangal Dosha*, as she had experienced a series of setbacks. So, Sam took Devi to Keshavan.

When they both met with him, Devi gave him her old *Jathakam*.

"Oh yes, I recognize this *Jathakam*. It is written in my own handwriting," said Keshavan.

"Okay, please tell me where do I stand now? We just suffered the tragic loss of our unborn child," said Devi in a very concerned tone.

"I am sorry to hear the sad news. You see, in those days, I used a horoscope chart, which was the only natal chart available to me at the time. That was given to me by my father. After his passing, I only learned that he had given me an incorrect natal chart with a printing error. Now, I have a corrected new chart I acquired 20 years ago, which I use today. I can study the corrected chart and verify whether you even had a *Mangal Dosha*. So, if you can wait a few minutes, I can bring my horoscope charts and quickly review them with you, Devi," said Keshavan.

"Yes, we will wait here. We are in no hurry. This is important for us," said Sam.

Keshavan returned with a worn-out file folder containing many old, faded astrological charts. Some fell apart due to overuse, and others were partially eaten by silverfish and had a musty, decaying odor. He opened the folder, put on his very old, broken eyeglasses with a cracked lens on one side, and started reading them with devotion and an air of charlatanry as if he were reading some sacred, old scripture that he only knew how to decipher. Such charlatanry often bamboozled credulous people, making them fall prey to it.

From childhood, through various experiences and cultural and religious orientation, Devi was conditioned to believe in the sacred nature of Vedic astrology. So, she started looking at Keshavan with admiration.

"Devi, I can't believe what the corrected chart tells me. The horoscope your parents received from me many years ago was developed based on the incorrect natal chart with a printing error. According to this corrected chart and based on your birthdate and time, no *Mangal Dosha* was evident in your horoscope. I'm sorry, Devi; your original *Jathakam* had an error because of the incorrect chart I used then. The great news is that you were not born with the *Mangal Dosha* and are not a *Manglik* after all. I can write a new *Jathakam* for you based on the corrected chart I have now without any trouble," said Keshavan.

Devi jumped up and down, cheering like a small child, and loudly said, "God is good! Thank you, Jesus, for your love, mercy, and blessings upon our families! Please revise the *Jathakam* for me. I want to share it with my parents, who often worry about it. Thank you, Keshavan," said Devi.

Then she sat down on the bench, became pensive momentarily, and asked, "What about Sam? He is also a *Manglik*, according to the *Jathakam* you wrote for him based on his birth date and star. Isn't he a *Manglik?*"

"That is okay because there is no baneful effect on you as a woman on your marriage because Sam is a man who was born with *Mangal Dosha*. It has no impact on a woman if the man is the *Manglik*. If you want to see it, I'll show you that in this chart," said Keshavan to convince Devi.

Keshavan's strategy to convince her beyond a shred of doubt worked! She did not want to look at Keshavan's dirty, old, stinky, and faded charts. She was overjoyed and relieved that she was no longer considered a *Manglik*. Being a *Manglik*, Sam did not have any bearing or baneful effects on their marriage either. That was all she wanted to hear. Keshavan advised them to return in the late afternoon and collect her revised *Jathakam*.

Late in the afternoon, Sam went alone and collected Devi's revised *Jathakam*, then paid Keshavan 2,000 rupees as promised. After receiving the revised *Jathakam*, Devi ran to her parents with it, like a small child, and showed it to Balan and Sarasu. But they were confused and did not know that a *Jathakam* could be rewritten. Devi informed them that, due to a printing error on the original natal chart Keshavan had used to write her original *Jathakam* at birth, her horoscope had been misread and mischaracterized in the narrative of her *Jathakam*.

The new *Jathakam* seemed to serve as the security blanket that finally ended Devi's unfounded worries about her *Mangal Dosha*, which they never mentioned again. It certainly acted as a placebo, allowing Devi to stop tormenting herself with her constant preoccupation.

Sam thought, sometimes, identifying the source of our worries and uprooting them from where they have taken hold can be the cure.

PART TWO

In Pursuit of an Inconvenient Truth

LOS ANGELES

CHAPTER 13

S am was conferred the degree of Doctor of Philosophy (Ph.D.) in Evolutionary Biology at commencement, and he was now known across the campus community as Dr. Sam Jacob. He received numerous accolades from his colleagues at the University and from the broader scholarly community for his high-caliber research and the new knowledge he contributed to the fields of Evolutionary Biology and Genetics. Many scholars from abroad requested an abstract of his dissertation.

As a result of his high-caliber research study, which raised the bar and brought exposure to the University as a center of excellence in Ecology and Evolutionary Biology, the Faculty Senate and the Vice Chancellor's Office passed resolutions honoring Dr. Sam Jacob. Immediately after earning his doctoral degree and publishing his research studies in scholarly publications, he was promoted to Associate Professor of Evolutionary Biology by the University of Cochin.

Sam did not want to stop there. He was a highly aspiring academic and scholar committed to doing advanced research in Evolutionary Biology and Genetics. He wanted to explore research opportunities in an American university, where they have high-tech laboratories, intellectual power, and more resources to conduct advanced research in Evolutionary Biology and Genetics.

However, Sam was growingly concerned about leaving Devi alone in Kerala should he get an opportunity to pursue postdoctoral studies in

America, because securing a dependent visa for a spouse of a postdoctoral student would take a couple of years. Devi would have to remain in an unfriendly, toxic, and risky environment as a Dalit in Kerala alone.

So, Sam often suppressed his dreams and reined in on his aspirations. He thought reconciling with how things are in their lives was much more potent than aiming for how his life ought to be. Sam held his aspirations of pursuing postdoctoral study abroad to himself. He did not share it with Devi for fear of making her uncomfortable.

———————————

Nearly five long years had passed since the cold, gut-wrenching, and wrongful arrest of Sam and the vulgar brutality of the police violence against Devi that killed their unborn child. They tried to put behind that diabolic and heinous incident, but it crept up on Devi and Sam from the deepest, darkest corners of their heart during the weakest and saddest moments of their lives. The more they tried to suppress its memories, the more they realized it had taken a permanent residence in their brains.

It was harder for Devi than for Sam, as her dream of bearing another child became an elusive one due to the damage inflicted on her uterus by police brutality. She had heard of surgical procedures in America that could repair such injuries and often wished she could go there to restore her ability to conceive. Her maternal instincts, along with the longing to have another child, kept resurfacing the painful memory of losing her most cherished and awaited baby to senseless violence—memories that remained raw and vivid even after five years.

She sometimes felt this was a cross she had to bear alone, even with her most empathetic, loving, and caring husband by her side. The painful memory continued to haunt her and made her deeply miserable. She longed to escape that environment, but there was nowhere to run—

nowhere she could go without leaving behind her beloved husband and her struggling parents. Besides, Sam was the only child of Elsy and Johnnie, and she couldn't bring herself to even entertain the thought of asking him to flee with her to some godforsaken, desolate place far from the pernicious climate of untouchability.

Devi privately contemplated ending her wretched life, but when she thought of her poor parents and the newfound meaning in her redeemed life, with the unconditional love and devotion of Sam, the thought of the pain she would inflict on him and her parents felt even more unbearable. It was no real solution.

In the darkest, deepest, and saddest moments of her existential crisis, Devi found profound meaning in choosing to live for the love of her life, Sam, and her most cherished parents. Moreover, her newly found, loving, and devoted in-laws, Elsy and Johnnie, added yet another layer of meaning and joy to her life.

Sam and Devi had a relaxed breakfast that Saturday morning, enjoying each other's company and engaging in casual conversations. As he sipped coffee, he thumbed through the daily newspaper, Indian Express Saturday Special Edition. He began reading the article about the fantastic mission of NASA's Space Shuttle Columbia, which took to the skies on April 12, 1981, from the Kennedy Space Center.

He was utterly fascinated by the unprecedented and mind-boggling scientific and technological advancements happening on the other side of the globe. What America was accomplishing was like science fiction to him. The feelings of awe inspired him, and an intense desire to pursue his scientific interests in such a highly scientifically and technologically advanced country overwhelmed him.

"Devi, I'm interested in applying for postdoctoral research opportunities in the U.S. I have learned that the Christian University of Los Angeles (CULA), has the best high-tech labs, resources, and intellectual environment that would offer me opportunities to grow and flourish in the field of Evolutionary Genetics," said Sam.

He then got up from his seat, went over to Devi, held her affectionately, and asked, "What do you think of living in America if there is an opportunity for me there? Will you be interested in living there for a while? Since you have a professional degree in physical therapy now, you'll have plenty of opportunities to work in America and get paid a much higher salary because there is a growing need and a severe shortage of physical therapists there," said Sam smilingly.

"I'm not sure, Sam. Do they have Untouchables in America? I know they have blacks, and I read that they have their share of racial tensions and discrimination. I learned about American slavery and the despicable Jim Crow laws that legalized racial segregation in public places and enforced racial order in one of the social science classes I took in college. But those practices are illegal there now," said Devi.

"Yes, both racism and its various manifestations are illegal now in America," said Sam.

"I'm convinced about one thing, though, dear: I don't want my children to grow up in this socially toxic environment of discrimination and bigotry. I'm baffled that even the Syrian Christians and their churches are tainted by bigotry, gender bias, and misogyny. I understand Christ's message was an egalitarian one. Still, the Syrian Christians seemed to have corrupted His message, as evident in their support for the oppression of Dalits and discrimination of even converted Christians like me and not allowing women in pastoral ministry," said Devi.

"Sweetheart, that is exactly what I was thinking, too. If we're fortunate enough to have any children, I don't want them to grow up among some of my fellow Syrian Christians, who are so misogynistic and bigoted. Some of them harbor so much animosity toward lower-caste people, especially the Untouchables, who have the same God-given dignity as we all do, because of their misguided belief that they are of Brahminic origin and, hence, the elites."

"You are right on, my love," replied Devi.

"Many of them are woefully bigoted, thinking their religion and God are the only truth and that all others are idolaters, pagans, and heathens. That lack of respect for the dignity of other humans, their religions, and gods is a manifestation of their religious bigotry. They flourish in that bigotry and fight each other to establish who is better than the other and whose God is the only true God," added Sam.

"Yes, I can't agree with you more," said Devi.

"What is much more important to me is that I don't want them to harass you and discriminate against you anymore. I'm getting tired of it. Wherever we turn, we need to look over our shoulders because you were unjustly and immorally affixed a stamp of untouchability for no fault of yours. For me and to those who look at you objectively, I can tell you are the most beautiful woman, who was also created in the image of our Creator with the same kind of God-given dignity that is possessed by Brahmins, Syrian Christians, or a White person."

"Thank you, Sam. I am the most fortunate girl in this world to have a husband like you," replied Devi.

"You look prettier than many Brahmins and Syrian Christians that I know. Still, I don't understand why they harbor animosity toward people like you based on your caste. That is not only so unchristian; it is also so ungodly of all other upper-caste people. They'll even discriminate against our children by saying their mother is an Untouchable," said Sam.

"Thank you! I love your analyses. You have a gift, dear, to articulate those same thoughts I have about the bigotry and racism I am experiencing much better than I can. Although we are all of the same brown race, many of them see the Dalits as some despicable race. So, please keep going," said Devi.

"I think it is time we look for opportunities in countries where they respect you as a human and for your worth rather than whether you belong to a certain race, caste, '*gotra*,' or religion. I had enough trauma already after experiencing the pain of their wickedness inflicted on you and me. They claim they are religious and loudly preach 'love thy neighbor' and recite that verse, 'Whatever you did for one of the least of these brothers and sisters of mine, you did for me.'"

"I agree with you, Sam. I am afraid to live here because of the manifestations of their misogyny and bigotry. But I will miss my parents and yours if we go to such a faraway country. If we ever go, can we come home often, at least once a year? I am unsure whether I can eat their food and speak English as well as they do. We recently had an American doctor speak at our hospital. I couldn't understand him well because of his American accent. I am sure we can learn those things, like how I learned to practice physical therapy," said Devi.

"Of course, we can come home every year as you please. If we get employment in America, they pay you well, so we'll have the resources to take a trip every year," said Sam.

"By the way, a few weeks ago, I saw a job opportunity posted in our departmental newsletter for a Physical Therapist at the St. Vincent Hospital in Los Angeles. I didn't even want to explore this opportunity, thinking that you didn't want to leave your parents and the University," said Devi.

"Oh no, dear, I am ready for a new adventure where we can grow to our fullest potential. I want to do advanced research in Genetics, and I think America is where I want to be," said Sam.

"May I apply for that opportunity in Los Angeles, then? The deadline to apply for that job might have passed. There was a phone number to call," said Devi.

"Go right ahead and find out whether the job is still open. I would be thrilled if you got that job because CULA is in Los Angeles, California. I would like to pursue postdoctoral research there," said Sam.

"Sam, can you please be on the call with me in case I don't understand what they are saying," asked Devi.

"Sure, I will be there to back you up. If we call tomorrow evening, it will be the morning for them as they are about 12 hours behind," said Sam.

On Monday evening, after returning from work, Devi called the St. Vincent Hospital as planned. The person who took the call connected Devi to another person named Kimberly Thomas. She told Devi that she could call her Kim. She told Devi that she was the head of the Physical Therapy Department. She asked Devi for details, such as where she completed her degree, how long she worked, and her specific skill sets.

After Devi's casual interview with Kim, she suggested that Devi conduct a formal job interview with a representative from a hospital in Cochin on a specific date. Kim advised her to bring all her original credentials, such as her degree certificates, transcripts, and employment history paperwork, to the interview. Upon her successful interview with that person, if Devi was selected by him for the job, Kim would then inform her of the next steps. She gave Devi the phone number and address of the interviewer in Cochin.

As directed by Kim, Sam took Devi for the interview with the designated person, an American-trained doctor at another hospital. He interviewed Devi, verified all her credentials, and asked for the name and phone number of her supervisor, as well as Devi's home phone number and address.

Two days after her interview with the doctor, Devi's supervisor at the hospital informed her that he had received a call from a hospital in Los Angeles requesting a reference check for her and had provided a positive reference. Devi knew that the hospital in Los Angeles was interested but did not think much about it.

Quite interestingly, Devi received a call a couple of days later in the evening from the Human Resources Department of the Hospital on behalf of Kim. To Devi's surprise, the HR Director offered Devi the Physical Therapist position at St. Vincent Hospital, accompanied by an annual salary of $50,000, retirement benefits, and family health insurance coverage.

He informed Devi that after the successful completion of her first year, they would review her job performance, and if everything went satisfactorily, she would receive a Cost-of-Living Adjustment (COLA) and a pay increase based on merit. If she accepted the job offer, she would have to call him back within two days, and at that time, they would advise her on the procedures for obtaining the visa papers for herself and her spouse. Devi agreed to call him back the very next day at the same time. The HR Director asked whether she could start her job within two months.

Devi was overwhelmed with mixed emotions and insecurities about going to another country and starting a new life. She wanted to cry with abundant happiness and joy from within and laugh her heart out at the incredible fortune that had fallen into her lap. Sam was listening to the entire conversation and couldn't believe what had happened, especially the salary and benefits they offered Devi.

If you convert the dollar value into Indian rupees, they did not make even half of that salary as highly educated and well-placed professionals. Sometimes, when a dream comes true, you are stunned and overwhelmed, and you don't know how to proceed. Devi and Sam were wonderstruck and wanted to ensure they were not dreaming.

Devi jumped up and down with joy so many times, then took Sam by his shoulder, shook him, and said, "Sam, say something. Wake up, my love. I don't know what to do or say. I need you to speak now and give me some direction."

He was so euphoric that he couldn't utter a word. He remained silent in awestruck for a few more minutes and then said, "Congratulations, my love! I am so incredibly proud of you! You handled the first interview and today's call with the HR Director so professionally. I'm not at all surprised that you got the job. You're a highly competent woman. I'm so proud of you, Devi. I suggest that you call back tomorrow and accept the job offer," replied Sam.

"Okay, I will," said Devi.

"Please don't resign from your job at the hospital until you receive all the employment papers, including the visa papers, from Los Angeles. There's so much for us to process here. I need time to think about this because all this is happening too quickly. I must apply for a leave of absence without pay for at least three years to do postdoctoral studies," Sam added.

"Okay, like you suggested, I'll call the HR Director tomorrow and accept the job. I am a little bit nervous; this is developing so rapidly. Do you think we can prepare ourselves to leave in two months?" Asked Devi.

"I'm sure we can get ready and leave in two months. As you are aware, I have now been promoted to tenured associate professor. So, I can take a leave of absence for up to five years without pay. I do not want to resign until I get another job in America. My application process for the leave of absence will take some time to complete. I'll apply for a leave of absence with the University right away. Once the leave is sanctioned, my job will be secure for the duration of my leave," said Sam.

Sam got up from his seat and hugged her tightly. He gave her a deep, wet kiss and kissed her again and again, and she was so jubilant. He wanted to scream out and say to the world, "We're going to America and leaving you and your bigotry behind…"

"Do you know, our life will drastically change from here on? I need to convince my *Appa* and *Amma* about going to America. *Appa* will not have any issues, but *Amma* is going to be very sad," said Sam.

"I don't know how my parents will take this news when I tell them. They can't fathom a world outside of here, much less America or the opportunities there. They're afraid of the police and will now be paranoid that someone will do us harm in America if we go there. All they know is that you must cross many oceans to reach America. They still think that crossing the ocean is a bad omen or something. Sam, I'd like you to speak with my parents. You know how to convince people; besides, they think the world of you. Either way, they will be terrified of our leaving," said Devi.

As promised to the HR Director, Devi called him back the next day. The director took the call after learning that the incoming call was international, although he was in the middle of a meeting. Devi accepted his job offer, thanked him, and then asked what the next steps were.

He congratulated Devi, thanked her, and informed her that his Office would send her the employment offer letter and a contract with the agreed-upon salary for her signature. The director requested that Devi return the signed contract the next day so that his Office could submit it to the Board of Directors for approval. The director also mentioned that he would send another packet with the immigration paperwork, which she should take to the nearest American Consulate to secure the necessary visas for them to enter the U.S. He advised Devi and Sam to obtain their passports before visiting the Consulate.

Neither Sam nor Devi had taken their passports, as there had been no occasion or need for international trips in their lives. Securing two passports within a few weeks would be a monumental task.

The next day, Sam and Devi went to the Regional Passport Office in Cochin to apply for their passports. By the end of the day, they had gathered all the required documents, obtained passport-sized photographs, and submitted them along with their passport applications. They were informed that a police verification would take place before their passports could be issued. To expedite the process and receive their passports within two weeks, they paid an additional fee.

That weekend, they had planned to make the trip to their home on Friday afternoon rather than wait until Saturday morning, as they had so many things to discuss with their parents and decisions to make before leaving the country for America. They did not know how their parents would react to the exciting news of them working and living in America, as they were both the only children of their respective parents.

Their unusual arrival at home on a Friday evening somewhat surprised their parents. Since they had some important and exciting matters to discuss with their parents, Sam and Devi picked up Balan and Sarasu and brought them over to Sam's house. Balan and Sarasu were pleasantly surprised to see them on a Friday evening. Elsy invited Balan and Sarasu to eat supper with them, and Devi and Sam had them all sit together.

"We have some important and very exciting news to share with you. We'll tell you, this is one of the best pieces of news we've had in a long time, but we're unsure how you'll take it. You know that Devi is a professional physical therapist with a degree and nearly five years of full-time experience now. As I'm interested in doing a postdoctoral study in America, I encouraged her to apply for a job opportunity in California because I have quite promising opportunities there in Los Angeles for doing advanced research in the field of Evolutionary Biology and Genetics that I'm interested in," Sam paused for a moment and locked eyes with Devi.

He looked very excited but anxious about telling their parents that they would soon be relocating to another country. He was stricken with a deep pang of guilt at once for leaving their parents.

"Come on! Go ahead and tell them," Devi gently prodded him.

"Believe it or not, Devi applied and got selected for employment in California with a much higher salary. Her job will start in two months, and we didn't want to miss this opportunity, so she accepted the job offer. I consider this as an enormous opportunity for both of us. So, we would like to emigrate to America and work there for a few years. We promise to visit you once a year and spend quality time with you. What are your thoughts?" Sam said this with a feeling of apprehension about whether his parents would like it or not.

Their parents looked stunned when they heard the news that their children were planning to leave the country! There was pin-drop silence. Although they were so proud of their children's success, they didn't want them to leave the country either. They seemed to have mixed feelings.

"Devi's *Appa* and *Amma* don't have to worry about anything. We will send you enough money to make a very comfortable living. You both can retire now. My *Appa* will find another overseer to do the farming, and we will send you the funds you need to live comfortably," said Sam.

After the initial shock from the news, Johnnie and Elsy recovered momentarily and felt both proud and happy. They understood what it meant—that their only son and daughter-in-law would be living in America for a while and would miss even their fortnightly visits. They experienced a bittersweet happiness, feeling incredibly proud of their children's outstanding achievements.

Although Balan and Sarasu were overjoyed and proud of their children and the good fortune this would bring, they also seemed saddened that their children were leaving for America.

"Devi and Sam, you are professionals and adult children. You have a whole life ahead of you. This is when you must explore the world and live life to its fullest potential. I am so overjoyed and extremely proud of your great accomplishments. Devi, you are an amazing and competent woman to land a job in America. As diligent and high-caliber persons, I think you both will have many more golden opportunities in America. Moreover, you don't have to deal with wicked and petty people like we have here. Congratulations, and good luck to you both," said Johnnie.

"Congratulations, Devi and Sam! I'm sad I won't be able to see you both often. But please promise me that you will come to visit us every year. Once people go to America, they never return. I support you. You shouldn't miss this opportunity," said Elsy.

"I am so afraid of the upper caste people here who illtreat the Dalits. I heard America is a great country with good people where women are respected, and they don't have untouchability and casteism there. I'm sad to see you leaving us, but we know you'll be happy wherever you go. Congratulations, Devi, my dearest daughter. I am very proud of you and Sam," said Balan.

"I am very proud of you, my children. I didn't even know Devi was interested in going to America. We are sad that we will not be able to see you often, but we know that you both will have a great future there. We look forward to your visit every year. Congratulations to both of you," said Sarasu.

"My *Appa* and *Amma* got a car, so they don't need another car. When we leave for America, we will leave our new Fiat car for Devi's *Amma* and *Appa*. We will arrange for a part-time driver to take you to the temple, shopping, or to the doctor's office and to visit your relatives. We will completely pay for your car expenses and the driver's salary," said Sam.

Devi was stunned by what Sam had offered her parents, which was quite generous. Devi thought no Dalits in her village had ever owned a car, and so that would be another reason for new upper caste outrage and animosity. Her parents were blown away by what Sam said. Their jaws dropped with shock and delight at the news that the Dalits were going to have a Fiat car with a driver. They had a whole lot to digest in such a short time.

"Son, that will be another reason for the upper caste to hate us and a direct reprisal against us. Watching the Untouchable parents going in a new Fiat car will cause so much animosity and anger against us from the upper caste thugs. They are already upset that we have a house built by you," said Sarasu.

"I am afraid they will burn our house down for going in a Fiat car. We don't need a car, son. We are Dalits, and we are used to walking everywhere. We can walk to the store to do the grocery shopping and see the doctor, or we can take the bus. Please keep the car here with your *Appa* and *Amma*. Your *Amma* can use a second car, son," said Balan.

"No, Balan, we don't need another car, but you need one! If anyone asks, you must tell them it is a gift from your daughter, who works in the United States. We have a car, and that is all we need. You should keep the car and park it proudly in front of your house as a gift from your daughter and son-in-law. When you go out, go with a driver and let them see it. I will have the local police surveil your house again. If anyone is going to have a problem, they will be arrested," said Johnnie.

"You both have worked so hard in your life. Now you are getting older. It is high time for you both to retire and enjoy some comfort you never had and now deserve. Your daughter is a well-placed professional with a very lucrative job in America. You should live proudly," said Elsy.

"Sam, thank you, my love. I am the most fortunate girl in this whole world to have you as my husband and the captain of our ship. You have a divine heart full of love and compassion. Thank you for the kindness we enjoy daily," said Devi.

After their meeting, they all had supper together. Later, Sam dropped Balan and Sarasu at their home and told them that they would come and stay with them on Saturday night.

A few days after they returned to Cochin, Johnnie called to tell them that the police had met with them to verify the information they provided for the issuance of their passports. After two weeks, Devi and Sam received their passports on special delivery.

Devi also received the official job offer letter and contract from Los Angeles that week. After signing the contract, Devi returned the original to the HR Director by registered mail. In the meantime, Sam applied for a three-year leave of absence from the University. However, he kept his plans to immigrate to America confidential from his colleagues and supervisors until they secured their immigrant visas.

A week after receiving her job offer and contract, Devi received a special delivery from St. Vincent Hospital that included all the necessary paperwork to process her immigration paperwork and visa to enter the U.S. She was advised to visit the American Consulate in Madras as soon as possible.

Two days after receiving the visa papers, they took a train to Madras City to secure their visas. After standing in a long line for three hours, they finally got to the counter of the American Consulate, where they submitted their immigration papers and applied for their visas. The Consulate Office gave them an appointment and advised them to wait for their turn. Late in the afternoon, they had their interview with the Consular Officer, who verified and validated all their necessary documents, issued their immigration documents, and stamped their passports with entry visas to travel to the United States.

As previously advised by the HR Director, they went to the Pan-Am Airlines Office in Madras City and booked the air tickets. Devi's air ticket had already been paid for by the hospital and was ready. They had to pay for Sam's air ticket from their own pocket. Reservations on Pan-Am flights were made for both of them, and they were advised to collect the tickets the following day.

Sam and Devi stayed in Madras City for one more day to confirm their air tickets, and then they returned home by train. Their air travel was scheduled to begin from Cochin on Indian Airlines exactly two weeks after their return from Madras. They were booked to fly from Cochin to Bombay on Indian Airlines, and from Bombay, they were scheduled to fly on Pan-Am Airways to Los Angeles via Frankfurt.

They had so much to do in two weeks before they departed for Los Angeles. Devi gave her supervisor a letter of resignation. They were sad to see Devi leave, as she was a valued and highly productive member of their staff. Devi's Office gave her a warm farewell party and invited Sam too for the occasion.

After obtaining his immigrant visa and taking a leave of absence, Sam informed his colleagues that he would be immigrating to the United States. His students were very disappointed that he was leaving the University. Sam was a popular and well-liked professor, and the University felt the loss, as he was a celebrated researcher with an excellent reputation. Although they regretted losing him to America, they wished him great success in his dedicated career and intellectual pursuits. They knew it was only a matter of time before a prosperous country like the United States would attract such a talented young researcher and scholar.

Sam gave their landlord a written notice to end their apartment lease. They sold their furniture to another couple who was moving into the building. The day after selling all their furniture, they loaded their car with their belongings and drove back home.

They got busy shopping for a few more essential items for their trip since they had only a week left. They had already bought clothes, essential cosmetic products, shoes, luggage, carry-on bags, and other essentials from Cochin.

Before they realized it, they noticed they had only five more days to go. They began packing their clothes into the luggage and their degree certificates and travel documents into their carry-on bags. Within two days, they finished packing and were ready for the trip.

Sam found a temporary driver to drive the car for Devi's *Appa* and *Amma* and set a fixed salary for his part-time driving services and car maintenance. He advised Balan to build a car shed to park the car.

Two days before their trip, Sam took the car to Devi's parents and parked it in front of their house. He told Balan and Sarasu that he had given the driver directions regarding his duties and details about his monthly salary, as well as additional monies for any extra services, such as filling the gas tank, changing tires, and taking the car for service in town. He assured Balan that if he had any emergencies or questions, his *Appa* and *Amma* were also there to help him and Sarasu.

The day before their trip, they revisited Devi's parents and spent time there. Sam and Devi then went to the lagoon, where it all began, and spent quite some time there reminiscing about their past and talking about the long journey ahead to the U.S. They were excited about the trip but, at the same time, aware of the long and tedious journey, which would cross three datelines and two oceans.

Balan and Sarasu chose not to accompany their children to the international airport, opting instead to stay home. They felt uneasy about traveling to the big city because of its size, and the thought of flying made them nervous. When Devi and Sam said their goodbyes, Sarasu began to sob, and tears welled up in Balan's eyes as he struggled to contain his emotions. Overcome with sorrow, Devi broke down and wept at the thought of leaving her beloved parents.

After giving Sam's parents a warm hug, they said goodbye to them with eyes full of tears and hearts full of sadness for leaving their older parents at home to fly away to a distant land in search of new opportunities and a much more affluent and productive life and future for them and their children. Sam was visibly sad about leaving his parents as he was the only child and his father's righthand man. Johnnie and Elsy, along with their driver, took them to the Cochin Airport.

Sam thought that sometimes a man had to do what he was supposed to do, which was to leave his nest and fly away in search of green pastures and gold mines. Only there would you find the good fortunes waiting for you.

They boarded their Indian Airlines flight to Bombay in the afternoon. When they reached Bombay, they were taken to a hotel because their Pan-Am flight left for Frankfurt only at 4:00 a.m. After resting at the hotel for a few hours, they returned to the Bombay Airport after midnight and boarded their flight to Frankfurt during the wee hours.

Right after their Immigration and Customs clearance in Los Angeles, when they exited the waiting area, a St. Vincent Hospital driver with a sign that read, "Devi and Sam Jacob, St. Vs.," picked them up and took them to their apartment.

As they approached their apartment complex, the driver showed them the nearby grocery stores and restaurants, all of which were within walking distance. Then he showed them the St. Vincent hospital building from a distance.

The two-bedroom, two-bath apartment had everything they needed, including utensils, silverware, furniture, linens, and other accessories. Someone had even done some essential grocery shopping, as their fridge was packed with bread, eggs, milk, cheese, vegetables, tomatoes, potatoes, and ketchup, and the kitchen counter had bananas, apples, oranges, and other fruits and vegetables. The St. V's hospital even installed a telephone in their apartment for them.

So tired and jet-lagged, they dragged their limbs around the apartment, eyes heavy and ready for bed. Devi stifled a yawn.

"I can't keep my eyes open," Devi mumbled, rubbing her temples.

Sam blinked hard, trying to clear the jet lag fog from his head. "We need to call home."

He fumbled with the rotary phone on the side table, squinting at the numbers as he turned the dial. "How do we even call India from here?"

After a few failed attempts and muttered curses, he picked up the receiver again and dialed zero. "Operator? I need help calling Kerala, India... yes, directory assistance, please."

He gave the operator his parents' phone number. The line crackled— and then, finally, a familiar voice came through. It was his father's. Relief swept over Sam like a wave.

"*Appa*! We have arrived safely in Los Angeles, California. We are now in our apartment. How is *Amma*?" asked Sam.

Johnnie's voice brightened. "Thank God! I'll tell Devi's parents right away. *Amma* is doing well. I will call her. How is Devi?" He called out, "Elsy, come quickly—Sam's on the line. They've reached Los Angeles!"

Elsy joined the call. "How was the flight and the journey? It's so nice to hear your voice. Devi, sweetheart, we'll go over to your parents now and tell them the great news. They'll be so happy to know you arrived safely."

Devi closed her eyes, tears welling. The ache of distance softened just a little.

They changed their clothes, showered, and figured out how to light the kitchen burner.

The egg omelet they made—along with some fruit, cheese, and milk— was the first meal they savored in America. They went to bed immediately afterward and slept until noon the next day, stricken with severe jet lag.

CHAPTER 14

———◆———

When they woke up, the only sounds and smells they noticed came from the air conditioner, humming softly and filling their apartment with cool, clean, and comfortable air. In Cochin, mornings broke with the blaring horns of cars and trucks struggling through congested streets or, when they were back in their village, with scripture readings blasting from loudspeakers at the nearby temple, accompanied by the earthy scent and sound of torrential rain. But the smells and sounds of their first morning in California were strikingly different. Despite the steady flow of traffic, everything was quiet; no honking, no chaos, just the orderly movement of cars along the side street.

As morning light spilled into their apartment's family room, the sun's rays felt even brighter than they had imagined. They had heard stories about California's blistering summers, when sweltering heat often drove temperatures into the triple digits. Although summer had just ended and fall was approaching, the sun still shone with a fierce, radiant intensity.

The first things they noticed through their family room's glass window were the bustling street running parallel to their building, with several lanes of speeding cars, and a large, tall, shimmering building across the street, directly opposite their apartment complex, bearing a big sign: "The St. Vincent Medical Center." They were thrilled that the hospital was hardly 800 feet away or about one block from their apartment.

"Devi, look, the hospital complex is only a few minutes' walk from our apartment. You don't even need a car; it is only a stone's throw away," said Sam.

Sam and Devi were relieved that the hospital was ideally located across from their apartment complex. She could walk to the hospital safely, regardless of the weather conditions or the time of day. Their apartment was centrally located, with restaurants, grocery stores, and a shopping mall nearby.

They quickly got ready and walked to a nearby restaurant for lunch. Although they could read the menu and understand the ingredients, they were unfamiliar with the flavors and tastes. The only familiar items that made sense to them were the hamburgers and the roasted chicken, served with mashed potatoes and beans.

Devi ordered the roasted chicken, served with mashed potatoes, and Sam ordered the hamburger. After paying the bill for their lunch, they walked out without leaving any tips for the waitress, who looked at them with resentment. Realizing his inadvertent mistake, Sam quickly returned and placed a few dollars of the balance she had brought back on the table for her. He apologized for his oversight, and the waitress thanked him.

Devi's meeting with Kim Thomas was scheduled for the next morning at 9:00 a.m. Kim had advised her to bring Sam along if he liked to join. Devi was also advised to obtain the originals of all her credentials, including degree certificates, immigration documents, and her passport, so she could complete all the employment-related paperwork at the Human Resources Office.

Kim indicated during their meeting that the first two weeks of orientation would be with her and her staff. Then Devi would be assigned to a senior Physical Therapist (PT) for two more weeks of training. During that time, she would learn about various procedures, the equipment used by physical therapists in America, occupational safety, patient rights, laws, rules, and regulations, as well as information related to malpractice. Devi's regular work schedule would commence one month after orientation and training, and her regular hours would be from 12:00 p.m. to 9:00 p.m., with a one-hour break.

After Devi's nearly one-hour meeting with Kim, she was advised to visit the Human Resources Office for fingerprinting and to complete all other necessary paperwork, including social security, federal and state tax, family health insurance, and term life insurance applications. Devi was advised to report back to her at 7:00 a.m. the following day. She was also reminded that her first month's orientation schedule would be 7:00 a.m. to 4:00 p.m., with a one-hour lunch break.

Sam was eager to learn the location of the CULA campus, so he asked Kim about the approximate distance from their apartment to the campus. Kim told him it was located in Westwood, less than a mile away and within walking distance from their apartment.

After meeting with the HR Office and completing all their paperwork, Sam and Devi took a stroll to the Christian University of Los Angeles (CULA), using a map. There were sidewalks from their apartment complex up to the campus.

It took them approximately 10 minutes to walk to the campus. While returning to their apartment, they stopped at a nearby grocery store and bought chicken, cabbage, onions, green peppers, garlic, ginger, and parboiled rice. They thought that the grocery stores were like a library of food, featuring displays of a variety of fruits, vegetables, bread, meat, poultry, fish, dairy, cheese, and eggs, along with many shelves full of essential canned and neatly packed food items necessary for the convenience of a busy working community.

When they got home, Sam cut up the whole chicken using a cleaver and shears from the drawer, but they did not know how to dispose of the chicken skin and other waste materials. After searching for a while, they found a trash bin under the kitchen sink for the waste, but the next challenge was figuring out how to dispose of the waste from the bin. They kept the waste in the bin to deal with it later. Sam sliced the cabbage for '*thoran*' and other ingredients necessary for making a pot of chicken curry.

They cooked the parboiled rice and made a relatively large amount of "cabbage *thoran*" and chicken curry. To prepare Malayalee cuisine, they brought all the necessary spices from Kerala. After making the spicy chicken curry, they enjoyed a sumptuous dinner together and felt life was great in America. Before bed, they stored the leftover food in the fridge for their meals over the next few days.

Since the alarm was set for 5:00 a.m., Devi got up when it went off. She made coffee and toast, cut some fruits, and they had a healthy breakfast by 6:00 a.m. After taking a shower, grooming her straight, silky black hair, applying makeup, and donning her best dress pants and matching top, she looked beautiful and professional, like any other staff member at the hospital. Devi was out the door to work by 6:30 a.m. and reported to Kim at 6:45 a.m. Kim was impressed by her punctuality.

Soon after Devi left, Sam donned his best trousers, dress shoes, shirt, and eyeglasses and took with him in a messenger bag a copy of his doctoral dissertation that outlined his research study, copies of his diplomas and his several major scholarly publications, including the ones published in referred international journals, and records of the classes he taught, and copies of his resume. He went to CULA to find out whether he could meet with the Department Head for Biological Sciences.

After walking around the campus for some time, he found the Biological Sciences Building. He asked the receptionist for the Office of the Department Head. Sam told her he was an associate professor at the University of Cochin and would like to meet with the department head. The receptionist called the Dean's office and asked her Administrative

Assistant whether the Dean had a few minutes to meet with a professor from abroad. The Admin Assistant advised her to send him over to her office.

The Dean welcomed him and introduced herself as Dr. Susan Cheney. After the self-introductions, Sam thanked her for seeing him and inquired whether there would be any postdoctoral research opportunities in her division soon. He shared his research interests, his four major publications in professional journals, his doctoral research study and dissertation, and his teaching record with her. Sam expressed his research interest, particularly in Evolutionary Genetics.

After reviewing the publications and doctoral thesis, Dean Cheney asked whether he could teach two undergraduate classes for the semester in addition to his research. Sam told her that he would love such an opportunity.

Dean Cheney asked him to wait there. Then, she went to the front desk and checked with her Administrative Assistant to see whether she had any one-hour appointment slots available that week. The Dean advised her assistant to invite Dr. George, the Department Head of Molecular Biology and Genetics, to a meeting to interview a candidate for a possible postdoctoral fellowship. The Administrative Assistant made appointments for all three of them for Friday of that week at 10:00 a.m.

The Dean asked Sam to go to the Graduate School, one floor below, and inform them that Dean Cheney had advised him to submit an application for a Postdoctoral Fellowship. The Graduate School Office provided him with an application, which he filled out immediately, and attached copies of the credentials he had brought to support his application. After walking around the campus for a while, Sam returned to his apartment.

He fell asleep on the couch due to the severe jetlag he experienced; he woke up only when Devi got home. They both shared their challenges and new experiences of the day with each other.

"Great news, dear! I got an interview for a Postdoctoral Fellowship. It is on Friday at 10:00 a.m. with the Dean of the Biological Sciences and the Department Head of Molecular Biology and Genetics. I have only two days to prepare for the interview. They asked whether I could teach two classes for the upcoming semester. I told Dean Cheney I would love to do that. I don't know how many hours of teaching that was per day. Anyway, let me see what pans out. She told me that all the funds for the Postdoctoral Fellowship had already been committed. But she said she would consult with the Department Head," said Sam.

"Congratulations, Sam! That is great news. Your dreams are coming true! I'm so proud of you," said Devi.

"Thank you! How was work today, dear?" Sam asked.

"I'm learning new things and meeting with some of our staff. They're all very nice. No one seems concerned about my caste, religion, or origin," said Devi.

"Great! I'm famished after walking around campus and strolling back to the apartment. Let us eat some of our leftover chicken curry and rice," said Sam.

After eating their supper, they figured out how to operate their television, watched some news and American sitcoms, relaxed for a while, and went to bed.

Sam did not go anywhere for two days. He stayed home, reviewed his research studies and scholarly articles, and mapped out his interests in future research areas.

On Friday, he arrived for the interview and reported to the Admin Assistant at 9:45 a.m. for his 10:00 a.m. scheduled interview. After the interview, they asked Sam to wait outside in the lobby.

Dean Cheney addressed the need for a Lecturer to teach the Freshman and Sophomore biology classes with Dr. George, the Department Head, and they thought Sam was a great candidate since they did not have funds to pay the salary and benefits of a full-fledged Assistant Professor.

Dr. George reminded the Dean about the grant they had recently been awarded from the National Biological Science Foundation (NBSF) and informed her that they were seeking a researcher; however, the Primary Investigators (PIs) of the grant project required that person to work full-time.

Dean Cheney suggested to Dr. George that they hire Sam for three semesters, including the summer session, as a Postdoctoral Fellow to teach Biology classes for freshmen and sophomores. Additionally, as a trial, they would engage him in research for 20 hours per week per semester and evaluate his performance in early Winter. They both agreed that if Sam performed well in research, the Primary Investigators of the grant could hire him full-time for research, and she would try hard to hire someone else to teach. However, she acknowledged the difficulty in hiring qualified faculty members with doctorates in Biological Sciences for low salaries.

After their meeting, Dean Cheney called Sam back to her office. She asked whether he had a work permit from Immigration and Naturalization Services to seek employment in America. He said he had an immigrant visa.

The Dean offered Sam a one-year contract to teach two classes per semester and 20 hours of research per week in Genetics and Genomics. She said they had only funds to offer him a stipend of $35,000 for a one-year postdoctoral fellowship. She added that, as part of his contract, he also needed to teach two additional summer classes.

Sam was delighted that he had gotten a foot at the door of the institution he had dreamed of participating in research. He gladly accepted the offer and thanked her immensely. Dean Cheney thanked him, welcomed him, and asked him to start work in two weeks when classes began. She then informed him that her Admin Assistant, Julia, at the front office would prepare all his paperwork for signature and assist him with his schedules, the courses he needed to teach, the location of his classrooms and buildings, and the syllabi. Julia also called Dr. George, the Department Head of Genetics and Genomics, and made another appointment for Sam to review the details of the research project and schedules.

After meeting with Dean Cheney and Dr. George, Sam went to the Graduate School and HR Offices to complete all the official paperwork relating to his postdoctoral fellowship and contract. Sam got home with the most fantastic news he had ever received—a fellowship he had dreamed of at CULA.

When Sam got home by late Friday afternoon, Devi was already home from work and had been waiting for Sam. He warmly embraced her, "Devi, I have great news for you. I was offered a Postdoctoral Fellowship for one year with a stipend of $35,000," said Sam.

"Thank God! Congratulations, dear! I am so proud of you! Things are working out for us," said Devi.

"Fortunately, I was there at the right time when they were looking for someone to teach two classes and assist them with research for a grant they recently received from the National Biological Science Foundation," said Sam excitedly.

"When do you start work," asked Devi.

"Two weeks from now," replied Sam.

Devi was overjoyed and pleased with the opportunity that opened up for Sam. She was happy that the week ended with Sam's most exciting news. But Devi felt homesick and wished to see her parents. Her thoughts of home and longing to see her parents began to fully occupy her mind, and she wanted to get over the homesickness that was coming upon her.

"Sam, it's Friday evening. Our chicken curry and cabbage '*thoran*' are all finished. Let us go out and explore some new cuisines. I'm famished," said Devi.

Considering the village life she had led in servitude for nearly three decades, the past week in America had been a sea change—a new life on the fast lane in one of the largest cities in the world. Sam loved this new adaptable, adventurous, and rapidly evolving Devi compared to the woman who was in doubt and fear, worrying about her *Mangal Dosha*.

They held hands for a while as they walked in the opulent area of Westwood near the CULA campus. As they were strolling through the area, Devi saw a Thai Restaurant with a menu and the day's specials posted on a menu board at its entrance. The red curry special must be delicious, she thought.

"Sam, would you like to eat at this Thai Restaurant? Please look! They have red curry and fried pompano fish. Did you see that?" Devi asked.

Sam knew she wanted to dine there. Sam never turned her down when she was in her comfort zone.

"Let us eat there," said Sam.

When they went in, there was a long line of people waiting to dine. The girl at the reception told them there was a 25-minute wait for a table of two to become available. She took Sam's name and told them they needed to return in 25 minutes. They decided to walk around the area near the restaurant.

Next door to the restaurant was a relatively large electronic retail store that immediately caught their attention with its loud, popular 1980s disco music featuring Michael Jackson's danceable rhythms and catchy lyrics. Devi was captivated by the kind of music they were playing and momentarily caught up in the magical rhythm of the American popular music.

Sam and Devi browsed around the store, awestruck by the electronic goods they sold, including cassette players, eight-track tapes, and various AM/FM and shortwave radios. They were attracted by the variety of portable cassette player cum AM/FM shortwave radios. Before long, they realized that they were late for their restaurant appointment and rushed to eat.

The Thai chicken curry tasted somewhat similar to the Kerala chicken curry, with coconut milk and the distinct flavors of lemongrass and fresh basil. They also loved the fresh pompano fried, which was so different from the fried fish she had at home. It was distinctly different in flavor, but was delicious.

Sam's assignment at CULA started with teaching two biology classes for freshman and sophomore students, as well as 20 hours of postdoctoral research per week. During the first semester, he sounded slightly unusual due to his Indian accent and mannerisms. Then, he gradually assimilated and adopted a new style as acculturation began to take hold; his Indianness slowly faded away. The students were attentive, and their critical thinking skills were remarkable, which he noticed when they asked many questions. They read the assigned chapters as indicated in the syllabus before class, so they were prepared and eager to discuss the subject matter with Sam. He loved this pedagogical style.

Students began to appreciate his breadth and depth of knowledge in the subject matter, as well as his patience, dedication to teaching, and concern for the welfare of his students. Before long, he became an excellent teacher with an Indian accent, and students rated him in their reviews as both an outstanding teacher and a harsh taskmaster.

His extra efforts enabled most of his students to perform well in his classes, and his teaching evaluations from students were consistently returned to the Department with very high ratings. They all loved this teacher, who had an Indian accent and genuinely wanted his students to learn the subject matter and succeed.

As unusual as it was, one of his students nominated him for even an Outstanding Teaching Award in the second semester. Dean Cheney and Dr. George were so pleased and wanted Sam to keep teaching.

Sam and Devi did not have much time to cook or do grocery shopping often. Their lives gradually changed to keep pace with their busy schedules. Even during the weekends, Sam had students' homework assignments to read, exam papers to grade, and experiments to set up in the laboratory.

Devi and Sam ate their lunch at the workplace canteen and began to pick up food to bring home for dinner most nights. As their palates evolved, they began to savor the diverse cuisines of other cultures and countries. Finally, they found a couple of Indian restaurants in the neighborhood to savor some native-tasting meals and frequented them on weekends.

No one at work was concerned about Devi's caste or her origins as an "Untouchable," nor did anyone care about Sam's Syrian Christian background or religious heritage, unlike back home. What truly mattered in their new environment was their individuality, integrity, and professional performance. Both Sam and Devi began to receive recognition for their strong job performance. As a result, their outlook and self-esteem improved, their confidence grew, and so did their sincere drive to excel further and realize their full potential.

Sam's postdoctoral research took place in the Department of Molecular Biology and Genetics. He was assigned to support ongoing genetics research, with a focus on evolutionary genetics, as part of a CULA team that had received a significant grant from the National Biological Science Foundation (NBSF) for gene mapping. Sam's specific duties involved assisting the CULA research team in the preliminary mapping of the human genome, particularly in identifying the DNA base pairs across human chromosomes.

During the summer term, Dr. George assigned Sam to conduct research in Evolutionary Genetics because of his keen aptitude and deep passion for the subject. To build on his skills and existing knowledge base, Sam enrolled in two courses in computer programming and data analysis, as well as a few doctoral-level courses taught by renowned UCLA scientists in the field of genetics. These courses he took were spread out during the academic year, including the summer and the following fall semester.

As an evolutionary biologist, Sam was especially interested in tracing the evolutionary lineage of hominids that migrated out of Africa. His research focused on evolutionary connections between the genera *Homo* and *Australopithecus*. Specifically, he examined the genetic similarities between *Homo sapiens* and *Homo erectus* within the genus *Homo*, as well as between *Australopithecus africanus* and *Australopithecus afarensis* within the genus *Australopithecus*.

Sam's fascination with this area was further fueled by the famous fossil "Lucy," an *Australopithecus afarensis* specimen. "Lucy" had a cranial capacity similar to that of chimpanzees but demonstrated clear evidence of bipedal locomotion. Both *Australopithecus afarensis* and *Australopithecus africanus* exhibited a combination of ape-like and human-like features. The anatomical evidence Sam analyzed supported the prevailing scientific consensus that species within the genus *Australopithecus* were either direct ancestors or closely related precursors to the genus *Homo*.

Additionally, since the DNA of humans and chimpanzees is approximately 96–98% identical, Sam's evolutionary findings further supported longstanding paleoanthropological evidence that *Australopithecus* belonged to the hominin lineage—that is, the evolutionary group leading to modern humans. These findings, along with newly emerging genetic data showing close genetic relationships between humans and chimpanzees, were among the compelling scientific interests addressed in the NBSF grant.

With newly acquired skills in computer programming and data analysis, as well as a deeper understanding of genetics and genomics, Sam became an indispensable member of the emerging Human Genome research team. Upon successful completion of his initial two years of postdoctoral training, Dean Cheney and Dr. George extended Sam's appointment, offering him an additional three-year contract to continue full-time postdoctoral research under the same grant.

As Sam delved deeply into the study of evolutionary ecology and genetics, his understanding of the human creation story, as described in the Book of Genesis, began to undergo significant changes.

He became convinced that the Earth was not created in seven days, as Genesis suggests. Instead, he found overwhelming scientific evidence indicating that the Earth is approximately 4.5 billion years old—far older than the roughly 6,000 years implied by a literal interpretation of biblical genealogies. The scientific data directly contradicted the account of creation in the Book of Genesis.

Mainstream scientists generally agree that Earth was a barren "hellscape" during its first 500 million years, with intense volcanic activity and a molten surface, long before plant life emerged on land. During the Hadean Eon, a Mars-sized body collided with Earth, ejecting material that eventually coalesced into the Moon. This widely accepted theory led Sam to conclude that the Moon was not created by divine forces but formed through natural processes.

These revelations led Sam to hypothesize that there was no scientific evidence for any divine or teleological intervention to make Earth habitable for human life. For billions of years, Earth remained hostile to complex life. As Sam noted, dinosaurs first appeared around 230 million years ago, long before humans, and their dominance rendered Earth inhospitable for human evolution—until a massive asteroid struck the Yucatán Peninsula roughly 66 million years ago, causing their extinction and paving the way for mammals to thrive.

Through his research in evolutionary ecology, Sam discovered that approximately 99.9% of all species that ever lived on Earth have gone extinct over millions of years. Contrary to Creationist beliefs, the planet was not explicitly designed for humans. Instead, evolution by natural selection—where traits that best fit an organism's environment enhance survival and reproduction—was the only scientifically supported explanation for the diversity and persistence of life. Those species unable to adapt went extinct.

Sam argued that Charles Darwin's theory of evolution was the most coherent and evidence-based explanation for the existence and development of life on Earth. He believed that both life and the universe were in a continuous process of change.

Sam spent five years in postdoctoral research focused on evolutionary ecology and genetics, which provided him with the interdisciplinary foundation necessary to explore the emerging field of Evolutionary Genomics in the 1990s.

Building on his early success, the Division of Biological Sciences and the newly formed Department of Human Genetics and Genomics at CULA offered Sam a three-year full-time research contract in Human Genomics with a six-figure salary. His curiosity and scientific inquiry led him to integrate insights from Evolutionary Ecology and Anthropology. These disciplines helped him explore the evolutionary paths of both human cultures and non-human primates. This interdisciplinary approach also opened new avenues in primatology, enriching his scientific perspective.

This diverse background gave Sam the insight to study the "3.1 billion base pairs" in the human genome—23 chromosome pairs (one set from each parent). He explored how even minor mutations or "misspellings" in the DNA sequence could lead to genetic disorders such as sickle cell anemia or FOXP2-linked speech and language impairments.

After eight years of research—five as a postdoctoral fellow and three under contract—Sam became one of the nation's leading scientists in Evolutionary Genomics and a scholar in the Human Genome Project at CULA.

He co-authored two books and published numerous peer-reviewed articles in top journals on Evolutionary Biology and Genomics. On the recommendation of the Academic Senate Committee on Privilege and Tenure, and with support from Dean Cheney and Dr. George, the Chancellor appointed Sam as a tenured Associate Professor of Evolutionary Genomics. In the mid-1990s, he officially joined CULA's faculty with a salary of $175,000 per year.

Sam's faculty role included teaching one graduate-level course per semester in the Department of Human Genetics and Genomics, conducting ongoing research in Evolutionary Genomics for the Human Genome Project, and supervising doctoral students in Evolutionary Biology, Genetics, and Genomics.

Devi had completed eight years at St. Vincent Hospital and became a highly valued and respected member of the Physical Therapy department. She was promoted to Assistant Director and earned the position as a senior Therapist.

After receiving their promotions, they purchased a home in a neighborhood near Santa Monica, Los Angeles. The home was four miles away from the CULA campus and three miles from Devi's hospital.

They drove to work every day for efficiency and convenience.

Devi, the Dalit village girl who was once very troubled as an Untouchable *Manglik*, turned out to be a highly liberated city girl who drove around in one of the busiest cities in the world. *Mangal* or Mars, which affected the unfortunate people in her village, did not torment her anymore in America, and no one knew about her Dalit status or untouchable origin or cared to even find out about it.

Devi had become a person of dignity and worth as a professional who helped heal patients, especially during their rehabilitation, and had become a revered member of American society, which valued individuality and personal freedom over caste and religious status.

Although they had planned to visit Kerala every year, due to their busy work schedules and Sam's hectic postdoctoral study and research, they had visited their home in Kerala only every other year.

During their previous visit, Sam insisted, despite Balan's resistance, that Devi's parents get a telephone connection so that Devi and Sam could speak to them every week. So, they applied for and secured a telephone at Balan's home. He initially feared talking on the phone but gradually got used to it. Sam's parents have had a telephone connection for many years now.

Sam and Devi called both homes every week, sometimes even more often, and spoke to their parents for at least one hour. This helped them check in on their aging parents frequently and update them on all their news and accomplishments, which they were eager to hear. Because of their weekly conversations, their parents did not miss them that much.

They started planning another trip to Kerala for the upcoming summer. Dean Cheney and Dr. George were informed of his plans early in the academic year. He told them he would take six weeks off during the summer when Devi became available to take her vacation.

CHAPTER 15

As Human Genome research progressed and flourished in the late 1990s, a few wealthy investors formed a private company to conduct gene sequencing and develop a comprehensive data bank. The new company they founded was called Genomics America, Inc., which partnered with the CULA Genome Project Team. When Genomics America got well underway, the Chief Scientist of the CULA Human Genome project resigned and joined the company as their lead scientist.

Since Sam was one of the leading scientists in Human Genomics in America, he was promoted to the position of Chief Scientist of the Human Genome Project at CULA. The University offered Sam a new contract with a salary of $250,000 per year, making his compensation commensurate with his new responsibilities as Chief Scientist of the Human Genome Project and Professor of Human Genetics and Genomics. They thought this increase would make his salary competitive and prevent a private company or another institution from luring him away. They also incorporated a non-compete clause in the partnership agreement with Genomics America and ratified it.

When the Human Genome Project began to wind down, Sam emerged as one of the most celebrated genomics scientists in the U.S. With his research load easing, his professorship required him to conduct academic research and teach one graduate course per semester at CULA. The course he taught in genomics had long been in high demand and consistently filled up as soon as enrollment opened. It was a point of pride for CULA that Sam was considered one of the most sought-after speakers in DNA sequencing and genomics nationwide.

Two of the most critical early findings Sam supported through his Evolutionary Genetics and Genomics research were: 1) the ancestors of our modern-day species, *Homo sapiens*, evolved in Africa based on fossil records from 200,000 to 300,000 years ago, and, therefore, humans were not a created species; and 2) as a species, all humans are genetically 99.9 percent identical when comparing their DNA, regardless of race, skin color, ethnicity, or national origin, with a low level of genetic diversity.

After eight years of careful and relentless research, Sam arrived at a profound and humbling realization: though human beings may differ in intellect, temperament, or experience, no system of caste, creed, race, gender, nationality, or religion, and certainly no cruel invention like 'untouchability' or bigotry, can ever justly declare one group inherently superior or inferior to another. Caste and race are not truths etched in human nature, but illusions crafted by history and sustained by bigotry. Fashioned for the convenience of those in power, they have been shaped and reinforced by history, solidifying into the oppressive chains that still bind the conscience of society.

These primary constructs postulated by Sam, based on his Evolutionary Ecological and Genomics research, validated the longstanding paleoanthropological evidence. However, they were not only at odds with the Christian fundamentalists and creationists in America but also with the caste-based religious fundamentalists in India. The Christian religious fundamentalists, Hindu religious fundamentalists, and casteists found Sam's research findings and his assertions offensive and as existential threats to their centuries-old belief systems rooted in creation myths.

Sam became very vocal and articulate about these inconvenient truths, such as the 99.9% genetic similarity among all humans, irrespective of their country, caste, race, gender, or ethnic origin. Another unsettling fact he revealed was that Homo sapiens share a common ancestor with chimpanzee-like, possibly bipedal primates from East Africa. These scientific truths, drawn from Sam's research in evolutionary ecology and genomics based on fossil records and genomic studies, challenged the core religious beliefs and worldviews of racists, Hindu casteists, creationists, and some Christian right-wing conservatives alike.

The extreme Christian and Hindu fundamentalists and creationists found Sam's findings about human ancestry sordid and blasphemous. And those facts ruffled the feathers of religious believers in both his native and the host countries.

The Board of Trustees of the CULA was troubled by the calls they were receiving from some of the Christian fundamentalists and the far-right conservatives, who were concerned and ashamed that Sam was perpetuating the unchristian lies that imply their believers were not created by God but evolved from primates. The President of CULA called Sam and conveyed their concerns to Sam; however, as a tenured professor, Sam was protected by academic freedom to express freely the findings of research funded by taxpayers.

As Sam's popularity increased among the scientific community worldwide, so did his scientific influence and his calls for social justice and human rights. He openly condemned all discrimination and subversion of human beings based on race, caste, gender, ethnicity, or skin color.

That Saturday evening was momentous for Sam and Devi. While listening to a lecture at CULA by Athol Fugard, a renowned South African playwright and novelist and an advocate of racial justice and dignity, they were both quite emotionally moved by Fugard's account of his early fight against apartheid and its social injustices through his plays. As Fugard articulated to the audience how his life's work was a fight for social justice and human dignity, tears began to roll down Devi's cheeks.

What was more disturbing to Devi and Sam was that when Fugard, as a white man raised by an Irish Father and an Afrikaner mother, publicly confronted the moral blindness inherent in the injustice of apartheid through his plays, how he was threatened with arrest and got in legal trouble. They seized his passport in London and tried to ban him from reentering the country. He emphasized the importance of valuing human dignity and the need for shared humanity.

Sam found Devi restless and anxious throughout the lecture and reliving her past. Devi turned to Sam and whispered in his ears, "Apartheid and its evil devices were the diabolical manifestations of bigotry like "untouchability" that exploited and subjugated the innocent and segregated them based on caste and ethnicity. I still feel the evil manifestations of that bigotry in my soul; I still feel the ache of it in every bone in my body, and it still wrenches my gut and my heart. Those are the scars I have, and I still live with, to prove that giant evil still exists and oppresses and subjugates over 160 million Dalits in India today."

Sam felt the wetness of Devi's post-traumatic tears as they flowed from her eyes onto his ear while she whispered to him. He had carried the weight of her pain for many years, and even now, he could still feel it. Yet in that moment, he clearly heard what Fugard said: *The pen is a more powerful weapon than the sword.* That message—and the moral imperative it carried—stayed with him throughout the lecture, leaving an indelible mark on his soul.

When they were returning home, Sam apologized to her, "I did not know that he was going to cut through our souls and drive home the message of the struggle for social justice and dignity for all humans. I am sorry, dear, to put you through reliving your trauma," said Sam.

"With your life and your very existence, by loving and marrying me, you found your essence and are calling attention to the same moral blindness and indignity of 'untouchability.' By loving me unconditionally, you are fighting that injustice. It was cathartic for me to listen to the lecture. Thank you for taking me to the lecture. I am inspired and aware of the injustice and the critical need for shared humanity. Love you with all my heart, dear," said Devi.

"Devi, did you hear what he said?" asked Sam.

"What," asked Devi

"Yes, '*Pen is a much more powerful weapon than the sword.*' I have been thinking of writing a nonfiction scientific book about the emptiness and baselessness of 'untouchability' and the falsehoods surrounding its bogus history, especially after spending eight years of full-time research in Evolutionary Ecology and Genetics," said Sam.

"Hooray! I am rooting for you, dear. You must write a book in layman's terms in a lucid style about the emptiness and baselessness of the superiority one group feels over another group to subjugate them and oppress them. A lot of people are morally blind to such injustices and can't see them, or they remain silent and hence are complicit in such oppression. If anyone can write such a book with scientific authority, it is you. You lived a life fighting alongside me. Go for it," said Dev.

———

Athol Fugard's inspiring lecture deepened Sam's moral awareness. He felt that it is our ethical duty to respect and uphold the *human dignity* of all people, regardless of caste, race, skin color, gender, religion, or ethnicity. His talk effectively conveyed the message that genuine respect for human dignity could only be achieved through social justice, where the equitable treatment of all individuals was ensured. As Fugard noted in his lecture, Sam was convinced that *"the pen was a much more powerful weapon than the sword"* in combating social injustice and bigotry and in exposing the 'moral blindness' that allows such injustices and fundamental human rights violations to persist.

His personal and professional interests began to turn to India's caste-based discrimination against 160 million Dalits, many of whom are of untouchable origin, living in squalor, bonded labor, and under oppression. Sam held the view that a brown-skinned Dalit with the Untouchable label affixed to them at birth for no fault of their own was, according to the data, genetically 99.9 percent identical to the brown-skinned upper-caste Brahmin.

He intensified his efforts to understand this hypothesis further; in other words, he hypothesized that there were no inherent biological, genotypic, or significant phenotypic differences between the 'brown-skinned' upper caste Brahmins and the 'brown-skinned' Untouchables, who are the modern-day Dalits.

Any phenotypic differences between the two groups were, by far, dictated by socioeconomic conditions, nutrition, and environment rather than genetics. Sam held the view that the caste system is primarily a social construct of convenience. He focused his research studies on the genetic, genomic, ecological, anthropological, and archeological developments relating to casteism in India.

Sam ascertained that the "hunter-gatherers," or the original inhabitants of India 65,000 years ago, were the *Homo sapiens* who emigrated to India from East Africa via the Middle East. They were believed to be the aboriginal tribes of India, later known as the Nagas, dating back to around 4,000 BCE, based on anthropometric measurements of their remains from the past.

He made many trips to India to study the DNA samples of various racial and ethnic groups from different regions in India. Then, he examined the history and anthropology of migration. These studies led him to ascertain that the original hunter-gatherers transitioned to live in social settlements for agriculture and animal husbandry around the Indus Valley.

However, due to dry and unfavorable weather conditions, a lack of rain, and ongoing famines, they relocated further south in search of more favorable weather conditions. When their agriculture flourished and the population expanded, they adopted their new methods of agriculture and then began moving back to the northern regions, populating all over India.

That was when social stratification began to emerge, leading to the division of labor. Through clever and complex social engineering that gradually gained its religious validation and imprimatur, the dominant castes might have built a viable social order into the social fabric, which later found meaningful expressions in religious narratives through theological convergences.

Thus, the dominant groups relegated polluting and filthy jobs, such as scavenging, skinning animals, and removing human waste, to socially and economically disadvantaged minorities, who became the groups performing these undesirable tasks; a caste structure was born.

Sam's findings from anthropological, archaeological, historical, and genomic studies provided him with compelling evidence that Brahmins and Dalits (formerly referred to as "Untouchables") belonged to the same ancestral population. These studies revealed no significant genotypic or phenotypic differences between the brown-skinned upper castes and the similarly pigmented Dalits who were labeled as "polluted" or of "untouchable" origin. They all shared common ancestry and descended from the same tribal and ethnic roots.

As social stratifications developed, the upper caste adopted and instituted another clever strategy of "endogamy" to keep their cultural and class purity. Sam hypothesized that, by far, this exclusionary social engineering that led to the practice of endogamy became the predominant reason for the social segregation of groups and later into a caste-based society.

Therefore, he postulated that the vast majority of people who inhabited the entire Indian subcontinent before the arrival of the Aryans were all from one caste called the Nagas, whose ethnicity was later characterized as "Dravidians," a term that, according to some legends, was a Sanskritized version of "Nagas." The Nagas were initially called by that name because they worshipped Naga (snake).

As many believed, the language of Nagas was Tamil, which dominated India from the deep South to the northern regions. Therefore, some scholars believe the lingua franca of the entire population of India once was the 'Tamil' language.

The Aryans, referred to as the "noble people," were foreigners who spoke Indo-European languages and were originally settlers of the Indus Valley and the Ganges Plains from approximately 1,800 to 1,500 BCE. They, along with others who followed them from Central Asia, likely began emigrating to India due to unfavorable agricultural conditions and famine.

As many believed, they began settling in India and intermingling with the indigenous Nagas of India. Those people spoke Sanskrit and were allegedly responsible for Sanskritizing the name of Nagas and converting their tribal identity into "Dravidians," allegedly the Sanskrit term for Nagas.

Sam argued that the Nagas, the later Dravidians, the Brahmins, and all the other upper-caste people were of the same stock but were later classified as different ethnic identities through clever social engineering. His anthropological and ecological studies led him to assert that the Aryans of the Vedic age (1500-500 BCE) created these classifications as the caste system. In essence, it emerged over time from this same stock in the prevailing dominant group's own existential self-interest, primarily by dividing society into four groups called the "*Varnas*": Brahmins (priests), Kshatriyas (warriors), Vaishyas (merchants), and Shudras (laborers). Although Shudras were part of the *Varnas*, they were considered lower caste and ceremonially impure.

Sam argued that the Vedic people claimed that the divisions were divinely ordained to lend their social engineering religious validation and credibility. Furthermore, earlier anthropological studies provided adequate evidence that the Vedic people began assigning menial jobs to the impoverished in their settlements, condemning those who performed such jobs as "polluting" humans. They established boundaries against these so-called polluting individuals and later labeled them "Untouchables."

These enlightening findings from Sam's research attracted considerable interest worldwide. Many wanted to know more about the evolutionary history of the *Homo Sapiens* who migrated to the Indian Subcontinent and how some of those millions eventually became the "Untouchables" of epic proportions—nearly 160 million people who still live under oppression.

Sam began to outline a book about the evolutionary ecology and anthropology of how a branch of Homo sapiens who emigrated to India over the millenniums became the oppressed Untouchables of epic proportions. Sam's book, *Homo Sapiens to Untouchables,* was written in a lucid and straightforward format that was easy to understand. A major publishing house in New York agreed to publish his book for a handsome royalty. When the book was released in New York, London, Paris, and New Delhi, it instantly became an international bestseller.

A couple of months after its publication, there was a big uproar in India from some of the far right and upper caste religious fundamentalists about the "inconvenient truths" in Sam's book that challenged their spiritual way of life and caste-based hierarchical setup for their living. The "inconvenient truths" that became evident through the book were considered by them as existential threats to "Hindus" and the "Syrian Christians" in Kerala.

Those hardline religious fundamentalists condemned America for publishing such a book. The fundamentalists bought hundreds of books and began to burn them publicly in India. And then, the violent mob started invading the bookstores; they grabbed Sam's books and burned them publicly. They have asked the publisher in New York to pull all the books from the shelves and threatened to boycott all their books in the future. The American publisher refused to withdraw Sam's book, resulting in a surge in worldwide book sales. India banned the book, and people smuggled Sam's book to India for them to read.

A group of fundamentalist Christian thugs attacked Sam's father, Johnnie, in Kerala and damaged his car as a warning. They tried to intimidate Balan and Sarasu by setting fire to their vehicle, which the police aborted. They arrested two thugs later for arson. Johnnie had to call for continuous police surveillance of their homes.

The protests against Sam's books continued for a few more weeks and eventually died down as the publisher refused to withdraw the book. The book continued to be a best-seller worldwide, except in India. Sam was being recognized by many scientific and literary societies from around the world for his outstanding work.

Then the Indian-American Foundation of the Upper Caste Coalition in America, which was supported by some tech billionaires and millionaires of Indian origin, offered the Christian University of Los Angeles, $5 million for an interdisciplinary endowed faculty position in "Sociology, Anthropology, and Evolutionary Genomics" to conduct research exclusively on races and caste. The Christian Fundamentalists of America and the Far Right supported the Upper Caste Coalition of India's initiative with their leadership and moral support.

The only condition the Foundation put on CULA in return for the $5 million was the termination of the atheist and anti-religious radical Dr. Sam Jacob from his job for perpetuating pseudoscientific theories of caste and race and attacking the sentiments of the religious people in

India and America.

Devi was petrified and startled by her colleagues' questions about her husband. Sam was nonchalant about the controversy and was determined not to back off. The President of CULA submitted the offer of a $5 million donation to the Board of Trustees for approval. They deliberated about the funding and approved accepting the endowment funds without their required condition to terminate Sam. The Foundation was still okay with their donation, even if CULA did not terminate Sam, since the Upper Cast Coalition of India wanted to gain a foothold at CULA to undermine Sam and his research.

Wherever Sam spoke, the Foundation arranged protesters who chanted, "Down with the caste hater and atheist," and disrupted his speech. The Faculty Senate of CULA unconditionally supported Sam and protected his academic freedom to disseminate the results of his studies. They requested that the University administration reject the donation and return the endowment fund to the Foundation.

However, the pressure on Sam and the disruption of his professional life continued. The Foundation paid people to disrupt Sam's speeches, and he began to receive death threats. Devi began to feel afraid again, even to go out shopping.

After considerable deliberation and thought, the Board of Trustees of CULA returned the $5 million to the Foundation due to pressure from the Faculty Senate. At that point, the students of Indian origin at CULA started a campaign to boycott Sam's graduate classes and gave him bad reviews. However, despite the negative reviews orchestrated by Indian students, his graduate classes continued to fill up on the first day of open enrollment itself, and the Department continued its usual practice of creating a 'waiting list' for his class in case students dropped out, allowing those vacated seats to be filled.

A few weeks later, Sam received an unusual call from the CULA President's Office to congratulate him. He was pleasantly surprised when the President informed him that his graduate students had nominated him for the Outstanding Teaching Award. The President indicated that the Outstanding Teacher Award Committee meritoriously chose him as that year's University's Outstanding Teacher! The President informed Sam that he would receive the award during the December Commencement Ceremony. Sam thanked the President.

After a couple of days, the President called him again to congratulate him on the University community's selection of him as the Keynote Speaker for the December Commencement Ceremony. He requested that Sam deliver the Keynote Speech at the Commencement Ceremony. Sam was delighted by the confidence the University community had bestowed upon him.

After 15 years of living in America as immigrants, Sam and Devi were finally sworn in as U.S. citizens that summer. American citizens of Indian origin were eligible to apply for a multiple-entry visitor's visa or a Person of Indian Origin (PIO) card, facilitating easy travel to India. So, Sam and Devi applied for their PIO cards and were waiting. It generally took 6 to 8 weeks to process the PIO Card. Even after eight weeks, they still had not received their PIO cards.

After nine weeks of waiting, Devi received her PIO card, but Sam did not receive any response. A few days later, Sam received an official letter from the Embassy denying him the PIO card and a visa for entry into India. The letter cited his research studies, lectures, speeches, and best-selling book, all of which addressed the socially constructed system of discrimination in India. The authorities alleged that the findings he presented constituted anti-India propaganda.

Sam immediately responded to the Embassy, stating that he was a scholar in the disinterested pursuit of truth in an unbiased manner. His findings were gathered using the widely accepted methods of scientific inquiry, and he was not motivated by politics or economic gain. He particularly mentioned that he loved his motherland but not the oppression of millions of innocent Dalits of untouchable origin. He stated that they were also Indians with the same dignity gifted by a God who created them in His image.

Banning Sam from entering India was the straw that broke the camel's back because Sam's elderly father, Johnnie, was bedridden with cognitive issues, and his health had been steadily declining due to old age. Over the past few years, Sam spent many days with his parents during every trip to India while researching and gathering data for his studies. During those visits, Johnnie was weak but stable and in good physical condition. However, his health declined gradually.

Since his father had expressed a desire to see him, Sam considered making a trip earlier than their usual visit planned for the upcoming summer. He felt disheartened by his mother country's rejection of his sincere pursuit of truth. Yet he found solace in the thought that a foreign nation, America, had embraced him as a celebrated scientist for his impartial quest for knowledge and discovery. Sam appeared to follow truth wherever it led him, regardless of the consequences.

The only option they had was for Devi to travel to India by herself in the summer. Sadly, every time Devi visited India, all their relatives asked was only one thing; whether they had any exciting news of a child on the horizon. Devi's desire to become a mother had not come to fruition, and that realization had taken away her joy for a while now. They have been trying to become parents for the past 15 years.

Devi had undergone another surgery for bearing a child in America in the hope of correcting her injury sustained from the past police violence. But the injury she suffered from the police violence seemed to have made her permanently infertile. That had been a cross they had been bearing for many years, regardless of their stellar professional and financial successes.

Johnnie and Elsy were so proud of Sam and rejoiced in the fame and fortune he had achieved worldwide within the scientific community in the past 15 years. However, they were also becoming increasingly concerned about their motherland's punitive sanctions against his research studies and best-selling book.

Sam called his father every other day and spoke with him for hours, which made him feel comfortable and calm. Sam finally told him about his visa being rejected for visiting India. Sam had to break this news to him; otherwise, during his final days, he would have thought his son had abandoned him.

In the meantime, Sam was informed by his publisher that his book had been nominated for the Pulitzer Prize as a distinguished nonfiction work that had opened the eyes of the world to the oppression and suffering of an epic proportion of mostly impoverished people in India.

After a few weeks of old age-related sickness, Johnnie was finally admitted to the hospital. Doctors told Sam over the phone that his condition was deteriorating. Sam spoke to him in the morning and afternoon.

In desperation, Sam made a final plea to the Embassy for a visa. He had one of the California Senators' offices send a special request, asking that he be granted a visa on humanitarian grounds to see his dying father. However, religious fundamentalist leaders influenced the Government's Foreign Affairs Office to deny Sam entry.

Sadly, Johnnie died peacefully in the hospital, knowing that his son stood and fought for what was moral and right in this troubled world. Sam was uncontrollably sad when his father passed away due to the realization that his own motherland did not even allow him to see his father for one last time or attend his funeral, even on humanitarian grounds, because of the inconvenient truths he brought to light.

This rejection by his motherland for standing up for what was right and for not doing anything wrong made him very sad. He felt rejected and betrayed by his own mother country in a manner somewhat similar to how they had rejected their native Untouchables and their human dignity.

Sam took one week off to grieve the death of his beloved father. On the second day morning of his bereavement leave, he received a call from the Office of the Chair of the Pulitzer Prize Committee. The secretary asked him to hold on for the Chair, Dr. Benjamin Dowd.

"Good morning, Dr. Sam Jacob. My name is Benjamin Dowd from the Pulitzer Prize Committee. How are you doing, Dr. Jacob? asked Dr. Dowd.

"I'm doing very well, Dr. Dowd," replied Sam.

"Dr. Jacob, I'm calling you with exciting news today. I'm delighted to inform you that you have been selected as a recipient of this year's Pulitzer Prize for Nonfiction. Congratulations! You will receive an Award letter with details of the Award and the Award Ceremony, which will be held at Columbia University in New York."

"Wow, thank you from the bottom of my heart. That is a great honor! I'll be there to receive the award," said Sam.

"I have read amazing things about you. I look forward to meeting you, your spouse, and your guests. Thank you for your time. Do you have any questions?" asked Dr. Dowd.

"No, thank you," replied Sam.

"Goodbye, Dr. Jacob," said Dr. Dowd.

"Goodbye, Dr. Dowd," said Sam.

Sam immediately called Devi at work. Devi was in her office and saw Sam's phone number on the dial. She picked up the phone and said,

"Hello, this is Devi."

"Hello, Devi. Are you sitting down? Guess what. I have been awarded the Pulitzer Prize for Nonfiction. Would you believe it," asked Sam.

"Oh my gosh! Sam, my heartfelt 'Congratulations' my love! You are the first Indian scientist and author to receive a Pulitzer Prize for Nonfiction. It is going to be international news. When is the Award Ceremony and where?" Asked Devi.

"It's going to be in New York. I will soon receive an award letter with the details of the Ceremony, including the date, time, and location. I want you to take a few days off to go to New York with me," said Sam.

"Sure, that will not be any problem," said Devi.

"I wish my father were alive to hear this great news. When I told him I had been nominated for the Pulitzer, he was thrilled and thanked God many times. I want to invite my mother to visit America and attend the ceremony. I know your parents refuse to travel even to the Cochin airport, so there's no point in inviting them. Why don't you come home? We'll go out to lunch together," said Sam.

Before Devi came home to go out to lunch with him, Sam called the CULA President's Office and shared the news with the President before he heard it through the media or from someone else. The President was ecstatic that one of his prominent scientists had won the Pulitzer. The President's Office invited Sam to the campus late that afternoon for a Press Conference.

Sam called Dean Cheney and Dr. George to share the great news. They were all overjoyed, congratulating him and expressing their pride in him. The CULA community was exuberant and jubilant over one of their professors receiving the Pulitzer Prize.

Then, he called his mother in India to inform her that he had won the prestigious Pulitzer Prize. She thanked Jesus loudly over the phone for all His blessings and mercies before congratulating her son. Elsy wished Johnnie was there to share this stellar achievement of their son, the proudest moment of the family and the country.

Sam invited Elsy to visit America for his Award Ceremony in New York. She informed him that she would have been thrilled to make the trip, but her health was not good enough for such a long and tedious international trip. She acknowledged to Sam that her son was the first Indian Scientist and author to receive a Pulitzer for nonfiction and expressed her pride and joy so loudly over the phone.

Next, he called Balan and Sarasu and told them he had won one of the most significant awards, the Pulitzer Prize. They knew little about the value or worth of the award, but they were genuinely happy and proud because Sam won it. They individually congratulated Sam and thanked *Bhagwan* for his blessings. It was their proudest moment, and they told him that they never heard of any other Indian scientists winning such an eminent award.

The next day, newspapers in India featured a headline on their cover pages: "Indian Scientist in America Awarded the Most Coveted Pulitzer Prize for Nonfiction." From Cape Comorin in the South to Kashmir in the North, all the newspapers and news outlets reported this story as their cover feature, taking pride in the unprecedented success of an Indian scientist. However, they failed to mention that the scientist, Dr. Sam Jacob, was banned from entering India even on humanitarian grounds – whether to visit his father on his deathbed or to attend his funeral.

His crime? A disinterested pursuit of truth and the dissemination of its findings, which became inconvenient truths that shook the foundations of the caste boundaries they had built and maintained for ages.

CHAPTER 16

Devi had completed over 15 years of praiseworthy service at the St. Vincent Hospital in Los Angeles. She received numerous accolades for providing outstanding services to help patients regain mobility and achieve some degree of normalcy in their daily lives after surgery or another life-changing event, such as a stroke. Recognizing her excellence in leadership and long service, she was promoted to the administrative position of Associate Director of the Physical Therapy (PT) Department, which offered her a six-figure salary. As a loyal and long-serving member of the hospital staff, she was considered a valuable asset by the hospital.

After 15 years at the Hospital, Devi, who was born Devika, gradually became known as Debbie due to cultural assimilation and the changing demographics of the City of Los Angeles. The name Debbie gradually evolved from a simple, anglicized, and logical transformation of her diminutive form, Devi.

The transformation of her name from Devi to Debbie occurred due to the strong influence of the sizable Hispanic population that spoke Spanish in Los Angeles. In Spanish, the letters "b" and "v" are pronounced identically, as they are not considered distinct phonemes but rather bilabial sounds. As a result, many Spanish speakers mispronounced and misconstrued Devi's name as "Debbie." Over time, due to both this mispronunciation and the gradual anglicization of her name by others, Devi's name gradually evolved into the popular American name "Debbie."

Incidentally, a few days after the announcement of Sam's Pulitzer Prize Award and Press Conference at CULA, the St. Vincent Hospital CEO's Office contacted the Physical Therapy Department requesting the best PT in the Department to provide services for a patron of St. Vincent Hospital and a distinguished patient who was scheduled for hip surgery at their hospital.

The Hospital President wanted the best physical therapist with good bedside manner and expertise to provide rehabilitation services for the patient after her hip replacement surgery. The PT Department, without any reservation, recommended Debbie (Devi) for the assignment, mainly because the patient was also a prominent Indian-American and a major benefactor of the St. Vincent Hospital.

The patient's name was Mrs. Priya Venugopal, a renowned astrophysicist who had retired in great eminence. She worked for the National Space Research Center (NSRC) in California for 30 years. Her husband, Mr. Venu Gopal, a technology entrepreneur from Los Angeles, owned a multinational technology company and was one of the earliest Indian tech billionaires. After his retirement, he became a philanthropist and a benefactor of St. Vincent Hospital. Mr. Venu Gopal served as the President of the St. Vincent Hospital Foundation and as a trustee on the hospital's Governing Council.

Venu and Priya lived in an estate home overlooking the Pacific Ocean with a private beach in Santa Monica. Since he was one of the neighborhood's wealthiest and most resourceful men, the hospital enlisted him to serve on its Foundation Board and the Governing Council. Ever since his association with the Hospital, Mr. Venugopal donated $40 million to St. Vincent's to build a new Surgery Center in their namesake.

The hospital welcomed Priya getting her surgery in their namesake "Venugopal Surgery Center." After Priya's scheduled hip surgery, she was moved to the luxurious private suite of the Venugopal Surgery Center, which was dedicated exclusively to patrons and VIPs. Debbie

(Devi) was assigned solely to be responsible for her rehabilitation and care during her hospital stay.

Devi trained Priya to perform everyday activities like bathing, changing clothes, getting out of bed safely, and walking while recovering at the Center. She also helped Priya learn range-of-motion exercises for her hip and use assistive devices such as walkers and crutches to regain some level of independence in daily activities.

During these sessions and between breaks, they spoke casually about personal and professional matters to break up the monotony of the repetitive and uncomfortable physical exercises. This type of interpersonal care can sometimes distract the patient from the discomfort. As usual, Debbie used her good bedside manner and listened attentively to what Priya had to say.

Devi discovered that Priya was originally from Kerala and had been one of the Chief Space Exploratory Scientists before retiring from NSRC. Priya was an Orthodox Brahmin who strictly adhered to traditional values, rituals, social customs, and above all, upheld the spiritual purity of Brahmins among all other upper caste groups. She had dark skin, stunningly beautiful looks, and an attractive body, even in her early 70s.

To Devi's surprise, Priya playfully asked for her zodiac sign and horoscope, just for fun, and to see whether, as a Christian, Debbie (Devi) ever had a *Jathakam*. Although Devi answered yes, she had no desire to become chummy with Priya or share anything more about her past.

"Since your name is Debbie and you have a light skin tone, I presume that you are a Christian from Kerala," asked Priya.

"Yes, I'm a Christian. We go to an Episcopal Church here in Los Angeles," said Devi.

When Priya took a break between her exercises, she said, "Debbie, I had a *Jathakam* that forecasted that I would become a celestial pundit or '*shastranjan*' (scientist). Well, that was accurately fulfilled in my life. I became a noted and well-accomplished astrophysicist. The *Jyolsyan* had also predicted that, since I was born a *Manglik* with a *Mangal Dosha*, I would encounter a stormy married life, my husband's health and life would be in danger, and he would have a lot of failures in his professional life," Priya paused to see Debbie's reaction.

"Okay, that sounds interesting," said Devi with a nod and a smile.

"You know, my husband is one of the most successful tech billionaires and a healthy dude. I lived in America for 45 years and was married to him for 40 years. We never had any marital problems, nor was he ever in danger of being hurt. So, that part of my *Jathakam's* forecast is still pending," said Priya jocularly.

"I know you're a renowned scientist who has always dealt with objective reality and empirical evidence, gathered through experiments and observation. As my husband would put it, you worked with *a posteriori* knowledge and inductive reasoning. So, may I ask, do you still believe in 'superstitions' like *Jathakam*?" asked Devi.

"Yes, I believe in *Jathakam*. I know you Christians don't think much of it. However, you see, there are many things we don't understand in this physical world of phenomenal reality and the metaphysical world beyond our sensory experiences. However, there are many things in this world that we do understand through '*a priori*' reasoning, which is independent of human sensory experiences. You see, mathematics is an excellent example of '*a priori*' reasoning independent of sensory experiences," said Priya.

"Wow, really? I'm surprised that a renowned scientist like you truly believes in such superstitions as *Jathakam*," said Devi.

"Look, we prove theorems and do mathematics without conducting empirical experiments. We utilize such mathematical theories with precision to conduct interplanetary explorations. So, *a priori* knowledge is independent of sensory experience, and mathematics is not only precise but also universally valid, though not empirical! A vast body of knowledge was considered divine and passed down to us through the scriptures. In that sense, it existed before humans came into being and was transmitted across generations. *Jathakam* and similar mythological knowledge were also passed down generationally, because they were rooted in observational traditions, *a priori* reasoning, and interpretive understanding," said Priya.

"So, do you think "*Mangal Dosha*" and its malefic effects would come true sometimes as forecasted?" asked Devi.

"Yes, they do. My marital life is going well, but that doesn't mean it will remain the same forever, and my husband will be insulated from any bodily harm. I'm sure our married life is okay now, but it is dynamic," said Priya.

"How do you mitigate the malefic effects of *Mangal Dosha?*" asked Devi.

"Listen, when I got married, I had to do a *Kumbha Vivah*, which was a symbolic marriage to a pot, before my real marriage with my fiancé, Venu Gopal, to mitigate the malefic effects of my *Mangal Dosha* (Mars defect). If I had married another *Manglik* like me, I wouldn't have encountered any baneful effects. However, Venu was not a *Manglik*, and we had been in love since college, so I could not marry another person who was a *Manglik*. You can also ward off the malefic effects of *Mangal Dosha* by worshipping 'Lord Hanuman' and performing *Mangal Dosha puja*. I still do all those things," said Priya.

"Are you serious? I am blown away to hear that a world-renowned scientist like you believes in a world beyond our sensory experiences or things outside of time and space," Devi asked.

"Yes, I do believe in a world beyond our sensory experiences. Listen, science and religion are separate magisteria. As we previously discussed, science is empirical and grounded in inductive reasoning. Metaphysics, however, is based on philosophical and '*a priori*' reasoning. I practice empiricism in my professional life and use '*a priori*' reasoning in my private life concerning matters of faith and religion because, I believe, there is a reality beyond our physical world," said Priya.

"How does a dead planet, Mars, orbiting over 150 million miles away from Earth, monitor and control the fate of insignificant little humans on Earth and keep tabs on their marital lives, behaviors, and future?" Devi asked.

"I don't fully understand how it works. But my lack of understanding doesn't mean that our observational traditions and the astrological predictions are all untrue. As a Christian, you probably know that even the wise men and kings practiced astrology during Jesus' days. If you take the case of the three Magi, namely Gaspar, Melchior, and Balthasar, they followed the 'Star of Bethlehem' that guided them to Jesus's birthplace. They were allegedly among the first people who worshipped Jesus. However, they were led by the 'Christmas Star' or the 'Star of Bethlehem' to Bethlehem from different parts of the world. How did the Star of Bethlehem know to guide those three Magi from three different continents to the City of Bethlehem?" asked Priya.

"That's a good point and begs the question, 'How did the Star of Bethlehem know to guide the three Magi,'" said Devi.

"As you know, nearly two billion Christians like you believe in the historical events surrounding the birth of Jesus. That star might not have a brain or a mind like the divine beings. However, I believe that this universe and its galaxies, suns, planets, stars, black holes, and all living beings are under the spell and command of the Almighty Universal God," said Priya.

Devi wanted to ask this famous astrophysicist one crucial question that Sam always asked for her own personal understanding.

"Priya, may I ask which God that is? Is that the Creator God Brahma, God the Father, Ahura Mazda, Zeus, Marduk, Inana, Aton, Amun, Enlil, Yahweh, El Elyon, Jesus Christ, or Allah?" Asked Devi.

"Wow, you are quite knowledgeable of the various names of these gods! He is the God of this Universe, the Demiurge. The names you mentioned are all the same God of this Universe, but with different identities of how humans have conceived Him over the millenniums," said Priya.

"Why is the Universal God always known as a 'He' rather than a 'She.' Historically, we had many goddesses, such as Ishtar, Tiamat, Nemesis, Minerva, Athena, Aphrodite, Lakshmi, Saraswathi, Parvathy, Kali, Kamakshi and others," asked Devi.

"That is because the Universal God chose a masculine form, and that was how he manifested Himself to us, humans," said Priya.

"If that is the objective truth, then why do we have different scriptures and images of these gods and different sorts of personifications of them, as my husband would ask, or why don't we agree on any of the details and nuances of Him?" Asked Devi.

"Scriptures are all human narratives of a deity who lived among us— or, in some cases, they reflect how we perceived an apophatic God, and in others, an amorphous one. That's probably why we can't agree on the details. It's like the story of the three blind men trying to comprehend and describe an elephant by feeling it. The elephant is too vast for them to comprehend without all the sensory tools of perception that provide experience," said Priya.

Devi slipped into a flashback of her past life as a *Manglik*, a traumatic time that caused her so much pain, anxiety, nervousness, and uncertainty. In her past life in Kerala, she feared the malefic effects of *Mangal Dosha*, also known as the Mars Defect. Eventually, when Devi came to America, she put them to rest and filed them away as superstitions in the deepest, darkest corners of her mind. There, in America, she found solace in her new life with Sam. However, after talking to Priya, a fundamentalist Brahmin woman who passionately defended her superstitions with logical theories and philosophy, Devi began to feel herself slipping back into the old Devika.

Devi was glad that the therapy for Priya ended that day successfully, but she felt a horrible sense of déjà vu. *Mangal Dosha* followed her to America, this time through the powerful words of a superstitious but world-renowned astrophysicist. She was glad that the day's work was over and that she could soon be with Sam, in whose arms she always found comfort, reassurance, and safety.

After dinner, she told Sam about her new patient, a world-renowned National Space Research Center astrophysicist named Priya, and her passionate and rational defense of the superstitious constructs of *Jathakam* and *Mangal Dosha*. Sam warned her to refrain from such conversations to safeguard her mental peace.

The next day, Priya's therapy started early in the morning. Even with assistive devices, such as a walker and crutches, the walking exercises were too tedious and painful for Priya. She had to take additional painkillers and rest between sessions, but she was a persistent lady. One thing Devi learned about Priya was that she loved sharing her superstitious cultural traditions and some of her conservative and prejudicial Brahmin worldview even after her liberating scientific education, professional career as a scientist, and 45 years of living in America.

"Debbie, you told me that your last name is Jacob. You must be a Syrian Christian. I had many Syrian Christian friends in college and now here in Los Angeles. Many Syrian Christian women have light skin tones like yours, but you are one of the most beautiful Kerala women I have met," said Priya.

"Yes, I am a Christian. Thank you for your kind words about me," replied Devi. She didn't want to elaborate and share personal details with her.

"I understand that the Syrian Christians have a Brahminic ancestry because the families that Apostle Thomas converted to Christianity in 52 A.D. when he landed in Kerala were all Brahmins. You see, Syrian Christians continued to maintain 100% of their purity by not marrying outside of their community or from lower and Dalit castes because they wanted to preserve the purity of their lineage. This is also the reason why the Syrian Christians have been strictly practicing endogamy, like us Brahmins," said Priya.

At that time, the nurse practitioner interrupted their conversation to perform a medical examination on Priya and administer the prescribed medications. Consequently, they paused their discussion.

What amazed Devi was Priya's feelings of caste superiority and her religious arrogance as a Brahmin, which she did not feel the need to inhibit or hide because of her status and wealth.

Meanwhile, Devi sat silently, lost in her past, and began to experience post-traumatic stress disorder (PTSD) stemming from the oppression she and her parents had endured for decades while living in servitude in Kerala as Dalits of untouchable origin. Dalits who live in servitude invariably suffer both psychological and physical oppression.

Devi's agony was a private symphony of torment that had begun playing again in her mind. The rest of America would not understand this particular form of "post-traumatic stress disorder (PTSD)" experienced by a Dalit woman with an untouchable past, made even more complex by her *Mangal Dosha*. Moreover, America was a technologically advanced country positioning itself for interplanetary travel to Mars. It had spent billions of dollars exploring Mars remotely. Still, the scientists did not know what "Mars defect" or "*Mangal Dosha*" meant—

knowledge that, ironically, only a high school dropout like Keshavan possessed, which had been passed down from his father.

Sam only could understand and empathize with Devi's torment since he knew that Devi, like many Dalits of untouchable origin, was a victim of years of oppression, servitude, and psychological trauma that manifested now as a typical "Dalit trauma."

Priya, a highly conservative Brahmin scientist, possessed advanced education, wealth, and higher social status. These privileges naturally developed a sense of superiority in her dealings with others. This sense of superiority she felt was also exacerbated by Priya's religious conditioning that they were 100% pure blood favored by God. The privileges they enjoyed as members of the priestly class (Brahmin), along with all its trappings, traditions, and superstitions, she felt must, therefore, be justified and defended with rational narratives, no matter how absurd they might sound.

Furthermore, some extremely wealthy individuals are often dismissive of the sensibilities and feelings of others because they perceive themselves as being at the top of the social hierarchy. So, when you have everything in life like Priya—money, advanced education, status, and immense wealth--your attitude and dismissiveness define you.

The hospital staff and the President were at Priya's beck and call, as her husband was their primary benefactor, having donated $40 million to build the surgical center where she was recovering. Whatever Priya said seemed to carry the weight of gospel, and she held nothing back—she was remarkably outspoken. Devi understood that the surgical center belonged to them, so she couldn't openly disagree with Priya, fearing she might lose her job.

When Devi returned after lunch, Priya was energetic and ready to go through another round of exercises. Devi worked with her for one long session and then gave her a break to rest. Devi stayed with Priya during the break. Priya thought she was amusing Debbie with topics of common interest in their Indian-American community.

"Debbie, there is a world-renowned Indian-American scientist at CULA who won the Pulitzer Prize a couple of weeks ago for his non-fiction book that lucidly synthesizes the outcomes of his research studies on the evolutionary ecology of indigenous populations in India. He concluded that the Brahmins and Untouchables are of the same stock and have no phenotypic or genotypic differences," said Priya.

"Okay, that is interesting," Devi nodded.

"His wife is an Untouchable, so he felt compelled to develop such dubious and pseudoscientific inferences and claims. But you know that the Untouchables were considered a polluted class of impoverished and slow-witted people who performed menial jobs for centuries. Still, he had the nerve to direct his research in that manner, concluding that they were of the same stock. It is an interesting book that you might want to read. The book is banned in India now, but it offers intriguing insights, albeit with questionable results," said Priya with indignance.

Devi was surprised that Priya had no clue. She didn't even suspect that the author, Dr. Sam Jacob, might be her husband or a relative, given their similar last names.

As a college-educated professional and a successful woman with multicultural life experiences, Devi had gained great insight over the years—both as an impoverished Dalit living in servitude in the gutters and now as a well-to-do professional woman living in an extravagant world of freedom and social justice. She had experienced the harsh realities of caste oppression and abuse, and she was now a highly productive member of an advanced industrial society in America.

Devi had learned that liking a person was often an instant visceral reaction. Similarly, loving someone usually depended on an action or a series of actions, most often without bearing on the past. Invariably, developing a romantic love for an individual was also based on the present. However, "hate" was more often connected to past conditioning. What we were told as children and how we were conditioned socially and religiously over the years trigger a "hate" mechanism in us instantly, like turning on an electric switch.

Devi thought that if she owned up and admitted to Priya that she was the Dalit woman married to Dr. Sam Jacob, she would immediately trigger that "hate" switch in Priya for no other reason than that Dalits were despised and because Priya was conditioned to believe the lie that they were impure and polluted humans. Devi was petrified of Priya marginalizing and reducing her to a "polluted" human devoid of dignity, if she revealed her identity.

Devi instinctively felt defensive about triggering Priya's "hate" mechanism against her for being in her impermissible proximity as a Dalit, which Priya would despise. Devi's primordial Hypersensitive Agency Detection Device (HADD) was in full gear, and she wanted to run for cover from the scene, fearing the raging bear in the bush.

As a conservative Brahmin, Priya had been conditioned to believe that Dalits were Untouchables and that they must keep a safe distance from Brahmins. So, Devi decided not to engage further in conversation with Priya. She did not want to admit to Priya that she was the Dalit woman who was the wife of the Pulitzer Prize-winning scientist.

Devi had an uncontrollable urge to heave from Priya's hurtful and bigoted words. Still, she knew without a doubt that whatever she would say would be taken against her. That was the power of the $40 million vested by the "Venugopal" in the surgical Center.

Priya was not even cognizant of what Devi was going through. As a professional, Devi had learned to mask her feelings and had become skilled at doing so over the years.

She felt nauseous and sick and wanted to go home. She never felt this traumatic before, even when she was bleeding from her womb due to the police violence. The mental trauma she had just experienced from Priya's hurtful words and attitude cut deeply through her entire being and was much worse than the physical injury she sustained from the police officer's kick in the groin.

Devi felt highly uncomfortable in Priya's presence and decided to quit the session and run for safety. She returned to her office and told her supervisor that she was coming down with a bug and feeling nauseous and unwell. Devi told him she did not want to pass her bug on to Priya and wanted to go home. She requested that someone else be assigned to care for Priya and said no further comment. She felt paranoid about re-opening the wounds of the past and rehashing her traumatic memories of living as an Untouchable in servitude in Kerala.

Lying on her bed, she began to toss and turn, grappling with a sort of post-traumatic stress disorder (PTSD) from the suffering she endured in her servitude under the oppression of the upper caste during her past life in Kerala. She felt lonely and distant from her parents, and she could not wait for the love of her life to return home to be near her.

By the time Sam came home, she had developed a mild fever but felt slightly relieved when she saw him. Sam asked her whether she wanted to go to the hospital emergency. She told him that she was exhausted and needed only some rest. She asked Sam to sit beside her. Devi updated Sam about what Priya told her. He tried to calm her down and asked her to call in sick for a couple of days and stay home even if she lost her job. Sam expressed his disdain for Priya's comments.

In his moral indignation, Sam said, "Devi, some of the conservative Brahmin scientists who came to America, which is, shall we say, a predominantly Christian nation, have issues with their identity. They don't fit into mainstream society due to their uniquely different religious belief systems and a whole host of superstitions of their culture that they wholeheartedly adhere to."

"That is true," Devi interrupted, putting in her two cents.

"As scientists, we all have to live by the evidence collected through scientific inquiry in everything we do professionally rather than the falsities of our superstitions or anecdotal evidence. The scientific evidence and 'a posteriori' knowledge that these scientists help to develop in their daily lives drastically shake the very foundations of their own faith, traditions, and superstitious practices, such as their caste system and their irrational trust in astrology," said Sam.

"True, indeed. I am baffled at her lack of intellectual honesty and hypocritical adherence to superstitions. What was more bothersome was her bigoted and intolerant attitude toward Dalits even after living in America for several decades," exclaimed Devi.

"I am not all surprised that some of them continued to be intolerant and dared to become intellectually dishonest and compartmentalize their professional and private lives. It is hard to shake India and some of its age-old superstitions from them, no matter how long they have lived in America. Priya is no exception; what she said to you was outrageously offensive," exclaimed Sam with indignation.

"Yes, I know, dear," exclaimed Devi.

"She seems to be an obnoxious and nasty woman without any intellectual integrity. So, please don't let those comments bother you. For your mental well-being, please ignore her offensive comments and try to get over your hurt. I am here with you. You have done an outstanding job of caring for her as your patient, even when she displayed a toxic attitude. Relax! I love you unconditionally with all my heart," said Sam.

Devi called in sick for two more days to extend her recovery through the weekend. She needed the entire weekend to recover from the psychological trauma she suffered from listening to the religiously arrogant and bigoted Brahmin, who lived in a free country, America, for 45 years but still lived in a bubble and disparaged the human dignity of Dalits with impunity.

The PT Department assigned another therapist to rehabilitate Priya. When Devi returned to work on Monday, Priya had already been discharged and gone home.

On Friday of that week, Sam and Devi were scheduled to fly to New York City. The Pulitzer Prize Award Ceremony was to be held at Columbia University on Saturday afternoon, when Sam would receive the Award, followed by dinner. They were booked to stay at the Ritz-Carlton Hotel on Friday and Saturday nights and were expected to return to Los Angeles on Sunday afternoon.

They flew out to New York City and arrived there on Friday afternoon. A representative from the Award Committee picked up Sam and Devi from John F. Kennedy International Airport in a limousine and took them to the Ritz-Carlton Hotel in the City. They stayed at the Hotel, had dinner there that night, and rested in their room until Saturday afternoon. During that time, Sam brushed up on his Pulitzer Prize acceptance speech, and Devi served as his audience for the practice.

Sam wanted to give his best award acceptance speech, and Devi was determined to prepare him well for it. She made him practice it several times before they left the Hotel for the Awards Ceremony on Saturday.

When they reached Columbia University, the host escorted Sam and Devi to the banquet hall through a special entrance. Dean Cheney and Dr. George were already there, waiting to join them. They were then directed to their designated seats in the hall.

Following the welcome speech by the Awards Committee Chair and remarks by the President of Columbia University, the committee announced 21 different categories of awards. Then, they invited each awardee to the stage and introduced them individually to the audience, presenting their brief biographies. Upon their introduction, they were awarded the Pulitzer Prize and were asked to deliver the acceptance speech. Sam was the second recipient of the Award.

Dean Cheney and Dr. George congratulated Sam after the awards ceremony. They praised him for the profound and meaningful acceptance speech he delivered. They made Sam and Devi aware that there were some protesters outside the venue on the street with offensive placards, such as "Dalit Lover," "Caste Hatemonger," and "Down with Atheist." Several campus police officers and city police officers were present. So, Sam was not bothered by the protesters; simultaneously, he felt they had a right to protest.

Sam and Devi had a great time at the Ceremony and Awards Dinner. More than Sam, Devi was just gleaming with pride at Sam receiving the coveted Pulitzer Prize. It was the proudest moment in their lives.

When the event was over, they were escorted out through the private entrance toward their limousine for the trip back to their Hotel. Sam could see the protesters, mostly students, at a safe distance, peacefully demonstrating at the main entrance of the banquet hall. The area was well-lit, and the campus police were directing traffic for an easy exit from the venue. As usual, Devi was vigilant because she had developed a sixth sense of the hidden dangers and always looked over her shoulders as a woman of untouchable origin, as they often fell victims to rape and violence.

Their limousine was parked on a side street, not far from the hall's exit. A hedge, with a dense row of shrubs running parallel to the sidewalk, obscured the view from the limousine. As they were getting in, Devi saw someone emerge from the shrubs and walk toward Sam—despite the presence of campus security—as if he were a friend wanting to talk to him.

Noticing the man approaching Sam, she instinctively felt a sense of danger. She quickly went around the car and rushed toward Sam to protect him from the intruder. Before Devi could alert him, the thug pulled a knife and was about to stab Sam when she leapt on him, grabbing the hand holding the weapon. In the struggle, Sam escaped, but in the heat of the moment, the thug slashed her left upper arm. Despite the stab wound, Devi's right hand maintained a firm grip on the thug's knife-wielding hand—the same kind of unyielding grip the Kerala police officer had been unable to break without a brutal kick, the day she lost her unborn baby.

With her firm hold, she tackled the thug by twisting his hand even when she was in pain and bleeding. He was a young man of Indian origin wearing a hoody and a fleece jacket. He yelled expletives at Sam: "Hindu-phobic," "Brahmin-hater," "atheist asshole," "infidel," and "Dalit lover"…

Her hold on him and the twist of his hand was so firm that the punk could not retain his balance; he was screaming with pain and fell to the ground. Police rushed to the scene, took him into custody, and whisked him away to the police car parked nearby for questioning. He was later arrested for felonious assault.

Devi's firm grip was something her father, Balan, taught her when she was a carefree teenager trying to climb trees like her father. When Balan climbed the tallest coconut trees on the farm, he had to grasp the tree trunk tightly to avoid falling to his death. Balan's father, Devi's grandfather, and his great-grandfather were all coconut tree climbers, possessing a unique skill that allowed them to climb the tallest coconut trees — 80 to 100 feet tall — without any special climbing gear, relying only on their bare hands.

Like Balan, they all routinely used their bare hands to climb such tall trees. They developed unique skills and adapted to climbing a 100-foot tree with such a firm grip that they never fell to their death. Over many generations, their tribe developed a firm grip, and their gene pool might have gradually evolved with this unique genetic ability for a firm grip—probably an evolutionary adaptation inherited by the coconut tree-climbing Dalits.

Devi was bleeding profusely from the gash on her upper left arm. Sam was taken aback, shocked, extremely saddened, and teary-eyed that Devi had once again been injured and was bleeding in her selfless efforts to protect him. Sam sat sobbing by her side on the street as they tried to stop the bleeding, with both of her arms outstretched for the paramedics to administer first aid—one hand for the IV and the other to treat the gash, as directed by the paramedics.

Her stretched arms seemed to tell Sam how deeply she loved him, even by risking her own life to save him. Devi had always been a true hero to Sam.

When paramedics stabilized Devi and told him that the injury was not life-threatening, Sam asked for a few moments with her. They asked him to be quick.

Sam whispered in her ears, "My love, this Pulitzer Prize truly belongs to you. But without you and your existential struggles, there would have been no story in my life. Honestly, I wouldn't have won this prestigious Award without you sustaining me with your unrelenting love and enriching my life. You truly saved my life today. I'm hurt and extremely sad that you got injured in protecting me once again. You are in every breath I take; your struggles and the existential struggles of innocent humans like you give my life meaning. And you motivate me to continue to be vocal about protecting our shared humanity, which makes us all human. Don't worry, we shall pass this test too," said Sam.

"Love you to the moon and back. I'm okay and feeling strong. Congratulations again, Sam! I am so proud of you!" said Devi.

She was rushed to the Presbyterian Hospital Emergency Room by ambulance after the paramedics gave first aid to stop her arterial bleeding. She needed multiple stitches for the stab wound she sustained on her left arm. Devi was out of danger after a few hours of treatment in the Emergency Room and was later released from the hospital.

The proudest and happiest day in their life was quickly turned into a traumatic day by the diabolical evil-doers who deny the truth and want to continue subjugating and oppressing innocent humans for their own advantage. To this end, Sam's disinterested pursuit of knowledge and dissemination of such truths posed an existential threat to their way of life.

When they returned to the Ritz-Carlton Hotel from the hospital, news reporters and TV channel anchors were in the lobby for an interview with the couple and were particularly interested in speaking with Devi. Sam begged for privacy for the family as they were pretty traumatized and shaken.

While resting in the hotel room that night, Devi realized that the lifeless planet Mars had no power over her; she had sprung into action to protect Sam. As the grifter Keshavan had predicted, Mars could not endanger Sam's life for marrying her. Even as a *Manglik*—one believed to carry the Mars Defect—she had stopped him from being killed by a human, not a planet. Mars had no baneful influence, nor any control over their destiny. Contrary to her horoscope, Devi had taken matters into her own hands and changed their destiny. In the end, she saw her *Jathakam* for what it was: a superstitious construct, worthless and false.

Sam told Devi that humans alone are the true evil forces, leading us to our own destruction through the relentless defilement of precious human creations. We humans—and only humans—control our collective destiny. Had Devi failed to stop the hateful thug's diabolical act at the crucial moment, Sam would have been stabbed, and it would have been seen as a self-fulfilling prophecy of her *Mangal Dosha*. That violent act would have been twisted by the purveyors and peddlers of meaningless superstitions into proof of the so-called malefic effects of the Mars Defect.

Devi had become disenchanted and disillusioned by the malefic influence once attributed to the *Mangal Dosha*. Her superstitious past had been laid bare and thoroughly debunked. Meanwhile, Mars continued its orbit—an immense, lifeless red planet made of dust and minerals.

However, the charlatanry of exploiting gullible people's credulity and profiting from it by invoking distant planets will persist as long as humans remain susceptible to irrational beliefs.

Similarly, the wickedness of cunning individuals who marginalize, subjugate, and exploit the impoverished—the "least of these brothers and sisters of mine"—will endure as long as we legitimize exploitation through religious narratives.

Only when morality becomes a 'categorical imperative,' an unconditional moral obligation, and social justice a fundamental duty, will such injustices begin to cease.

AFTERWORD

by Henry D'Souza, Ph.D.

A fter reading my original response to his novel, *Broken Chains*, the author, Matthew K. Isaac, invited me to adapt this critique as an "Afterword."

I thoroughly enjoyed reading *Broken Chains*. The novel opens in Kerala—a place where I grew up—and resonated deeply with me. My wife, Lizzie, is a Syrian Catholic. I am a *Konkani* secular Roman Catholic. This background helped me recognize and relate to the novel's tone, customs, and themes. The portrayal of caste, religion, and astrology in Kerala's social fabric is textured and unflinching.

After completing my Master's degree in social work, I worked closely with Dalit communities. My Ph.D. dissertation focused on a Christian Dalit movement in Tamil Nadu. During my years of academic and social work, I encountered firsthand the forms of exclusion, humiliation, and resistance that define the Dalit experience. The movement I studied drew inspiration from Paulo Freire's *Pedagogy of the Oppressed*, emphasizing that education must be emancipatory in nature. They used street theater and community animators to raise awareness and "conscientize" Dalits in their segregated, impoverished communities.

The ultimate goal was social empowerment, transformation, and liberation. Yet even radical movements are often de-radicalized over time. External pressures, such as state repression or dependence on foreign funding, also play a role. Internal challenges include leadership failures or entrenched sexism and patriarchy. My scholarly and lived background shaped my reading of *Broken Chains* and deepened my appreciation of its themes.

Faith, Myth, and Scholarship

The St. Thomas tradition is central to the identity of Syrian Christians, lending the novel historical and theological weight. Although there is no definitive archaeological or historical evidence from the 1st century, the tradition is supported by a long-standing communal belief and a plausible historical context. The story remains foundational despite scholarly skepticism. Readers unfamiliar with Indian Christian history would benefit from more context. Bart Ehrman's work on scriptural reliability is useful, as it places sacred narratives within broader questions of accuracy, tradition, and belief.

Astrology and Rational Dismantling

The novel's treatment of astrology is bold and provocative. The motif of *Mangal Dosha* and Sam's logical critique of its fatalism feels both intellectually satisfying and sometimes blisteringly funny. At times, the critique nears caricature, especially in the depiction of the *Jyolsyan*. Despite its lack of empirical basis, astrology maintains a profound emotional and cultural hold across all backgrounds.

During my fieldwork with the *Koragas,* a tribal community in *Dakshina* Kannada, I encountered similar belief systems involving *daivas* (folk deities) and local *poojaris* (priests). These traditions provided spiritual solace, social order, and psychological resilience—a form of psycho-cultural scaffolding for communities enduring systemic violence. Even in so-called rational societies, astrology persists. Nancy Reagan, for example, famously consulted astrologers.

For a powerful visual critique of such pseudoscience, I recommend the NOVA documentary *Secrets of the Psychics*, featuring James "The Amazing" Randi. He exposed the fraudulence of spoon-bending magicians who claimed that by wishing hard enough, one could shape reality with mental power. These same performers posed as mind readers, dramatically describing drawings created by audience members—always under highly controlled conditions—and attributed their performances to divine or supernatural gifts.

In one classroom experiment, Randi handed out an identical horoscope to every student. He asked them to rate how well the description matched their personality. Most students found it highly accurate. This shows how vague claims can seem personal when presented as astrology. Although astrology and religion offer relief from existential anxiety, they become a kind of "after-life insurance"—a promise of salvation that no normal "policy" can match. Religious institutions have amassed great wealth by marketing these "policies," sometimes surpassing even the most profitable insurers.

Sam's Integrity: Savior or Sympathizer?

Sam is courageous and principled, but his choices complicate our perception of him. He bribes the astrologer to change Devi's *Jathakam* and later to forge his own with *Mangal Dosha*. Love may drive these decisions, but they remain deceptive. He never confides in Devi. While his actions are understandable, they raise ethical questions. As an old *Konkani* saying puts it, "God forgives a father's thousand lies to get his daughter married." This sentiment extends to desperate lovers like Sam. Though such folklore expresses love and sacrifice, it does not literally endorse deception. It may be culturally resonant, but it does not excuse dishonesty. Sam is both liberator and manipulator, fighting superstition as he exploits it. This duality deepens his character and reflects a larger theme in the novel. Even well-meaning liberation often employs terms established by the privileged.

Power and Gratitude

The final acts of generosity, gifting land and building a house, are heartening and redemptive. These gestures were not initiated by Sam but by his parents, who offered them to Devi's parents as the families were about to be united through marriage. While noble on the surface, they subtly reinforce the very social hierarchies they appear to challenge. Sam himself offers a gift of his own: their newly purchased car, handed over to Devi's parents just before the couple leaves for America. The in-laws, who do not drive and had never imagined owning a car, are moved and grateful. Recognizing that the gift is of limited use without the ability to operate it, Sam generously offers to cover the cost of a chauffeur whenever and for as long as needed. The emotional power of these gestures is undeniable. Yet they mirror familiar patterns in Bollywood cinema—cathartic and satisfying but ultimately reinforcing patronizing narratives. If dignity and freedom must be granted by those in power, can they ever be truly earned or equal? The novel presents this tension without resolving it, inviting readers to grapple with its deeper implications.

On Priya and the Return of Trauma

One of the most poignant scenes is the conversation between Devi and Priya, the retired astrophysicist (pp. 257–260). Priya offers a calm, philosophical defense of astrology, without mockery. And yet, her words trigger a profound trauma in Devi. This scene illustrates how even rational, gentle speech can reopen old wounds—a testament to how deeply trauma lives in the body and mind. It's one of the novel's most emotionally intelligent moments.

Final Reflections

As I followed Sam and Devi's journey to the United States—earning graduate degrees, achieving professional success, and in Sam's case, winning a Pulitzer Prize—I felt a quiet unease. It's a familiar arc: freedom and dignity achieved only once validated by Western institutions. Yet this trope feels increasingly out of step in today's world.

The banning of Sam's Pulitzer Prize-winning book in India, and the subsequent revocation of his Person of Indian Origin (PIO) card—effectively denying him permanent entry—underscore how entrenched casteism remains. Even a secular government that claims to be modern resists narratives of caste liberation when they threaten dominant ideologies. The vitriol hurled at him—being labeled "Hindu-phobic," "Brahmin-hater," "atheist asshole," "infidel," and "Dalit lover"—exposes the ferocity of caste defenders. The eventual knife attack on Sam and Devi's courageous intervention that leaves her hospitalized offers a chilling reminder: caste domination is not just stubborn, it is violently enforced.

Devi's heroism is greater than it first seems. She saves Sam twice. First, during a brutal police encounter in India, she shields him from violence and is injured herself, losing her baby. She is rushed to intensive care. This moment is gut-wrenching and morally seismic. It foreshadows when she saves him again outside his Pulitzer Prize ceremony. These are not just acts of sacrifice—they show agency and strength. Despite being doubly marginalized as a Dalit woman, Devi becomes the novel's moral spine. Her resistance is not symbolic; it is embodied and life-risking.

Even Devi's renaming to "Debbie" is symbolic. It finalizes her "Americanization," but it does so with a multicultural twist. The Spanish "v" shifts to a "b." This subtle phonetic change reflects how immigrant identities are reshaped in the U.S. Despite white nationalism, the cultural blender still accommodates multiplicity. It's an ironic nod to survival through reinvention.

In revising this "Afterword," I was struck by something I had overlooked in my initial draft: Devi's valiant interventions to save Sam's life—first during a violent police encounter and again during the Pulitzer ceremony—are not simply plot points. They are acts of radical courage and moral clarity. It took me some time to realize that these moments eclipse Sam's own struggles to "save" Devi from caste oppression. Such is the invisible grip of caste ideology—even for someone like myself, with years of anti-caste work and scholarship. Antonio Gramsci reminds us that hegemonic cultural structures shape not only what we believe, but what we *see*. Even with cognitive awareness of injustice, our perceptual apparatus can be conditioned to overlook the most obvious truths. Recognizing this blind spot was humbling—and necessary.

Caste has not disappeared in the diaspora; it has traveled with them. The caste-discrimination law passed in Washington State reminds us that these structures endure. In 2020, Dalit female engineers at Microsoft, Google, and Apple broke their silence about casteism in the tech sector. In 2021, the California State University student government passed a resolution opposing caste-based discrimination. Caste doesn't dissolve across borders—it mutates.

The struggles against racism in the U.S. have long inspired movements in India. The Dalit Panthers explicitly borrowed their name, tactics, and ideological framing from the Black Panthers. And yet, even after decades of civil rights advocacy, racism in the U.S. persists through police brutality, residential segregation, and mass incarceration. The 13th Amendment outlawed slavery "except as a punishment for crime," creating a loophole that allows penal slave labor to flourish in the prison-industrial complex. Ava DuVernay's documentary "*13th*" offers an essential overview of this system. The Black Lives Matter movement is a testament to the fact that resistance must be constant and enduring.

Broken Chains is not merely a love story or a political novel. It is a moral investigation into how freedom is defined, who grants it, and what it ultimately costs. It confronts religion, caste, patriarchy, and institutional power with fearless honesty. It moved me, disturbed me, and reminded me that the work of liberation—anywhere—is never complete.

It deserves to be read widely. It deserves to be argued with. And above all, it deserves to be taken seriously.

Henry D'Souza, Ph.D.
Professor of Social Work, Grace Abbott School of Social Work
University of Nebraska at Omaha
Nebraska, USA
August 2025

ACKNOWLEDGEMENTS

The true inspiration to continue writing *Broken Chains* came from my beloved daughter, Sonya Mahajan, who read the first draft and immediately grasped the nuanced portrayal of bigotry as explored through the lenses of theology, philosophy, and science.

The next major turning point came when Mr. Shiva Ramaswamy, a former colleague and English lecturer at the University of Toledo, rigorously critiqued the manuscript. I am deeply grateful to both Sonya and Shiva for their insightful encouragement.

A subsequent review came from Dr. Dale Lanigan, Professor Emeritus of Sociology at Lourdes University in Ohio. He was captivated by the novel's treatment of theology, faith, and science—areas of deep personal and academic interest to him. Dr. Lanigan posed thought-provoking questions, and I thank him for his critical insights.

I am especially indebted to Dr. Henry D'Souza, Professor of Social Work at the University of Nebraska at Omaha, who found the novel profoundly compelling and admired its intellectual honesty in confronting religious bigotry, faith, science, and the systemic oppression of Dalits. Having lived and worked with Dalits during his doctoral research, Dr. D'Souza brought both scholarly depth and a practitioner's empathy to his reading. He understood the cultural nuances, ethos, and pathos of the Dalit community, and read *Broken Chains* critically—yet with devotion. His thoughtful analyses and heartfelt appreciation were invaluable sources of encouragement on this journey.

Another distinguished individual who generously gave her time in reviewing *Broken Chains* was Ms. Brenda Pickleman, a highly talented Hollywood actress and filmmaker from Chicago. I am deeply grateful for her warm encouragement and support.

I must also acknowledge the generous support of my friend, Mr. Bala Sriraghavan, CEO and Co-Founder of DataNetiix (Irvine, CA), a global software company. Recognizing the literary and social significance of this work, he wholeheartedly supported my efforts. His design team, led by Ms. Arpitha Sukumaran, created the striking cover for *Broken Chains*. I am thankful to Mr. Sriraghavan and his talented staff for their creative contributions.

I also thank Dr. A.K.B. Pillai, former Professor of Comparative Literature and Anthropology and Founder and Chairperson of the New York Institute of Integral Human Development Inc., New York, for his generous words of appreciation quoted earlier in this book.

Finally, I owe immense gratitude to my wife, Bina Susan, and my son, Shawn, who selflessly shouldered many responsibilities while I was fully immersed in writing. Without their unwavering support, I could not have completed the research or brought this novel to fruition.

About the Author

 **Matthew K. Isaac** was born in Kerala, India, to the late Mr. Mathunny Isaac, an American-educated professor and Principal of Titus II Teachers' College (Thiruvalla), and Mrs. Thankama Isaac, whose steadfast support and nurturing presence profoundly shaped his upbringing and career.

After completing a Bachelor of Science (B.S.) degree in Biology from Mar Thoma College, University of Kerala, and a Master of Arts (M.A.) from Christ Church College, Isaac was admitted to the University of Toledo in the United States to pursue graduate studies. He earned a second M.A. in English Language and Literature, a third master's degree (M.A.E.), and a Ph.D. from the University of Toledo, Ohio, where he received the 1984 John J. Turin Memorial Service Award for outstanding leadership and service to the university community while maintaining high academic standing.

He began his professional career at the University of Toledo (UT) as an academic advisor and faculty member in the Humanities, where he advised students and taught courses in writing and humanities. Shortly after launching his teaching career, he was promoted to Director and later Divisional Director of various academic programs at UT's University College.

Isaac later relocated to California, where he held senior leadership positions, including District Director and Executive Director of Economic and Workforce Development at the San Bernardino District Chancellor's Office. During his tenure, Dr. Isaac played a key role in securing over $25 million in state and federal competitive grants for workforce and economic development initiatives in the Inland Empire. He retired as Associate Vice Chancellor of Economic Development and Corporate Training.

Dr. Isaac received numerous accolades throughout his career, including statewide awards for "Excellence in Leadership" from both Ohio and California, in recognition of his contributions to workforce development and economic progress.

He is the author of the literary novel *Touched by Redeeming Love* (2018). When not writing, he enjoys recreational golf, reading, singing, and listening to music. He currently resides in Southern California with his wife, Bina Susan.